I0653064

Lord Skyler and The Earth Defense Force

By

Matt T. Schott

Copyright © 2009 by **Matt T Schott**

All rights reserved by the author. No part of this publication may be reproduced, stored in a retrieval system or transmitted in any form or by any means electronic, mechanical, photocopying, recording or otherwise, without the prior written permission of the author.

ISBN: 978-0-578-01418-0

I want to thank friends and family for not turning me over to an insane asylum. I would especially like to thank Terry "Leo" McGuire, who has been to Flarconea with me.

Chapter 1

"Hey, where do you think you're going? I want to talk to you."

Charlie Skyler just got home from work and his son, Jacob, nearly made it to the front door without being noticed.

Jacob recognized the arrogant lecture tone in his father's voice and decided it was time to make himself scarce. He got the benefit of one of his father's enlightened life speeches every once in a while: whenever he fought with his sister Liann, or when his grades in school started slipping. He stood by the front door and waited impatiently for another time-to-grow-up-and-be-a-man speech.

Charlie was still in office mode. He moved in stiff, rigid, rehearsed movements across the living room to the hallway closet. He stopped and released an over emphasized sigh, a standard before the daddy speech. Jacob dropped his head in anticipation of the onslaught to come. "What's this I hear? Your mom tells me you're not going out for the school baseball team. You're going to screw up your college opportunities if you don't go out for the school team."

Jacob peered out the door, avoiding his father's eyes. "I've got a lot of wrong decisions ahead of me," he mumbled. "I've got to make them myself." Jacob's tone was calm. He didn't want to upset his father any more than he already had but he wanted his opinion known. "I just want to take a little time off this spring for myself."

Jacob's father rubbed his forehead with the palm of his hand and shook his head trying to stay calm. He watched Jacob put on his long, dark blue Navy pea coat, which he had bought at the Army and Navy store on Central Avenue.

"You look like a wannabe hoodlum with that coat."

Jacob's father refocused his argument. "I'm trying to help you not make the same mistakes I did. Not going out for baseball your junior year is a mistake. Colleges look for that kind of thing. They want to see commitment, responsibility."

Jacob opened the front door and examined his old tan Chevy Impala through the porch screen. The car was speckled with early spring mud. It was three years younger than Jacob but life was a lot tougher on its rusted body than it was on its owner. The Impala was getting more dings and deteriorating more every year; meanwhile, Jacob had grown four inches in less than a year, putting him over six-foot-two. Playing football, wrestling, and baseball all year for the last four years kept his body lean and muscular. The baby fat on his face was all gone. The rugged chiseled features he inherited from his father were starting to come to the surface, the classic square chin and high forehead. The only thing Jacob now had in common with his car was the increasing cost of maintenance they both demanded.

"I'm going to play in the state league this summer. When we win, I could go to Puerto Rico."

Charlie turned his back on his son and eased off his tailored, dark blue, business jacket. Careful not to wrinkle it, he put his jacket on a hanger. He smoothed it out with the palm of his hand as if it was a suit of shiny armor. He treated the blue jacket like a trophy he earned and fought for.

Then he barked over is shoulder, "Nobody pays attention to those small-town leagues. You're just thinking about the trip to Puerto Rico. You're not thinking long term."

Jacob smiled as a new angle to the argument entered his head. "I've made good mistakes all by myself." Jacob ran his fingers through his well-groomed blond hair. "Look at my car. Buying that broken down hunk a junk taught me how to repair cars. Who knows what Puerto Rico will teach me?"

A sly, greasy smile leaked onto Charlie's face. "I know what it will teach you and your mother wouldn't approve."

Charlie proceeded to disentangle his expensive tie viciously as if the it had clamped hold of his throat and refused to be taken off.

He stopped and stabbed a finger in Jacob's direction halfway through the struggle. "That's another thing. Your car... you get that muffler fixed before this weekend is over or you're not driving it to school on Monday."

Jacob stared down at the Victorian house's polished oak wood floor, thick and impenetrable like his father's will. He squeezed the edge of the front door, venting his anger through his fingers instead of his mouth.

His father was trying to make another point on how to run his life. Jacob barked back in retaliation. "That's not fair. I don't get paid until next Friday. I don't have the money to fix it now."

Jacob's father folded his arms and shook his head side to side. "That's not my problem son, it's yours. That car has been running with a hole in the muffler for two weeks. You're lucky the police haven't pulled you over yet."

Jacob clenched his fist so tight his pinkie knuckle cracked. "How come every time you try to prove a point I have to suffer?"

Charlie's eyes almost popped out of his head. Jacob knew he crossed the line.

Jacob put up his hands to calm his father before he over reacted and grounded him. "Sorry dad, I know you're just trying to help me. I'll clean up my act, I promise. Give me some time to think about joining the school team."

Jacob's father rubbed his neck where his tie irritated his skin all day. "Get that car fixed."

Jacob looked at his primer-ridden car again. Dark brown primer dotted the exterior in patches, especially the dented fenders. The tan-colored car looked like a middle-class suburban commando vehicle. Jacob thought it had character and the hole in the muffler added personality.

Jacob stepped out the door. "I have to go, dad. Doug's waiting for me in the car and I told Leo I would pick him up after bagpipe practice and bring him to the movies."

Jacob's father walked up to the door to watch Jacob leave. He was still simmering down. "You be home right after the movie. Remember, we have to have this place cleaned up first thing tomorrow, before your mother and sister get back from Pop-Pop and Nanny's house. Your mother will ground us both if those dishes aren't done and the living room isn't picked up."

Jacob was hoping to end the conversation soon as he watched his friend Doug waiting impatiently in the car.

Doug Marcoux was tapping his fingers on his kneecap inside Jacob's car. He rested his sneakers on the dash and had a disturbed, anxious look blanketed across his face. As he watched Jacob approaching, he made pointing motions to where his watch should have been if he had one.

Jacob nodded to Doug and turned back to his father. "No problem, have to go."

Jacob shuffled to his car, shaking his head. His father knew exactly what he should be doing with his life all the time.

"Hey, where are your brothers?" Jacob asked Doug as he walked towards the car. Doug was a little huskier than his two older brothers, but he had the family brown eyes and the thin blond hair of the Marcoux clan.

Doug rolled down the window. "Dad caught them arguing over something again. Gram was playing with Ian's nunchuks or something. You know how Ian is so possessive about his things. So dad took them to the do-jo to duke it out and teach them both a lesson."

Jacob walked around the front of the car and opened the door on the driver's side. It made the usual crunching noise as the door rubbed against the fender. Doug rolled his window back up and smiled to himself. "My bros won't be around tonight."

Jacob started the car and backed out of the driveway. "My dad says I've got to fix my muffler before Monday or I can't drive it to school."

Doug frisked himself for money. "Sorry man, I'm broke."

The maple trees along the Hudson River were about to start budding if it would just stay warm for a couple days in a row. It was only March, but thoughts of spring and some warm weather had come early put the feeling of summer freedom into the boys' hearts.

Jacob drove to North Rockland High School to pick up Terry

McGuire. Leo, as everyone called him, was of dark, Irish decent. His dad owned an Irish pub and still talked with an Irish brogue. He made Leo start bagpipe lessons as a young kid as it was a family tradition going back ten generations. Leo had explained to Jacob one day that they weren't actually the bagpipes. They were the uilleann pipes, the Irish equivalent of the Scottish folk instrument.

When Jacob pulled up in front of the school, Leo was sitting on the curb with his pipes. He was straining his neck staring into the school trying to catch a glimpse of the girls on the basketball team.

Jacob and Doug smiled at Leo's blatant perverted attitude. Doug yelled out the car door window to him. "How did it go tonight, Leo?"

Leo opened the door to the back of the car and slid his pipes inside. "Not bad, we'll be ready next week for the St. Patrick's Day parade."

Rubbing his belly, he added, "I just hope I can walk the whole parade route without collapsing."

Doug played with the car radio, "Why do you do it, man?"

Jacob smiled and said, "He likes wearing a dress down Main Street."

Doug and Jacob laughed out loud and Leo patted his thighs, "At least I got the legs for it. I'm secure in my manhood."

Leo sat up in his seat. "Speaking of manhood, where are your brothers, Doug?"

Doug turned around in his seat and explained again why his brothers would not be joining them.

Leo shook his head in disappointment. "Pig-headed idiots. So, what else is new?"

Jacob drove his car up the old mountain road to the next town, New City. The pothole-ridden road was dark and curved slowly up and around Hi-Tor Mountain. The stacked rock wall close to the side of the road held back the earth from washing over the road. Jacob always thought it looked like it was going to crumble under the weight of the mountain.

All the movie theaters on the riverside along the mountain had shut down when video stores started opening up. It was the end of an era for small-town movie palaces in the area.

Halfway up the mountain road, the boys noticed a white glow up around the next bend. Jacob leaned forward over the dashboard, "Looks like another cop stop up ahead and me with a hole in my muffler."

Doug slammed his fist onto the dashboard then crossed his arms in a huff. "Those uniform geeks are always harassing us."

Jacob sat up in his seat. "Hey, don't sweat it. We got no beer and I'm doing the speed limit."

Doug reached over and grabbed Jacob's arm in a tight grip. His eyes bugged out in horror. "Jacob, they could put us away for having bagpipes in the car."

The boys laughed and Leo added, "If I play a tune they could arrest me for assault with a deadly weapon."

When the car turned the corner, Jacob put his forearm up over his eyes to block out the intensity of the light. The light was so bright he felt the nerve twitch in his eye running back to his brain. He jammed on the brakes, throwing the other two forward in their seats. The car skidded to a stop in the center of the road.

The motor turned off, the radio went dead, and then the car lights went out. The boys stared at each other with their jaws dropped and their eyes wide in fear.

Doug screamed at Jacob. "What are you doing, man, start this pig back up and get us out of here."

Jacob slammed the steering wheel with his palms. "It wasn't me. The car went dead by itself."

Jacob tried starting the car. He turned the keys three times but there was no response. They all peered out the dirty windshield and looked up with their mouths gaping open. They were all stunned by the hovering white light.

Leo finally spoke very slowly, thinking carefully between each word: "What, the hell is it? A helicopter?"

A surge of intense green light struck the car and engulfed it. The whole automobile down to the frame started shaking back and forth, throwing the boys around inside the car. They curled up into the fetal position, shaking with fear. They could hear a deep rumbling noise that grew more intense with every moment that passed. It felt as if a freight train was running over them. Leo grabbed his pipes tightly and wrapped himself around them like an old security blanket, just before he lost consciousness.

Chapter 2

"Captain, Titan war ships are coming out of warp near the fourth planet."

The bridge of the Flarconean cruiser, the_Cambree, went into full alert. Lights glowed red and the sound of bells echoed throughout the ship. The human-looking aliens inside the ship stopped in their tracks and changed direction. They focused like monks on their way to prayer and stayed calm.

The dark blue Flarconean space cruiser was twice as long and thick as a nuclear submarine. It had long rods sticking out of the hull like a spiked fish. The battle cruiser had four laser cannons mounted in spheres that clung on it like a chameleon's eyes. Two cannons were mounted in the front of the cruiser and two in the back. A quarter of the way back from the front of the cruiser was a round pyramid that rose above and below the cruiser like a pick axe. Underneath the cruiser stretched a long laser cannon running from the front of the ship to the pyramid section of the ship.

The bridge of the Cambree was located in the pyramid section towards the back of the ship. Captain Se Toris looked down to one of his lieutenants in charge of the first tier. Like all Flarconeans, the captain was bald with bronze colored skin. Lieutenant Tama instantly felt the captain's glare of annoyance.

The captain pointed a long thin finger at the arrogant, long nosed lieutenant "Tell that last transport to leave Earth now. Tell them the Titans are here early."

Lieutenant Tama sent the message instantly.

The bridge layout was shaped like an ice cream cone within the center of the pyramid. It was 20 feet between the inside wall of the ship and the cone shape platform. Four walkways came off the platform leading off the bridge like spokes of a wheel. The captain sat in the center of the room on top of a third tier of the bridge.

The entire bridge was in the middle of a holo deck. The captain had a complete view of space around his ship. From his perch, he was able to see technical read outs from all the console screens on the two other platforms, which tiered off below him.

The captain peered through his double eyelids towards the muscle bound Lieutenant Ra Sat, who was in charge of the third tier, "Call in the Aderain fighters. Tell them to form the stargate near Earth's moon."

The lieutenant acknowledged the captain with a quick nod.

Captain Se Toris scratched his extended leathery skinned chin as he studied the stars in front of him. "Inform the other transports that the Cambree and the Dezain will hold off the Titans as long as possible. The Pen Ta and the Zig Ta will escort the transports back to the stargate coordinates near Earth's moon."

Lieutenant Lu Silo was a young officer in charge of the second tier of the bridge. He looked at the captain and tilted his head questionably.

The captain caught his look. "I know, Lieutenant Silo, two Flarconean cruisers can't think of winning against a Titan invasion force, even with two Aderain fighters backing them up."

The captain sat back in his command chair and pointed to the spot in space where the Titan ships would be coming from. "We'll meet the Titan invasion force there, sector H-40. We'll distract the Titans so the transports and the other cruisers can escape."

A corporal manning a console received a message and turned to the officer manning her tier. Lieutenant Ra Sat looked up at the captain. "Sir, all the transports have left Earth."

The captain looked down and to his right and saw a holographic image of four Flarconean transports leaving the blue planet and heading towards the moon.

Lieutenant Tama was second in charge and he monitored the first tier, close to the captain. "Why do we bother with these primitives, captain? Their fate has already been sealed by the

Titans."

The bridge crew stopped and watched a large ball of white light appear out of dark space. It streaked towards Earth. The Titan battleship was directly in front of the captain on the holo deck. "The Titans have started their bombardment of the planet."

Lieutenant Silo reported, "Captain, fifteen Titan cruisers and two Titan battleships in sector H-40 are now in range. Zero point three AU's away. They're taking a low Earth orbit but they are firing at us."

The Flarconean cruiser started rocking back and forth when several green laser shots hit its shields.

Lieutenant Tama looked up at the captain. "Sir, six Titan cruisers have broken away from the main fleet and are on an intercept course with us."

The captain gestured a finger over a keypad and intensified the magnification on the room screen. The Titan cruiser was shaped like a robotic octopus with its tentacles pointed directly in front of it.

Tama studied the read out on the Titan ships. "Captain, they're sectional." The new Titan space ships were designed to break apart to form smaller space ships. He saw the Titan cruisers heading straight at them.

A stronger bolt of red light burst out of each of the three Titan cruisers, seconds apart from each other.

The captain looked to Tama. "Evasive maneuvers." Tama tapped a lieutenant's shoulder lightly. "Fire starboard thrusters, hit main engines with a burst of power. With that, two massive balls of red light roared down the cruiser's starboard side.

The third shot skimmed off the top of the Cambree's shields along the upper decks in the midsection of the ship, shaking the space ship violently. The Flarconean cruiser started to spin.

Some of the Flarconeans grabbed onto handrails to steady themselves. The ships gravity kept them from falling to the ceiling of the ship.

The captain focused in front of him as the holographic stars started to spin.

"Fire port thrusters, stop the ship from spinning."

The captain studied his playing field.

"Tama, head to sector X-75; get us away from the planet and position the Earth's moon behind us."

Captain Se Toris looked down at Lieutenant Silo.

"We'll draw their fire away from the moon and the planet. Then we'll circle around to the stargate."

"Very well, captain, I'll inform the other captains." The lieutenant turned away from the captain and gave the order to an ensign.

Lieutenant Ra Sat looked up at the captain.

"Main shield capacity down to seventy-five percent. We have two damaged defense rods. Section "C" upper shield grid is down to twenty-five percent. "

The Cambree stopped spinning with one short blast from the thrusters.

The captain looked at Tama.

"Full thrusters, take us to section L-85 and fire starboard batteries."

The two starboard laser cannons started spraying green laser balls at one of the Titan cruisers. The Titans intercepted a couple of shots with small defense guns. Several more shots were absorbed into the Titan shield, rocking the ship in several different directions.

Lieutenant Ra Sat checked his console again and tapped his ear com link.

"We're getting reports of an electrical fire on deck three."

Captain Se Toris never took his eyes off the Titan cruisers.

"Remove all nonessential personal from the top five decks of section "C" and send in damage control."

The captain checked the position of the Dezain. She was coming up quickly on the Cambree's aft side. "Bring us around to fire the main gun."

The Dezain passed underneath the Cambree firing its main gun. A red ball of electricity shot across space and hit the Titan cruiser head on. It's forward shields flashed and the weakened shield made the damaged Titan cruiser look hazy. The Titan cruiser took an evasive maneuver and veered off from the main group.

The Cambree's main laser cannon charged up and spat out another fiery ball of red light. The shot hit the retreating Titan cruiser along its side. A small part of the cruiser exploded out into space.

The Dezain's forward laser cannons peppered the wounded Titan cruisers. The shields flashed on the first three hits then the Titan's shields disappeared.

The next three shots from the Dezain were caught by small defense laser fire.

The fourth shot hit just behind the tentacles of the Titan ship. It caused a small explosion, blowing out the whole midsection of the space ship. The back part of the Titan cruiser instantly broke away from the rest of the ship and flew off on it's own.

A domino of explosions rolled towards the front of the tentacles of the Titan cruiser. Five tentacles exploded at the same time. The nine other tentacles of the cruiser were able to detach and become separate space ships.

Lieutenant Tama glanced at the captain.

"The Titan cruisers are scattering."

A rainbow swirling vortex appeared above the Flarconean captain's head.

Lieutenant Silo pointed to it.

"Captain, a tackyon field is forming right above the Cambree."

Two Aderain fighters flashed by the captain's face; they headed straight towards the Titan force. The Flarconeans on the bridge all ducked, as if to avoid the surprise arrival.

A searing white ball of electricity from the Aderain fighter streaked at one of the Titan cruisers that attacked the Flarconean cruisers. The Titan's shields absorb it.

The lights on the Titan cruiser flickered, and then the ship went dark.

The second Aderain fighter fired three rapid green balls of electricity right through the cruiser. A large explosion blew the cruiser apart into thousands of small lifeless pieces of metal. No section of the cruiser survived.

The Aderain fighters flipped around and headed right for the Titan armada. They swayed around each other like two dolphins flying through the water playing tag. They kept a constant bombardment of green laser fire on the oncoming Titan fighters as they flew right by them.

As they approached the Titan armada, the Aderain fighters banked away from the Titan ships. They exited away from Earth and the Titans. They were out of range before the Titans could lock onto them.

The young Lieutenant Silo turned towards the Captain with a look of disappointment.

"Sir, the Aderain fighters are off the screen again. They must have hyped back out of the quadrant."

Lieutenant Tama caught the captain's eyes.

"Sir, two Titan fighter squads have entered our sector. The Titan battleships are deploying more of their fighters."

Lieutenant Silo looked back down at his screen console then waved his hand towards the captain.

"Sir, the Aderain fighters have reappeared behind the moon. They are ready to form another stargate behind Earth's moon."

The captain nodded at Lieutenant Tama.

"Get us out of here, lieutenant"

The captain looked up at his upper left side. The Dezain had taken up a defensive position to protect the Cambree from three oncoming Titan cruisers. The cruisers peppered the Dezain up and down its hull with green laser fire. Two of the Titan cruisers suffered direct hits on the Dezain with red balls of electricity, close to the bridge area.

"Sir, Captain Re Tom of the Dezain is hailing us"

Captain Se Toris stood up.

"Captain Re Tom, retreat to the far side of the moon."

A small holographic picture flickered in front of Captain Se Toris

"Leave us to our glory." Captain Re Tom put his hand over his mouth muffling a cough. "Fight another day."

Lieutenant Tama reported to the Captain.

"Sir, the Dezain is reversing course towards the Titan cruisers."

Under his breath, Captain Se Toris prayed.

"Give it to them, Re."

The Dezain exchanged fire with the Titan cruisers using all her batteries. It peppered the first two cruisers, shaking them back and forth.

The Titans returned fire with two red laser shots.

The Dezain instantly burst into million points of light, disappearing into the vastness of space. Her explosion covered the Cambree's exit from the area.

As the Cambree emerged from behind Earth's moon, the rest of the Titan warships turned back towards the blue planet.

Lieutenant Silo reported to the captain.

"Sir, we are approaching the Aderain fighters' stargate."

With a deep, soulful sadness, the Captain sighed: "Go"

Chapter 3

"Commander Godon, we have locked onto the first Earth city."

With that, the towering Titan commander stomped around the center of the bridge of the Titan battleship Ritan, he circled around the blue glow of the holographic table like a starving vulture. The bridge lights were dim, which gave the room a feeling of being underground. The glimmering glow from the computer consoles that lined the perimeter of the square bridge flickered against black steel bulkheads like a crackling fire in a cave.

Commander Godon leaned down on the holographic table and scrutinized the shapes of Earth's landmasses. He studied the images like a strange jigsaw puzzle. "I hear the weather is hot." The commander looked up at Major Nabeeto.

"The ice on the planet is mostly liquid."

Major Nabeeto was in charge of the ground forces for the invasion. His black soft body armor wasn't as shiny or as big as that of the ten-foot commander, but he was just as feared by the crew.

Major Nabeeto got up from one of the computer consoles and walked towards the holographic table.

"Why do you care, commander? You'll be resting comfortably at the moon base."

The commander looked up and glared at the Major with annoyance.

"That's right, major, and if you make me come down to that boiling planet you better be dead."

The commander stood straight up, towering over the major by a foot. He looked towards the large screen positioned at the front of the bridge where the captain of the *Ritan* stood.

"Captain Tandom, fire the main laser cannon."

Captain Tandom nodded indiscreetly to the commander then turned to his lieutenant.

"Fire the main laser cannon."

A lieutenant sitting at one of the computer consoles shouted back: "Sir, fire the main laser cannon, yes sir."

A twenty-two foot diameter white ball of electricity fired out of the laser cannon mounted underneath the Titan battleship. It streaked towards Earth like a falling star. As the white ball of charged electrical particles passed through Earth's atmosphere it shaved off a layer of energy and the ball turned red.

To the Parisians around the Eiffel Tower, it looked as if a meteor was heading toward their city. For a long moment they watched, stared, and wondered what was coming at them. When the red ball of charged particles collided with the Earth, it exploded with an earsplitting thunderclap. It ripped a hole in the ground two miles in diameter. Buildings miles away exploded from the serge of electricity through the electrical lines and pipes. The Earth grumbled in pain.

Commander Godon nodded his head with approval.

"Tell the rest of the ships to proceed with the bombardment."

Major Targ was standing on the other side of the holographic map.

"Commander Godon, two Flarconean cruisers are in sector 45 by 20 by 20 units. It's some kind of ambush."

Godon marched around the table and shoved Captain Targ in the chest.

"Don't be a fool Targ, intelligence says the Flarconeans recruit aliens just before we invade a planet. They train them on how to fight us then send them back to annoy us."

Commander Godon turned to Captain Tandom.

"Captain, intensify your scan on the planet."

Godon returned to pacing around the holographic table. The bluish holographic image of space around the Earth doubled in size.

"Major Targ, send six cruisers to destroy the Flarconean ships."

Captain Tandom turned to the commander.

"Sir, we have detected seventy-eight missiles launched from Earth. Several Earth-orbiting satellites have also targeted us."

Commander Godon walked over to Major Targ.

"Don't have our ships destroy any missiles in the plant's atmosphere. We don't want to spoil the goods."

Godon scratched his flat head and looked at major Nabeeto.

"Major, contact Captain Chata at the Earth jamming station; order him to start jamming all Earth signals."

Captain Tandom stepped up next to commander Godon.

"We have one Flarconean transport leaving Earth's atmosphere. Our sensors have picked up three more transports and two more Flarconean cruisers heading towards the moon."

Commander Godon slapped the back of Major Targ.

"You see Targ, no threat."

The Titan battleship shot out another ball of white lighting crashing down into Earth's atmosphere. The blast leveled the city of Berlin. The second battleship targeted Tokyo. Titan cruisers circled the planet in a low Earth orbit, bombarding military installations around the targeted cities. The humans' defensives had no effect on the Titan battleships.

Major Nabeeto tapped a communication device mounted around his ear.

"Sir, Captain Chata reports a Flarconean transport landed and took off five minutes ago, sixty miles east of their position. He's requesting support troops in case of a ground assault.

Commander Godon was disgusted by his officer's lack of judgment in the Flarconean's movements.

"Doesn't anybody read the intelligence reports? Tell Captain Chata to hold tight. Our ground assault doesn't start for another week. Tell him we will monitor all activity in his area and will send reinforcements at the first sign of trouble."

Major Targ pointed to a spot away from the planet. "Sir, our cruisers have engaged two Flarconean cruisers here. Captain Sunto of the *Ravage* reports heavy damage."

Commander Godon walked next to Major Targ.

"What are the other two Flarconean cruisers doing?"

Major Targ checked the numbers from the console read outs.

"The other two Flarconean cruisers are escorting the four Flarconean transports towards the Earth's moon."

Major Targ rechecked his numbers then gripped the console tight. He pointed where the cruisers were battling.

"Stargate opening! We have a stargate opening right by the two Flarconean cruisers engaging with our cruisers.

Commander Godon pushed his way to the holographic table.

"Evasive maneuvers, order the fleet to form around us."

The other Titan battleship, the *Slin*, came around alongside the *Ritan*. Commander Godon stared at the hologram. The lengthy rainbow vortex stretched out for about a mile in space.

Commander Godon pushed around the table until he was able to look down into the vortex.

"Nothing but white light; wait, I see something, Adrian fighters! Put the fleet in a defensive formation. Deploy two squads of fighters to protect the *Ritan*.

Major Targ tapped his ear communication.

"Commander, they've knocked out one of our cruisers."

Captain Chuckdon was in charge of supply and establishing a Titan base on Earth's moon. He slammed the table with his fist.

"They'll be coming after us next."

The commander glared at the captain.

"Idiot, they'll make one swoop at us then form another stargate so the Flarconeans can escape."

The commander turned away from the table and put his hands behind his back.

"They're only here to get the Flarconeans out."

Captain Chuckdon glared back at the commander.

"One of them will form the gate while the other fires on us."

Commander Godon shook his head confidently.

"I don't think so. I personally wouldn't jump into space without having my main gun online."

Captain Tandom pointed to the two Aderain fighters.

"The Aderain fighters have taken an attack vector on the fleet, commander."

Major Targ leaned further over the table. He pressed several more buttons to focus the hologram in on the two Aderain fighters and the battleship.

"They're coming in for the kill."

Godon pushed the major away from the table.

"Fool, watch what they do."

The two egg-shaped Aderain fighters moved twice as quick as any other alien vessel in space. They zig-zagged and rolled towards the Titan fleet, constantly firing green laser blasts.

Just as fast as they appeared, they turned sharply and shot away from Earth and the Titan fleet.

Captain Tandom checked the numbers on his console: "The Aderain fighters are out of range and seem to be heading towards the solar system's asteroid belt."

Commander Godon threw his arms up in the air.

"You see, major?"

Major Targ bowed his head. "You were right, commander."

The commander studied the hologram image again.

"Major, don't stop giving me your stupid opinions. They remind me how right I am about things. Now, Captain Tandom, send your fighters to support the cruisers attacking the Flarconeans. Major Targ, resume the bombardment on Earth."

Major Targ studied his console screen.

"Sir, we destroyed one of the Flarconean cruisers. The other one is running towards the moon."

Major Nabeeto slapped his big hands together.

"Let's eat them up."

Commander Godon shook his head in disappointment. "No Captain, the Flarconean cruiser is meeting up with the other Flarconean cruisers and the transports, and the two Aderain fighters. I don't want to lose more ships if I don't have to. Who knows when I'll get replacements?"

Commander Godon walked up to Major Targ.

"Order the cruisers and the fighters attacking the Flarconean cruiser to stand down. Have them follow the Flarconeans at a safe distance. Tell them not to engage, just watch them and report to us."

The commander looked at all his officers.

"Once the Flarconeans have left the system, we'll step up our bombardment of the planet. We've lost two cruisers and our ships have taken on damage that we didn't count on. We can't fall behind our invasion schedule."

The commander walked around his officers.

"I want mining camps up and running in thirty days. I want all of you to figure out how we are going to get back on schedule."

Commander Godon walked towards the door off the bridge.

"Major Nabeeto, coordinate with Major Targ on your ground assault. I want you two to show me in one hour how we are going to be back on schedule. If anything comes up before then, I'll be in my quarters."

Chapter 4

Jacob had to rub the eye crust off his eyelids just to open his eyes. His eyes fluttered open and the white light around him felt sharp. He sat up grabbing the top of the bench he was laying on. He felt disoriented and a bit queasy. His mouth tasted like a pasty film was growing in it, like the time he was in the hospital for his appendix. He put his elbows on his knees holding his head between his hands. The joints in his shoulders and elbows ached.

Jacob was sitting on a long silver metal bench secured to the floor. He looked at Leo and Doug lying five feet across from him sleeping on the same type of bench. Doug's head was by the end of the bench and Leo's head rested on Doug's feet. The bench was just long enough for the two boys to lie on.

Jacob took a deep breath and thought they looked comfortable and cozy with the dark blue blankets draped over them. Leo was sprawled out on his back. His arms and legs spread out in different directions like an old hound dog sunning himself on a warm summer day. In his hand, resting on the floor, he gripped the case that had held his pipes.

Jacob smiled at Leo's comical snore. He made a low gurgling noise, sucking in a breath and breathing out. He was whimpering like Curly on The Three Stooges.

"Doug." Jacob sat up with the blanket wrapped around his shoulders rubbing his eyes, "Doug wake up."

Jacob took his first good look around; the ceiling beveled up sixty feet above his head. He was in the middle of a long row of benches that stretched half a football field long and fifty feet wide. Hundreds of people were sleeping on the benches. It looked like a bum convention.

"Doug, where are we? Some kind of gymnasium?"

Doug startled awake, kicking Leo in the head.

Leo flared his arms and legs in the air in circling motions trying to regain his balance. He fell off the bench with a groan and sat on the floor rubbing his head.

Doug sat up, yawned, and stretched like he just awoke from a long winter's nap. After he finally regained control of his muscles, he scanned the room. "What the… who are all these people? There must be hundreds of them."

Leo was groggy rubbing his butt from his fall. "What the hell is going on? Where are we?"

Jacob stood up and stared at the ceiling. It looked as high as any indoor sports arena. The walls were light silver with a fluorescent green accenting the corners. The air had a bland hospital feeling to it; cold and sterile.

He looked at everybody sleeping on the benches around him.

"Was there an earthquake or something?"

Doug and Leo stood up and looked around. Other people started stirring and waking up around them. Doug stretched his arms again high into the air.

"All I can remember is driving to the movies."

Leo stretched both his arms and looked around.

"It was right after my pipes practice. Thank God I still got them. My father would kill me if I lost his old pipes."

Memories flashed in Jacob's head. He remembered things as he spoke.

"We were driving on Old Mountain road when," Jacob looked both boys straight in the eyes," there was that bright light."

Leo, still scratching himself, asked, "Then what happened?"

Doug pointed to one of the far walls with an unbelieving look on his face.

"Look, a message."

In big letters on a twenty-foot screen a message read:

Earth has been invaded by the Titans
The human race has been enslaved.
We are the Flarconeans. We offer you
refuge. We abducted you so your species
would not be totally destroyed.

People around the room started noticing the message and pointing towards it. They started crying and hugging the friends that were with them. Others passed out and fell to the floor.

Two guys jumped up on the benches and screamed. "Show yourselves."

One of them looked familiar to Jacob. He was wearing a North Rockland High School wrestling jacket.

Doug threw down the soft blue blanket. He stomped back and forth staring at the floor.

"It's a lie! It's a lie. I don't remember any bombs going off."Doug stopped and grabbed Jacob by the shoulder. Doug's eyebrows raised and his eyes started to glaze over. A feeling of desperation consumed him.

"Where's my family?"

Jacob grabbed Doug by both shoulders and stared right into his eyes.

"Of course it's a lie."

He grabbed Leo and Doug by their jackets and pulled the two boys closer.

"Take it easy guys. I can't see any doors here and I don't think we're close to home anymore."

Doug's mood changed. He chewed on his lip and his expression turned to a glare of anger. He grabbed Jacob's jacket by the chest as if he was ready to throw down.

"What are you saying? You don't want us to try to escape?"

Jacob grabbed Doug by the arm. Then he gently slapped him on the cheek with an open palm.

"Listen and concentrate."

Jacob backed away from Doug and looked at Leo.

"I'm just saying I don't want to be the first one shot like the ones who panic in all those movies. We've got to play this smart. Let's get some more info before we storm the castle."

Two hours after the humans first read the message, most of them had calmed down and started clicking into small groups. Some were still in a state of shock. They stood by themselves staring into space with blank looks on their faces.

Leo tapped Jacob on the shoulder and pointed towards the message board.

"Look Jacob, here comes somebody."

A tall, lanky alien emerged from under the message board. Jacob noticed as soon as he walked a few steps the door behind him disappeared.

He wore a long, white-hooded robe covering most of his face. What could be seen of his skin was the color of bronze. He walked to the center of the room right passed Jacob, who caught a warm, fatherly smile partially hidden behind the alien's hood and the refreshing scent of a sea breeze as he passed.

Jacob motioned to the others with his head.

"He must be seven feet tall."

The alien raised his arms above his head to get the attention of all the humans in the room. Then he lowered them slowly, pulling back his hood to reveal his smooth, bald head. He had human features except that his nose was a little wider than that of any human. His ears were the size of quarters and not too noticeable on his long face. When the alien looked at Jacob, he almost fell over backwards. The alien's eyes were a fluorescent orange and they glowed.

"I am called De Naris; and I am a Flarconean. Be assured, we are your friends." His voice was a soft tenor and he seemed to sing his words when he talked.

Doug and Leo pushed Jacob forward until he almost bumped into the tall alien. Jacob looked up and stared into the alien's eyes. He swallowed the fear that was clogging his throat.

"If you are our friends, then bring us back to our homes."

Everybody in the room mumbled their approval to the demand.

De Naris smiled proudly at Jacob's courage, and then looked

out to the crowd.

"Your homes no longer exist. Two Earth days have passed since the time you were rescued. If your families have survived the Titan invasion, they will live in the wild or a Titan slave camp."

A geeky-looking boy with thin-wired glasses across from Jacob shouted: "No! No, that's not true. We want to be with our families."

He rushed De Naris as if to tackle him to the ground.

De Naris gracefully stepped to one side. The boy stumbled forward and fell to the hard metallic floor and started blubbering incoherently.

De Naris knelt down on one knee and cupped the boy's head with his hand. The Flarconean looked into the boy's eyes and glared into his sadden soul. The boy took a deep breath and hung his head.

De Naris stood up.

"It's a strange confusing time for all of you. Try to focus on this thought: you are traveling through space at great speed to the planet Flarconea. You must decide when you get there whether to learn how to fight the Titans or settle on one of the planets the Flarconeans protect."

De Naris motioned towards the far wall where he first appeared. The dark crease appeared like a burning fuse. A door slid opened and more Flarconeans walked out.

De Naris swung his long arms over the top of the teenagers around him.

"My brothers and sisters will walk among you to help you understand and answer your questions."

The Flarconeans filtered through the crowd helping those in shock; their movements and mannerisms were calming. They put the people at ease with their tone of voice and they listened intently to incoherent babbling, nodding their heads with understanding. Whenever someone slowed down and took a breath, the Flarconean would give a gentle smile and take a deep breath. They handled themselves like wise old monks.

De Naris walked over to Jacob, prompting Doug to step aggressively between them.

"What gives you guys the right to take us from our planet?"

Still speaking in a soft tone of voice like a monk in church, De Naris said: "The Flarconeans are like galaxy police. We protect peaceful societies in this part of the galaxy. It was an act of kindness that we took you from your planet."

Spinning around to anyone who was listening, he continued.

"The Titans are ruthless beings. We lost one of our battle cruisers in our escape from Earth."

Jacob moved Doug out of his way and asked: "Why are you doing this?"

De Naris turned to Jacob and flashed what looked like a satisfied grin.

"Every life form is unique. The Titans will destroy every human they come in contact with sooner or later. We are trying to preserve the human species."

Leo looked at the kids standing around listening.

"Great, we're on the universe's endangered species list."

Jacob looked skeptically at the Flarconean.

"Will we ever get back to Earth?"

De Naris turned away from Jacob.

"We are hoping that some of you might return back to Earth to fight the Titans. Our resources are spread very thin and we need all the help we can get to fight the Titans."

Jacob grabbed De Naris's arm just above the elbow before he could move it. He released his grip and asked with a touch of sincerity in his voice: "What's happened to Earth?"

De Naris's face went solemn. He put his hand on Jacob's shoulder and looked out over the crowd.

"A large Titan armada invaded Earth's solar system at the same moment we abducted you. That's why we lost one battle cruiser in our escape."

De Naris paused and clasped his hands together like he was praying.

"The Titans will proceed to fire on Earth from a high orbit for a week, keeping a constant bombardment on the major cities around your world."

The group moved in closer around De Naris. Several started

crying on each other's shoulder.

De Naris continued: "Titan fighters will follow up and finish the destruction of the cities and the small communities that surround the cities. They show no mercy, accepting no surrender. "

A young girl with tear-filled blue eyes and curly long blond hair tugged on De Naris's robe.

"Why did they do it?" She broke down and started crying. An older girl let her rest her head on her shoulder.

De Naris sighed and looked back on the grieving group.

"The Titans will mine and farm the Earth, sucking up all the planet's resources for its galactic war effort."

De Naris turned back to face Jacob.

"After the second week, the Titans will build marble buildings and towers around your old communities, turning them into harvesting camps. Titan soldiers will search the countryside for human survivors to act as slave labor."

Jacob stood next to De Naris and looked at his friends with tears in their eyes. With a burst of pride and commitment he said to the group.

"I'll be going back to Earth."

Jacob turned to De Naris.

"Start training me now. The quicker I'm done, the sooner I get back to my family."

Doug shouted out: "Yea, teach us now!"

All the other kids started shouting and asking to be trained. De Naris waved his arms to calm down the group.

"We can start your education and training tomorrow.

Leo raised his hand to get the Flarconean's attention.

"Excuse me, Mr. Naris," Leo said, rubbing his stomach. "I'm getting a little hungry. How about a pizza?"

Leo tried to put his arm around De Naris's shoulder, but the alien was too tall.

He looked at Jacob and winked. He then looked back up at De Naris.

"I know this great little pizza place down on Main Street in Haverstraw."

Leo scratched his chin as if pondering the idea for the first time.

"I got it, you lend me one of those fancy little space shuttles you got and I'll be right back with a couple large pies with extra cheese."

The crowd of kids all chuckled away their tears while De Naris had a bewildered look on his face.

"I can get you some food if you are hungry."

De Naris gave the small group a gentle smile and walked back to the disappearing door. Ten minutes later, more Flarconeans walked in carrying bowls of fruit that they placed all around the room.

Four familiar faces walked up to Jacob with red apples stuffed in their mouths. Three of the boys were wearing North Rockland high-school wrestling jackets. The pretty brown-haired girl was wearing a short black leather jacket.

The shortest boy was five-and-a-half feet tall but had the physique of a professional body builder. He swallowed some apple and said to Jacob: "They're not Mackintosh but they'll do."

He reached out and shook hands with Jacob.

"I'm Jim Kelly." Gesturing with his apple to his two male companions, he said: "This is Phil Ruzzi and Matt Byrne."

The two boys were a little taller but not as thick as Jim Kelly. Jim put his arm around the girl in the leather jacket.

"This lovely thing is my girlfriend, Cathy Michelea."

Cathy pushed Jim away. She gave Jacob a big smile that almost melted his heart.

"I'm not his girlfriend, he's my boyfriend."

Jacob stammered a bit.

"Hi, I'm Jacob Skyler." Jacob looked at Cathy and thought she could be a toothpaste model with such a beautiful smile.

Jacob smiled at Jimmy: "You were All-County Wrestler last year for North Rockland. I know who you are."

Jim Kelly looked around the room.

"Have you noticed that everyone here is under twenty?"

Matt stepped up behind Jim.

"I heard one of the Flarconeans saying they wanted to make

sure they had young healthy humans to help keep our race going."

Leo walked up to Phil Ruzzi and shook his hand.

"You play trombone in band, don't you?"

Phil grabbed Leo's hand excitingly: "Yea, that's right. You play the sax."

Leo pointed to his case on the bench.

"I also play the bag pipes. I guess they couldn't pry the pipes out of my hands when they knocked me out."

Jim Kelly gave Leo a friendly slap on his shoulder.

"A piper with his pipes."

A smile spread out on Jim's face.

"Could you play us a little tune? My dad used to put on pipe music every Sunday in the house."

Leo lumbered over to his pipes. They were his only link to home now. He opened the black case as if it had turned into a sacred religious artifact. He took more care than usual strapping on the ancient instrument.

A small crowd gathered around him that kept growing. Leo stared at the ceiling. He could see his parents looking back at him with pride.

Leo stepped up onto the bench. Jacob noticed a change in Leo's face. His friend had a thousand-mile stare in his eyes; he had become really serous.

Leo straightened to his full height, throwing his shoulders back. He held back his tears and glared out into space just above the kids' heads. The assembled masses gathered even closer around him as he started playing a soft, haunting note that grew in intensity. All the humans easily recognized the familiar sadness of hope in the melody. Two sisters thirty feet away turned towards Leo and started singing.

"Amazing grace, how sweet the sound
To save a wretch like me.
I once was lost but now I'm found
Was blind but now I see"

The last line seemed to take on a whole new meaning. Everybody stopped eating and helped the two girls finish the song.

The rest of the day, the youths mingled and then ate again. The Flarconeans brought out more blankets and dimmed the lights.

The next morning, the humans were served a simple fruit breakfast while De Naris walked to the center of the room and addressed the whole group.

"I believe the Earth expression is *good morning*. I'm sorry about the sleeping arrangements but these transports were the only ones available. We will try and make you as comfortable as possible. It will take us thirty Earth days to reach Flarconea. So, anything you can think of that you need we will try to accommodate you."

De Naris slowly turned to a different section of the crowd.

"I'm going to tell you a little about Flarconea. The Flarconean race is a warrior race; a race whose main religion is a pledge. This is a pledge to protect our sector of the universe from tyranny; it is a tradition taught to us by an old ancient race called the Aderains."

De Naris waved his arms as the ceiling slowly slid open. A large door opened up to a window. Bright streaks of light wiping by the ship held everyone's attention.

De Naris went on as everyone seemed stunned at what was happening to them.

"The Aderain race died out a thousand years ago. Their world was destroyed by the Titans. When the Titans discovered stargate technology, they launched a major surprise attack on the planet of Aderain."

De Naris lowered his head and sighed.

"All life on the planet was destroyed. All that was left of the Aderain race were the warriors who were fighting some where else in the universe when their planet was destroyed. These survivors were invited to live on Flarconea."

De Naris looked back up at the stars.

"After a thousand years, all that was left of the race were traces of their blood in all Flarconeans; it was their special gift to us."

De Naris pointed out to the stars and said: "Aderain fighter space ships are scattered throughout the galaxy. Their whereabouts are only known by the religious caste of the Flarconeans."

Jacob shrugged his shoulders.

"Thousand-year-old fighters? They must be hunks of junks by now."

De Naris shook his head side to side.

"Far from it, Jacob Skyler."

Jacob smiled and looked at Doug.

"He remembered my name."

Doug whispered to Leo: "I wouldn't be happy about that."

De Naris turned and faced another part of the group. He looked at the humans and said louder and with a little pride: "For over a thousand years, nobody has been able to duplicate the Aderain fighters' fighting and flying superiority. They are the only spaceships capable of forming their own stargate."

De Naris walked through the group.

"Other civilizations make stargates that are miles wide and need a large amount of energy to form tackyon tunnels."

Jacob asked: "Why not build a whole bunch of these fighters?"

De Naris once again shook his head.

"The secret to the technology behind the Aderain fighters died with the planet. The only Aderain fighters in existence are the ones that weren't on the planet when it was destroyed."

Jim Kelly asked: "Why not dissect one of these fighters? See what makes them tick."

De Naris frowned at the strong little man.

"The Titans tried that a couple of times. The Aderain fighter blew itself up. The Aderain fighters are sanctioned beings; they are alive. They are a silicone life form. They would not allow themselves to be dissected."

As he listened, Jacob couldn't help but think that these Aderain space fighters were arrogant beings.

De Naris went on: "They are very mindful about who will be their captain. They have designed a deadly test to select beings just to be interviewed. If your race is deemed worthy, some of you will have the choice to take the test."

Jacob and Jim looked at each other and nodded.

De Naris raised a hand of caution.

"Remember this: for the last thousand years, only Flarconeans have been chosen as captains. You could pass the deadly test and still not be chosen as a captain of an Aderain space fighter."

After breakfast, twelve more Flarconeans entered the room. They broke the humans into small groups and led them in exercises. They did basic calisthenics, push-ups, sit-ups and jumping jacks. Then they ran around the outside of the room. Some of the youths didn't join in at first, but most of them eventually acquiesced as there wasn't much else to do.

The Flarconeans were curious about human culture. They initiated conversations and tried to learn everybody's name. De Naris and other Flarconeans kept everyone emotionally stable. Out of the blue, some people started to cry; they missed home and wondered if their parents had survived the onslaught of the Titans.

The Flarconeans had a way of calming them down. They kept the humans thinking of what was happening in the present rather than grieving about what happened in the past. They had a soothing voice and had a remarkable understanding of all human emotions except for one: revenge. To the humans, Titans were a disease to be exterminated. It became obvious that the group had become fanatical about killing all Titans.

Two weeks later, De Naris finished explaining how the Titans had invaded from the outer ring of the Milky Way galaxy towards the center of the Galaxy when Jacob turned to Jim, Cathy, Phil, Matt, Leo and Doug.

"We have to stop the Titans."

De Naris stopped talking and looked at Jacob. He put one of his hands on Jacob's shoulder.

"I find the human anger towards the Titans to be extreme. It is not your responsibility, Jacob Skyler. The Galactic Community will stop them."

Jacob shoved De Naris's hand off his shoulder.

"That may be so, De Naris, but I will have revenge."

De Naris tilted his head to one side and the skin above his eye wrinkled up.

"What do you mean by revenge?"

"I can't speak for all the rest, but I know I will hunt Titans for the rest of my life for what they did to the human race. Even after we kick them off our planet, they'll pay for what they did."

Scratching his chin, De Naris questioned Jacob.

"Why would you go after them when you know it would mean certain death for you eventually? You could live in peace if the Titans leave your sector."

Jacob stared De Naris straight in the eye.

"I couldn't live in peace knowing they were still out there. My life has only one purpose now: revenge."

The youths all slapped Jacob on the back in agreement. Jacob was buoyed by the fact that they all seemed to have the same hunger to go after the Titans.

"Most beings would rather live in peace," De Naris said.

For the rest of the month, the young human children exercised, learned and remembered their families. Jacob was sure they missed their lives on Earth. When the kids got to Flarconea, they all seemed to accept their fate and the Titan reality.

Chapter 5

When the Flarconean transports emerged out of warp space for the last time, they were half an AU away from the planet Flarconea. Jacob and his friends had formed a small clique with Jim Kelly and his friends during the month-long journey through space. They trained together, ate together, and discussed their plans for the future, even though they had no idea of knowing exactly what the future would hold.

The Flarconeans flashed an image of their home planet onto the big screen. Leo turned to Cathy, who was standing next to him.

"It looks more orange than blue."

A Flarconean hovered behind Leo, who looked almost hypnotized by the image.

"Every planet has its differences as well as similarities," said the alien.

Cathy turned to the Flarconean and put her hands on her hips.

"What other differences are there?"

The Flarconean smiled as memories of fluorescent, rolling landscapes tickled his brain. He thought of sunsets that magically changed the color of the land, as if a new sky artist had taken over.

"Flarconea has one yellow sun close to it, like your Earth does, but it also has a distant red sun that shines after the yellow one has set beyond the horizon. To describe it would only be an insult to it. You'll have to experience it to absorb it."

Tension and excitement gripped the air when the transports entered the Flarconean atmosphere. Most of the young humans were standing in awe or murmuring to each other at the wonder of the sight before them.

Jacob shook his head in disbelief. The great adventure they had embarked on had started to sink in.

"Traveling to another planet, meeting aliens; a month ago I was concerned with zits and getting caught by my parents for not doing my homework, but this is a whole new ball game."

Jim Kelly patted Jacob on the back.

"Be strong, Jacob. I have a feeling only the strong will survive."

When the transport was about to land, everyone took their seats. They all waited for the transport to touch down on the planet, but there was no shudder or sounds to signal contact. The Flarconean transport landing was unnoticeable. The whole procedure happened without the feeling of descent.

As the humans walked off the ramp of the transport, some of the humans stumbled.

"Something seems strange here." Matt turned to a Flarconean as he held onto a railing while walking down the ramp. "What's going on?"

The Flarconean grabbed Matt under his shoulders to help him down the ramp.

"The gravity is slightly different on our planet than it is on yours. So is our planet's magnetic field. Some of you might feel sick for the first day until we help your bodies adjust to the new environment."

Jim Kelly stepped up and asked: "How will you adjust our bodies?"

The Flarconean raised a hand to ease Jim's concern.

"Don't worry, Jim Kelly. We will not harm you in any way. We will introduce your body to a new type of anti-virus technology; a small-computerized machine. It will search out dysfunctions in your body and cure them. It can alter your DNA ever so slightly that you would never know it to look at you. Your body will be able to change and adapt to different environments on different planets. It's like having your immune system enhanced."

Leo raised his eyebrow as he looked at Cathy and Jimmy.

"Sounds good to me."

Cathy smiled at Leo: "That's easy for you to say, you need

improvement."

The hidden door opened up and everybody moved towards it. A long dark tunnel emerged before them with a glowing light at the end of it. Jacob walked off the transport, shielding his eyes with his forearm. The Flarconean sky was a bright fluorescent orange.

Jacob's eyes adjusted and he scanned the horizon from the top of the ramp.

"This planet is unreal. It's like we've landed on a fantasy planet out of the movies. The color of everything is enhanced. Everything's got a fluorescent type of glow to it".

An Aderain monk was waiting at the bottom of the ramp.

"Please get into the hover vehicles. We will take you to the Aderain monastery."

All three hundred humans piled into a dozen open hover vehicles. The long, roomy vehicles rode the breeze as graceful as birds towards a large tan building. The shape and texture of the building made it blend into the natural landscape. It was as if the building grew there.

One of the humans pointed to the horizon. "Look, two suns!"

All the humans turned and gasped at the incredible sight. The bright yellow sun was almost beyond the horizon. Its domination over the day was giving way to the smaller red sun higher in the sky.

The sky became a deep maroon color. Everything became two shades darker right before the eyes of the mesmerized humans. Even their skins seemed to tan instantly.

The Flarconean driver smiled at the humans' fascination and said: "Our red sun doesn't reflect light as sharply than our yellow sun."

The humans were flown a short distance to a brown building that looked like a plane hanger. They carefully climbed off the hover vehicles and gathered around the entrance to a large stone building. The inside of the building looked like a large auditorium: the ceilings were two stories high and domed; and the walls were white and gave off a soft light that always kept the room lit. In the middle of each wall was a large video screen with pictures depicting different parts of the planet.

Jacob noticed the Flarconeans using an elevator. He whispered to Jim Kelly.

"There is no upstairs here. The main part of the building must be underground."

The group was led to cots in a section of the room that looked like a makeshift military hospital. Once all of the humans had an assigned cot, the Aderain monks injected them with *nanites* and asked them to lie down and rest.

For the first hour, everybody felt sick. Cathy, Phil and Doug threw-up. Three Aderain monks tended to them, making them more comfortable.

The humans watched videos images of the planet for most of the day. Flarconea had birds, wild beasts, and fish, just like the Earth. Some of the creatures even resembled the species on Earth.

By the end of the day, all the youths felt better than ever. They started remembering things from their early childhood they hadn't thought about for years. They sat and thought about the special moments in their lives that made them the people they had become.

The next several days were full of self-analysis, personal revelations, and life realizations. The humans absorbed everything that had happened to them in their lives and accepted it. A new type of wisdom swept over them.

The Aderain monks gave the youths lectures on the Titans and other related subjects. The humans learned about the boundaries in the universe and galactic politics.

The group learned that the Flarconean civilization has existed for ten thousand years. The Flarconeans became a major military power a thousand years ago when the last of the Aderain race settled on Flarconea.

A month after their arrival, the humans gained more agility and easily adapted to the lighter gravity. They exercised harder than ever and saw quick results in their body growth. The Flarconeans explained it as a second puberty. The Flarconean gravity and the *nanites* worked on maintaining the human body and allow it to work as proficiently as possible.

They exercised intensely and practiced daily on how to kill Titans with assorted weapons. Their days were full of lectures on new technology and training on how to beat the Titans. Part of their learning was on concepts in mathematics, philosophy, military tactics, and galactic politics. They were all trained in healing and treating laser burns and other injuries.

For a year, all the humans trained hard. The first three months were filled with dangerous physical training. Three people broke their legs and two others broke their arms in the obstacle course. But the *nanites* repaired them within a week.

Six months into the program, two people tragically fell to their deaths during a week-long survival course. The course was optional and the humans didn't hold the Flarconeans responsible.

During the eleventh month, some of the humans developed telekinesis. Some of them were trained to use it as a tool, while others got the ability to pick up feelings or push certain emotions onto other people.

Those who didn't develop telekinesis powers pursued the secrets of the universe. Their reasoning capabilities and problem-solving abilities sharpened to staggering degrees. Any one of the humans could build great weapons out of almost anything.

The youths learned all the best fighting strategies to use against the Titans. All the humans watched great space and land battles on Flarconean monitors. The Titans showed no mercy and were not afraid to die in battle.

Eleven months after their arrival, all the humans had grown physically larger. Some had grown ten inches taller and put on a hundred pounds. Their weight gain showed no fat, it was all bone and muscle. They were in better shape than any professional athlete back on Earth.

One morning before a lesson, a Flarconean teacher of history mentioned how amazed he was about the mental and physical growth of the humans. The teacher, Dez Rroyer, was a Flarconean teacher of history with direct Aderain descent.

"You have adapted very well to the *nanites*; better than any species has ever adapted."

Dez Royer was old, even for a Flarconean, who often lived well beyond three centuries. He stared out into the skies and began to recollect like he often did.

"The Aderains were the greatest warriors in the Galactic Community a thousand years ago. They also grew and adapted well, like you. I remember the stories my grandfather used to tell me about them."

He turned to the class and pointed at them.

"You know, it wasn't the fact that they studied every military tactic in the galaxy that made the Aderains great fighters, it was the special space craft technology they inherited from another ancient race long since died out."

Dez Royer leaned back and folded his arms across his chest.

"They invented a space craft that had it's own personality. The ships would develop personalities as they were being built; the Aderains would raise them like children. They had a sense of self-preservation; they became, and still are after a thousand years, the deadliest weapons in the galaxy.

These great space fighters were taught basic philosophy and the ways of the sciences of the universe. They went through special military training learning about all types of warfare. They learned from their mistakes and how the truth could be different to each individual. They were taught all this as they were being put together."

Dez Royer stood and strutted around the room like a proud peacock.

"The Aderain fighter chooses one individual to be its captain. One Aderain fighter here on Flarconea currently has no captain. The Flarconean council has agreed with the high Aderain priest that out of the two hundred and ninety-eight humans, five will be aloud to take the Flarconean trial."

Jacob turned to the others and smiled. He had heard rumors of the great Aderain fighters; their deadly force could greatly help them take back Earth.

Jim Kelly stood up and shrugged his shoulders.

"What is this Flarconean trial?"

Dez Royer waved a finger at him.

"Good question Jim Kelly."

The teacher gripped two chairs and looked at the class of humans.

"It's a test of will and physical endurance. Many alien races have tried the Flarconean test but only Flarconeans have past it and earned the right to be interviewed by the Aderain fighters."

Dez Royer waved his long, thin arm towards Jim.

"The council has chosen you and four others for the honor of taking the test. The others are Jacob Skyler, Cathy Michela, Tim Romano and Mike Paquette."

The humans rushed around the selected and patted them on the back.

Dez Royer broke the excitement.

"Leave them alone. Gaze carefully at their faces and remember them. For this trial could kill them all."

Looking directly at the chosen, Dez Royer added: "The physical and mental endurance you will take will push you to your limits. You may all die."

Dez Royer looked to the rest of his class.

"We will leave the chosen ones alone to decide if they want this honor."

Cathy and Tim stood up in protest. Jimmy and Jacob grabbed their arms. Jimmy put one finger across his lips to get Cathy to stay quiet. Jimmy looked up at the two and whispered to them.

"Let's discuss this among ourselves first."

Dez Royer ushered the rest of the class out of the room. Jimmy closed the door behind the Flarconean and then turned to the group.

"Listen, we've got to come up with a strategy."

Cathy walked over to Jimmy.

"Dez Royer says no other alien race has ever completed the obstacle course before."

Jacob stared out the window.

"I've heard a lot of aliens have tried to get through the course and just survive."

Jimmy had his positive attitude in full tilt. He walked over to

Jacob and said.

"The course must favor Flarconeans."

Mike asked: "What's this obstacle course like?"

Jacob turned to the group.

"It's an all-night hike to the top of a mountain filled with Flarconean wild life and Flarconean booby traps. Alien races don't succeed because the Flarconeans don't want them to."

Jim looked at Jacob totally taken back by the suggestion that the Flarconeans could be corrupt.

"How could you say that? After all they've done for us."

Jacob put his hands up to calm Jimmy.

"Listen, I'm not saying they're evil and I'm thankful they saved our lives and taught us how to fight. They are honorable and noble people, but even the Flarconeans have a bad side."

Jacob looked at the bewildered looks from the others.

"Look, the Flarconeans are a major player in the Galactic Community because they control the Aderain fighters. Before the Aderains arrived a thousand years ago, the Flarconeans were the Switzerland of the Galactic Community. They didn't choose sides. I looked it up."

Jacob turned back to face the window. The building was surrounded by electric blue grass. The sun made the bushes a fluorescent orange and when the wind blew them, they would turn a dark green then back to orange again.

"That's why the Flarconeans are great warriors; they don't like to fight. Doesn't Sun Tsu say: "A good solider avoids the fight"?"

Jacob turned back to the group.

"The Flarconeans are blackmailing the Galactic Community by using the Aderain fighters sparingly. This way, they keep their power in the Galactic Community. They don't want to end the war or they will end their usefulness."

The group took in the logic slowly. No one said a word. Jimmy walked around the room.

"Alright listen, we have to get hold of one of these fighters. It's the only chance we have to save our families back on Earth."

Jacob stepped away from the window, grabbing Jim's shoulder.

"We should choose one person now to be interviewed by the fighter before we go through the test. We should work together to get one person through the course."

Mike pointed at Jim Kelly: "Jim should be the one."

Jim looked at Cathy: "Why me?"

Cathy walked over to Jim and wrapped her arms around him and gave him a big kiss on the cheek.

"Because you're the cutest man on the planet."

Tim smiled and put an arm on Jim's shoulder.

"Jim, you are a natural leader. You're the strongest."

Jimmy added: "I'm not the smartest. I don't know how to lead a revolution."

Jacob smiled at Jimmy.

"You do what you do best. You solve the problems we get into. We'll be with you and give you plenty of useless advice the whole time."

Mike added: "Most importantly, we choose you to lead us."

Jim smiled."Thanks guys, I accept. And I know I'll regret it."

Chapter 6

The next evening, just before the red sun dominated the sky, all the humans gathered around for the start of the test course. Dez Royer was given the honor of starting the humans off.

"The end of the test course is twenty miles west towards the setting sun on top of Mount Aderain."

Jacob noticed the mountaintop was surrounded by a strange glow in the sky. The yellow setting sun's last rays of light filtered through the Flarconean atmosphere, making the mountain explode in a rainbow of fluorescent colors.

The chosen humans stood in a line on a small platform in front of Dez Royer. Cathy turned away from the crowd and smiled at the sunset.

"What's going on, Jacob?"

Jacob leaned over towards Cathy and whispered: "It's some kind of religious ceremony for us."

Michael whispered to Jimmy: "I'm not converting to their religion."

Jacob chuckled to himself then whispered back to Michael: "They're not converting you, Mike. They're just wishing us luck and presenting each of us with a traditional Aderain sword."

Five Aderain monks walked in front of each chosen human and bowed. They gracefully laid a beautiful, shiny sword across their forearms and presented them to the humans.

They were long double-edged swords with ancient Aderain inscriptions artistically crafted in the tan foot-long handle. The three-and-a-half foot long blade was the color of a blue sky on Earth.

Dez Royer walked past the chosen and explained the swords to the crowd of humans.

"The metal from these blades come from the Aderain home planet. Legend has it that the sword can absorb light and give a warrior a powerful aura of protection."

Dez Royer turned back to the chosen.

"These swords will be the only weapons you will have to defend yourselves."

The chosen humans raised their swords high into the air. The group of young humans roared with pride.

Leo began to play a soft lament on his pipes called Skyler Boat Song. It was a slow, uplifting tune that caused all the humans to reflect on the moment. It foreshadowed the long, dangerous perils the chosen were about to undertake and reminded everyone of what was at stake.

Jacob and the rest of the group put the swords in their sheaths and strapped them to their backs. They walked off the platform towards the stone trail, adjusting what little gear they had. They shook hands with Dez Royer and started down the path. The crowd of humans cheered again as the chosen started the test.

The small group started with a brisk jog. A mile down the path, the stone disappeared and the path became nothing more than an overgrown footpath.

Flarconean shrubbery, mostly large leafed bushes with thick branches, practically erased the path.

As the path got narrower, the group formed a single line. Jacob was at the front, followed by Cathy, Jimmy, Timmy and Mike. They stopped jogging but kept on walking at a fast clip.

Jimmy looked up at Cathy's back a few yards in front of him.

"Cathy, tell them what you found out about the wildlife we might encounter."

Cathy took a moment to catch her breath and think, but never slowed her pace.

"A deadly cat-like animal roams the wilderness that can weigh up to a hundred and fifty pounds. It lives in these mountains and it's called a swoota. It has a slender smooth body which gives it quick mobility through the underbrush. It's got dark green leathery skin and it's said to have lightning speed. From the pictures I saw, it looks like a prehistoric panther."

Making a motion with her hand like a cat scratching the thin air, Cathy said: "It has long, sharp claws to tear through the bush and its prey. It's said that if you encounter a swoota you should keep absolutely still and it won't attack."

Jacob stopped and looked at his friends and smiled.

"Patience is a time to plan. That's a Flarconean virtue."

The brush started getting thicker. Vines four inches thick blocked parts of the path, prompting Jacob cut a path open by slashing the vines with his Aderain sword.

Jimmy turned to Jacob.

"Don't let yourself get worn out slicing through the brush Jacob. Let me take a turn."

Cathy stopped in her tracks and grabbed Jim by the shoulders.

"Stay where you are, Jimmy. You have to store all your strength for the end of the test."

Mike jogged to the front of the line.

"I'll chop for a while guys."

The brush had reached a height of twenty feet on either side of them. The yellow sulfur moon reflected some strange yellowish glow into the top of the brush, but the visibility wasn't more than a few yards.

The group came upon a fork in the path and they all stopped for a breather. Jimmy sat on a thick vine and looked at the group.

"Anybody have any suggestions?"

Jacob stepped up.

"The Flarconeans aren't the type to try to trick us. They might use booby traps and wild animals, but not a direct deception. The path is a chance to turn away without losing face."

Timmy was kneeling and wiping the sweat from his brow.

"What do you mean?"

Jacob pointed to the path bearing left, leading away from the top of the mountain.

"You can turn away from the mountain now and say you got

lost. The perils ahead are lethal. Here's a chance to turn away without losing face." Nobody said a word. They gathered themselves back up to their feet and headed down the path towards the mountain.

The path got steeper and became more of a climb than a hike, but the chosen kept the pace up. In the distance, a sinister snarl echoed down the valley.

Mike looked up quickly with his eyes wide open. Timmy casually commented.

"Let me guess. The howl of the swoota sounds just like that."

Cathy looked at Jimmy.

"Sounds just like that on the video footage. Better let me lead for a while. I think I might be able to spot its trail."

Two hours into their journey, the trail got very rough. Towering sharp rocks bordered the trail and the vines reached across from rock to rock, blocking out all moonlight. The *nanites* helped sharpen their vision to the darkened path.

They came to a rock wall with two steps cut into the rock. Cathy turned to Jacob.

"I don't get it. What's with the steps?"

Jacob walked up to the wall and placed a foot on a small ledge and reached up for a handhold on a rock.

"I guess the next part of the journey requires a bit of climbing."

The group climbed for an hour. Each step was a calculation of weight and balance. They climbed over a hundred feet of cliff and ledges before reaching the last plateau.

When Jacob made it to the top he reached for the sword strapped to his back. He scanned the area and saw nothing, but still stayed at a ready position.

"Hurry up, guys. I can sense something's not right here."

Everything was quiet. The small scurrying sounds Jacob heard had stopped and the strange squeaking of the local chee-chee bird had disappeared.

Cathy and Jimmy climbed up and moved close to Jacob, drawing their swords. They were on an old road that had become overgrown. Jimmy directed his sword down the path.

"I heard something down this way."

A swoota leaped from the darkness over the three humans and dived into Timmy's chest as he was climbing onto the road from the edge of the cliff.

The swoota sunk his teeth into Timmy's neck as both of them fell over the edge of the cliff. Timmy never had the chance to yell.

Cathy scurried to the edge of the cliff and looked down.

"Timmy, Timmy!"

Mike quickly climbed up over the edge of the cliff and rolled onto the road.

Another noise came from the brush. The four backed up against each other, staring out into the darkness.

Another swoota poked his head out of the darkness right in front of Mike. Mike caught the animal's eye right away and both went into a trance, eyes locked together.

"Go on, you guys, I'll hold him off." Mike's voice had a little tremble in it but his eyes never left the cat.

Jimmy turned to face the creature.

"No, Mike, we won't leave you alone." Jimmy moved towards the cat with his sword in his hand. The closer Jimmy moved towards the cat the louder the deep throat growl of the wild beast.

Mike took in a deep breath and let it out slowly. He regained his composure and calmly responded.

"Stop moving, Jim. Don't worry about me. We're running out of time. You still have a long way and you're running out of moonlight."

Cathy started down the path.

"Don't worry, Mike. In about five or ten minutes the swoota will lie down and take a nap."

Jacob patted Jimmy on the back. He's not just doing this for you, Jim. He's doing it for his sister."

Jacob, Jimmy and Cathy moved on, sure in the knowledge that Mike could handle it. Jacob retook the lead down the path. They walked and climbed for another hour. Near another peak in the road, Jacob spotted a trap.

"Nobody move! There's an avalanche waiting to happen. It's

just waiting for one of us to trip the switch."

Jimmy tried to look around Jacob.

"I don't see it."

Jacob pointed up towards the right.

"There, up that slope; the rocks that are piled up go into that cave."

Jacob slowly moved his finger down the slope at a pile of rocks.

"See this line of rocks. Something is hidden behind those rocks. They trail down the slope to that large bush up ahead."

Jimmy looked at Jacob.

"Anything in the rule book about going off the trail?"

Cathy shrugged her shoulders. Jacob smiled and said:

"Not in the one that I didn't get."

Jacob hacked a small path around the trap away from the rock pile. When they got back on the trail they walked and climbed another hundred yards to reach the very top of the mountain. The top was fifty feet in diameter with a cavern at the center of it.

Cathy put her hand on Jimmy's shoulder.

"All this to reach a hole in the ground."

The two men smiled and scanned the area. Jimmy stretched and pointed to the far side of the cavern.

"Something is moving in the brush."

A red blast of light shot across the hole and blasted Jimmy square in the chest. The shot knocked him off his feet. Once he hit the ground, he slid another two yards on his back with smoke coming from his chest.

Jacob and Cathy dove for cover in different directions on the ground.

Five more shots blasted the rocky terrain around them. They crawled on their stomachs back to Jimmy. Cathy reached him first.

"He's alive!"

Jacob crawled up closer and looked at Jimmy's chest. The blood was dark and flowing. The wound was fatal. Jimmy coughed twice and his leg kept twitching.

He smiled at Cathy and said: "Not for long babe."

Cathy cradled his head and started yelling and cursing at the person firing at them.

Jimmy looked at Jacob with glassy eyes.

"I guess we know why no other alien race has made it all the way through the course."

Jacob shook his head in bewilderment: "Those bastards will pay, Jimmy. I swear it."

Jimmy reached up for Jacob's hand.

"Go on Jacob. It's up to you."

Jacob looked at Cathy, then back at Jimmy.

"Why me?"

Jimmy coughed and chuckled a little bit.

"Ask her, go ahead and ask Cathy why."

Jacob stared at Cathy, whose eyes watered up and bottom lip trembled.

"I won't leave him."

Jacob looked at the ground then at both of his comrades. He flashed a look towards the direction of his enemy.

"I will kill the bastard who did this to you, Jimmy."

Jimmy grimaced with the pain as he leaned toward Jacob.

"First the fighter, Jacob. First the fighter."

Jacob bit his lip then whispered to Cathy: "Give me thirty seconds, and then cause a distraction."

Jacob slid back down the hill and disappeared out of Cathy's sight. Five more shots peppered the ground around Cathy and Jimmy.

Cathy reached for a vine lying next to her. She chopped off a foot and flung it into the brush twenty feet towards her right.

The killer fired three more random shots into the brush, in the direction of the vine Cathy threw.

Jacob scurried on his stomach up to the edge of the cavern. He swung his legs over the edge and started climbing down. He reached blindly with his feet, finding small footholds. He was able to grab onto some vines that had grown into the cavern.

The attacker spotted Jacob as he disappeared over the edge into the darkness of the cavern.

The shadowed alien figure was exposed when he ran up to the

edge of the cavern and shot several blasts down at Jacob.

Jacob curled himself into a ball. He was nearly hit twice before a red laser from below ricocheted off the walls, up the cavern, and blasted the attacker dead on in the head.

Jacob looked down and yelled: "Thanks, nice shot."

A soft, white glow pulsed thirty feet down below him. Jacob proceeded to climb down. He jumped the last five feet to the ground.

"Greetings, earthman. I am Demock. I'm glad you have survived the test." The Aderain fighter spoke to Jacob slowly with a Flarconean accent.

Jacob gazed at the Aderain fighter then started to walk around it. He stepped slightly back from the alien spacecraft and took a good look at it. It was forty feet long and fifteen feet wide. The surface was an off-white and smooth. The walls of the ship looked three-dimensional to Jacob.

"Glad I survived the test? The test is rigged for Flarconeans to win only. I bet they don't fire on Flarconean warriors who take the test."

"Yes, you're right, human. When the Flarconean fired down the hole, he hit me. I defended myself and fired back."

Jacob smiled to himself, amused that he was having a conversation with an alien spacecraft.

Demock continued: "The test was not my idea or even an Aderain idea. It was the Flarconean government's idea."

Jacob stopped walking around the fighter and shook his head. He raised a finger as if he was about to lay into Demock. Then Demock said: "I have one question for you, human."

Jacob dropped his finger and took a deep breath. "Go ahead, give it your best shot."

Demock glowed brighter. "Why do you want to fight the Titans?"

Jacob rubbed his freshly-grown beard and thought. He started to walk around Demock again.

"Love," he said. "Love of my planet and my people."

The backside of the Aderain fighter opened up with a metallic cha-chung. A big section of the back lowered itself like a drawbridge. Jacob walked up the white glowing ramp into the craft. The door slowly closed as Jacob reached the top of the ramp.

Demock's voice was soft and encouraging.

"Walk to the front of the ship, Jacob Skyler. Take a seat in your new command chair."

Jacob smiled.

"I did it? That was it? I'm your new captain? That was easy."

"I've been watching the humans since they arrived, Jacob Skyler. Let's just say that was the last question of your interview."

Jacob walked around the craft, slowly taking in the smooth roundness of this killing machine. The back ten feet of the ship was a small cargo bay with white walls that glowed.

Jacob mumbled: "Twenty people could fit in here." A door slid open to the bridge of Demock. A large black chair stood at the center of the room like an island of refuge from the sea of technology around it. The chair was surrounded by a semicircle of panels full of colorful buttons, screens, and flashing lights.

Demock's voice was still quite inviting.

"Please, Jacob Skyler, take a seat and relax."

Jacob walked down a catwalk that ran around the outside of the room and extended to the chair. The chair looked fluffy and comfortable. Jacob noticed the soft but firm touch of the material of the chair as he sat down. The chair seemed to absorb around his body.

"Wow, nice chair."

Demock seemed pleased with Jacob's response.

"It adapts to the captain's body. It listens to your body and gives it what it wants."

Jacob said: "It hears me loud and clear."

Jacob sat up and said: "I have to go get my friends. They're not safe. The Flarconeans are going to kill them."

Demock responded assuredly.

"I can take care of that, Jacob Skyler. I am in touch with the Aderain religious leaders. They hold a different view of the test than the Flarconean government. They will pick up your friends in the jungle and protect the humans at the training complex."

Jacob relaxed back into the chair.

"Thank you, Demock. You are kind."

Demock quickly added: "And dangerous."

Jacob smiled.

"Alright Demock, why don't you show me what you're made of. Let's go for a ride."

Demock's mood seemed to have lightened; he seemed pleased with himself.

"Your wish is my command, captain."

The outside of the fighter started spinning to the right, revolving slowly at first, then faster. Jacob's position in the chair never changed. The space fighter looked like a child's toy top spinning in reverse. As the ship gained momentum, the front of the Aderain fighter tilted straight up. In the blink of an eye, the Aderain fighter shot out of the mountain, breaking the sound barrier a half-mile outside the mouth of the cavern. Demock streaked up into the Flarconean night sky.

Jacob couldn't believe his eyes. He gripped the chair tightly until his knuckles were as white as the interior of the ship.

Demock sensed Jacob's stress.

"Is everything all right, Jacob Skyler? Your heart rate has picked up since lift off."

Jacob felt no "G" forces, but the thought of being catapulted out of the atmosphere made him feel a little uneasy.

"Nothing a barf bag can't handle."

Jacob took in slow, deep breaths through his nose and was soon relaxed as they streaked by Flarconea's yellow moon.

The inner wall of the Aderain fighter turned transparent. Jacob could see the space all around him. It was as if the walls had fallen away from the ship. A sense of total freedom overwhelmed Jacob.

"This is truly amazing and scary; to be able to fly among the stars."

Jacob shook his head and a small smile appeared on his face.

"How do you feel, Jacob? Demock sounded very worried. "Can you handle this?"

Jacob almost laughed when he responded.

"Demock, you are capable of walking in the Heavens but instead you keep your head buried in the sands of Flarconea, like an ostrich."

Demock's voice was solemn.

"I've seen a lot of death out in space, Jacob Skyler. It's been a while since I've been able to notice any beauty or love."

Jacob sighed and ran his hand through his hair.

"I guess it goes with the job. Ignorance is a bliss I no longer have. I'll have to concentrate more on what's happening now, then thinking about what was or what will be."

Jacob looked back at the sharp image of the yellow moon and shook his head in disbelief.

"Why Demock? Why me? It couldn't have been just that one question."

Demock flew further away from the planet and returned the color back to the walls of the ship, except for directly in front of Jacob.

"I've watched the invasion of your planet. Humans fought even though they had no chance of winning. I've watched you train here on Flarconea. Your spirit suits me."

Jacob smiled and pushed himself deep into the chair again.

Demock interrupted with a report.

"Jacob, I have received a transmission from a fellow Aderain fighter. He's flying escort for three Galactic Community transports and four Galactic Cruisers. They're on their way to the planet Debarria. He needs some assistance in fighting off a Titan ambush."

Something gnawed at Jacob's stomach. He gripped the chair with his hands and focused his thoughts.

"Fight Titans, this is the moment I've been waiting for. Lets go."

A tunnel of light shot out in front of the Aderain fighter like a headlight of a car. It grew in diameter and started circling at an incredible speed. The fighter pushed forward and disappeared into the light. The light exploded then closed in on itself and was gone.

Jacob blinked and it was all over. He was surrounded now by a different set of stars.

"Demock, can other space ships make their own stargate?"

Demock turned towards the galactic space ships.

"Not yet, other space ships have to use a stargate."

In front of him, Jacob could see four Galactic Cruisers had squared off around the three transports. Five Titan fighters dived at the galactic ships then broke away. The Aderain fighter went after the five Titan fighters. The craft fired six red laser blasts at the last Titan fighter that broke away from the transport ships. The fighter exploded into a bright fireball. The rest of the Titan fighters led the Aderain fighter away from the rest of the galactic ships.

Two more squads of Titan fighters swooped down on the galactic ships. They flew circles around the Galactic Cruisers like a swarm of bees, peppering the transports with a dozen or more red laser blasts.

Jacob sat up in his chair. His heart was pounding in his chest.

"Where are those fighters coming from?"

Demock calmly responded.

"A Titan battleship is hiding one AU away. It's near the fifth planet, with two Titan cruisers circling it."

Jacob wiggled into the comfortable chair and chewed on his bottom lip.

"Alright Demock, let's go for the battleship."Demock didn't move.

"What about protecting the Galactic Cruisers and transports?"

Jacob focused on the fight going on around him. He broke out of his concentration with a deep breath.

"Once we engage the battleship, the fighters will break off their attack to defend it. Relay the message to your Aderain fighter friend, target the Titan battleship."

Demock took control of the navigation. He joined the other Aderain fighter in a cat-and-mouse aerial aerobatics routine heading towards the battleship. The two Aderain fighters made their approach on the Titan battleship from behind the planet. They hugged the planet until the planet was directly behind them and the battleship was directly above them.

The two Aderain fighters darted away from the planet directly towards the battleship. Jacob swallowed the lump in his throat.

"Those Titan battleships are really big."

The Titan battleship was a massive four-mile cylindrical space vessel. A quarter mile in diameter, it could shoot out hundreds of Titan fighters at either end.

The Aderain fighters banked around back towards the battleship. They each shot one white laser blast at the belly of Titan battleship. The battleship's electronic field absorbed most of the power of the shot.

The two Aderain fighters took on a fierce amount of laser fire as they darted away from the battleship. They dodged back and forth avoiding most of the bombardment.

The Aderain fighters swooped back around and fired two more white laser blasts at the midsection of the battleship. Demock's shot was absorbed by the shields again. The Titan battleship's electrical system flickered off and on a half a dozen times.

The other Aderain fighter's shot was blocked by one of the cruisers. It sacrificed itself for the battleship. The Titan cruiser took the shot broadside and went dark spinning out of control.

More Titan fighters emerged from the battleship.

Jacob started hyperventilating. He sat on the edge of his chair.

"Demock, can you form a stargate right in the battleship's path?"Demock was puzzled and answered.

"Yes, but its risky. We could collide with the battleship."

Jacob rubbed his hands together.

"We have to get that battleship somewhere else."

After a moment of silence, Demock responded more cheerfully.

"Jacob Skyler, that is a good strategy. I am impressed."

Demock spun himself around and headed straight for the Titan battleship, stopping dead a mile away from it. Demock spit out his spinning light of tackyon particles right in the battleship's path.

Two heartbeats after the Titan war machine entered the stargate, Jacob stood up.

"Shut the gate now."

The stargate blasted shut. A quarter of the colossal battleship cut off like a hot knife through butter. Explosions on the open decks worked themselves back through the ship.

Titan fighters by the dozens started spitting out of the hanger bays precariously at the far end. Several fighters collided and exploded in their rush to escape the sinking ship.

A large explosion in the center of the ship shattered the battleship into eight massive chunks. They spun aimlessly away from each other.

The two Titan cruisers and twenty-four fighters headed out of the solar system. Three of the Galactic Cruisers pursued them.

"Jacob you have an incoming call from Captain Rye Ter of the Galactic Community force."

Jacob raised his hand up. "Hold that call a second Demock."

Jacob took a deep reality breath and rubbed his head in the palm of his hands. He looked back up and took another deep breath. "Ok Demock put him through."

The image of a alien with a bear's head and the body of a human appeared in front of Jacob. He recognized the alien from the Flarconean archives as a Debarrian. "I am Captain Rye Ter of the Cenor cruiser. Captain are you and your fighter all right?"

Jacob sat up straight in his chair. "I am Jacob Skyler of Earth. I am a human being."

Surprised, the Debarrian smiled with his sharp teeth and bobbed his bear head back and forth.

"A human being in a Aderain fighter. I don't understand, but I am grateful. If there is anything I can do for you, Jacob Skyler of Earth, please contact the Galactic Government building on Senta. Ask for me, Captain Rye Ter of Debarria. I am at your disposal."

Jacob cleared his throat. "As a matter of fact, captain, I could use your transports once you empty them."

The captain stopped smiling and got defensive. "What for?"

Jacob explained, "Now that a human has passed the Flarconean test and is captain of an Aderain fighter, I believe the rest of the human lives on Flarconea are in danger."

Captain Rye Ter answered back thoughtfully, "Very interesting Jacob Skyler. I believe the Galactic Community would favor the humans as allies. I also believe they would like to do a favor for a captain of an Aderain fighter. Once we unload our cargo I will patrician my superiors to send you the assistance you seek."

Chapter 7

Demock cut through the Flarconean atmosphere and headed straight for the Aderain monastery. "Jacob the Aderain monks inform me all the humans have taken up refuse at the monastery. A group of Flarconean citizens, who think a human doesn't deserve the privilege to captain an Aderain fighter, have surrounded the monastery. The humans are under the protection of the Aderain monks."

It was an ugly day around the monastery on the southern continent. Rain clouds had blocked the yellow sun from lighting up the usual colorful landscape. The walls of the Aderain monastery were a drab gray instead of the usual inviting tan. The humans inside didn't seem to mind. They looked out the windows searching the sky for Jacob Skyler's return.

Demock hovered over the monastery slowly before descending into the courtyard. Jacob could see from his see through walls that a large crowd of Flarconean civilians had started to gather around the outside the walls of the monastery.

Demock landed softly in the monastery courtyard. He lowered the back door and Jacob walked out with a soft rain tickling the smile on his face.

Doug ran towards Jacob splashing carelessly through puddles. He grabbed Jacob's shoulders and gave him a slight shake.

"You did it man. You got the fighter. The first alien ever to be accepted by an Aderain fighter."

Jacob shrugged his shoulders. "No big deal, Doug. I was in the right place at the right time and I did what I had to do."

Doug smiled at the small group starting to surround Jacob. "Yea right, Demock kept in constant contact with the Aderain monks during the battle with the Titans. He transmitted the space battle to the monastery for all of us to watch."

Jacob walked towards the rest of the group out of the rain. They had gathered under a jade stone overhang that extended from one of the Aderain temples. It was large enough to cover all three hundred humans. Jacob turned to them and raised his arms up with his palms out calming them down. "The Flarconeans rigged all the tests so only Flarconeans would be the ones to past the test. They were cheating."

The crowd of humans started yelling and cursing the Flarconeans. Doug was standing next to Jacob when he pointed to Cathy a few feet away behind Phil Ruzzi. "Yea we know Jacob. Cathy told us what happened at the mouth of the cavern."

Jacob pushed towards Cathy grabbing her arm. "Cathy how's Jim? Is he all right?"

Cathy looked at the ground and rubbed her nose with a sniffle. She slowly lifted her head up and cleared her throat. She looked up towards the sudden cloudburst that poured over the compound. She looked Jacob right in the eyes. The raindrops ran down her face like tears. "Jim's dead Jacob."

She drew in a deep breath and looked back up at the clouds. "He died moments after you went down the cavern. He smiled and at me and said that we did it, then he closed his eyes and died."

Jacob wrapped his arms around Cathy and hugged her for a quick moment. He whispered to her softly. "I'm so sorry Cathy. I should have known. I should have stopped it from happening."

Cathy pushed Jacob back at arms length and stared at him fiercely. "His dying wasn't your fault Jacob Skyler. There was no way of telling the Flarconeans would stoop so low."

Cathy shook off her hostility and wiped the rain off her face. She squeaked out a small smile. "No Jacob, Jim Kelly died for the cause. He knew the risk and thought it was worth his life to save the human race. I think we all feel that way now."

Jacob looked at the crowd. "How much danger are we in now, here, in this monastery?"

Matt walked up to Jacob from the crowd and put his hand on his shoulder. "We're all safe for now, as long as we stay in here. The Flarconeans have too much respect for the Aderain religious cast to break in to their monastery. But I'm afraid that the idea of losing control over the Aderain fighters will make them do things they never would have thought of doing before."

Jacob climbed on a bench so everyone could see him. He looked at the crowd that surrounded him. "Listen, we are getting out of here tomorrow at day break. My first mission with Demock has proven to be beneficial. Two transport ships donated from the Galactic Community will be in orbit in twelve hours."

The crowd all mumbled and Leo shouted out. "Where are we going now?"

Jacob looked at Leo and smiled. He looked back at the crowd. "We're going home." The crowd cheered and everyone started hugging each other. Cathy tapped Jacob on the shoulder. "What do we do when we get there?"

Jacob's smiled disappeared and his look became intense. He looked back out at the crowd and yelled, "We will organize the surviving humans left on Earth then kill every Titan on the planet."

The crowd roared with enthusiasm throwing their fist up in the air. Matt tapped Jacob on the other shoulder and whispered in his ear.

"Of course Jacob, but Cathy means how do we kill all the Titans? How do we take back Earth?"

A tall shadowed figure walked away from one of the dark green pillars that were holding up the pavilion. "Maybe I can help you. I am called Ces Ision a humble Aderain monk."

Jacob smiled at the older Flarconean and waved him to step closer. Ces Ision threw back his hood revealing his bald Flarconean head and talked to the whole crowd. "When the Titans enslave a planet the first thing they do is set up a communication jamming station. It's able to block out all signals around the planet. It is also the center of their communications. I would suggest this be your first target."

Jacob looked to his comrades and smiled. "Thank you Ces Ision. I think we should talk more before it's time for us to leave."

Ces Ision put his hood back up and turned away from the crowd. "I think we should talk more too, but I will insist we talk inside out of the rain and only to a few of you. The few can communicate the information to the rest."

Mike, Cathy, Doug and Leo followed Jacob inside one of the small Aderain temples. The rest of the crowd waited anxiously while the others talked.

Matt stepped up on the bench and spoke to the crowd. "I think you would agree we need someone to lead us; someone to make the tough decisions and keep the main objective through the war with the Titans."

Phil stepped up on the bench next to Matt. "Someone with a military mind and can formulate a strategy to beat the Titans."

The crowd started grumbling, until someone in the crowd shouted, "Jacob Skyler is our leader." The crowd shouted out in agreement. Phil turned to Matt and smiled. Phil raised his arms to quiet the crowd. "Lets all give him the bad news when he comes out."

Two hours went by before the group came back out side from talking with the Aderain monk. Jacob raised his hands to get the crowds attention. "Ces Ision has given us much information about the way Titans enslave a planet. We will walk among you and tell you what we've learned. We will have to plan our strategy on our way back to Earth, I'm afraid there's no time now to do it."

Jacob motioned to Cathy, Leo and Doug to spread out among the crowd. "We will tell you what we have learned. I want everyone to form into small groups and brainstorm some strategy."

Matt and Phil walked up on either side of Jacob and helped him up stand up on a bench seat. Matt smiled and looked out into the group.

"And now for the bad news, Jacob."

Jacob looked down at Matt in bewilderment. Phil was on the other side of Jacob, patting him on the back then swept his arm towards the crowd.

"We have decided that Jacob Skyler should lead us in our fight to take back Earth."

Jacob looked at Phil and growled under his breath. Matt started patting Jacob on the back and Jacob shot the same expression at him. The crowd started chanting, "Jacob, Jacob, Jacob..."

Jacob looked at the crowd of friends and a shiver went down his back. He thought to himself, I'm supposed to tell them how to die. This is no honor it's a curse.

Jacob nodded in agreement. He walked into the crowd reluctantly. He was warmly greeted with smiles and pats on his back.

A few hours later two stolen Titan transports sent by the Galactic Community arrived in orbit around Flarconea. Tension in the crowd outside the monastery began to flare up. Flarconean police arrived before the Flarconean civilians committed any action. They surrounded the monastery keeping the crowd away from the walls.

The two Titan transports dropped out of the sky from a high altitude. They landed in the Aderain monastery like two sky elevators. The dark green drab coloring of the transports was a contrast to the rich fluorescent coloring of the Flarconean planet, even on a rainy day. The insect looking space ship had a long triangular head. It straddled a long rectangular cargo box large enough for all the humans to fit in.

The Flarconeans outside the monastery began shouting at the humans. They had infected their planet with Titan ships. They should all leave now and without the Aderain fighter.

Two Debarrians disembarked from each Titan transport. They had the head and fur of a bear but their bodies were the same shape as humans. They were two feet taller than any human on the planet.

Jacob walked up to greet them. "I'm Jacob Skyler from Earth."

The Debarrians bowed and the shorter one of the two stepped forward. "I am Zailback and this is Orge. We are your servants Jacob Skyler from Earth. We will fly the Titan transports to Earth for you and be your voice to the Galactic Community."

Jacob smiled and put his arm around Doug and Cathy. "Will you teach my people how to fly a Titan transport?"

Zailback bowed politely. "We will gladly teach humans how to fly a Titan transport."

Jacob put a hand on Leo and Cathy's shoulders. Then stood up straight at attention. "You two have volunteered, like I did, to take control of the transports. The people in your transport are your responsibility. Make up squads of five amongst them. That should give each of you around fourteen to fifteen squads a piece. Pick out three people to control five squads a piece, they'll be your captains."

Jacob slapped each of them softly on the cheek. "You guys are now Majors and I'm the general. Will start off with that as a command structure. Once we get to Earth every body becomes a captain. They will have to recruit their squads from survivors." Jacob paused, scratched his chin and added, "Any questions? Or better yet. Any suggestions?"

Leo and Cathy clicked their heels together and saluted Jacob. They turned and started loading every one up in the two transports. Jacob climbed back in Demock and all three ships took off immediately to the shouts of the Flarconeans protesters.

Once in orbit Jacob asked Demock, "Demock can you form a stargate large enough to fit yourself and two transports through?"

The walls of the spacecraft rippled to a cooler shade of white. "Yes Jacob Skyler, I can transport up to five ships at once as long as it's not as big as a battleship."

Jacob sat back in his comfortable chair and watched the two transports in front of him. "Let's get started Demock. Inform the other transports of your stargate coordinates then form your stargate. We are heading towards Earth."

Demock pulled in front of the two transports and projected his tackyon particles forming a stargate. The two transports and the Aderain fighter started their three-month journey to Earth.

During the trip, the humans took turns learning the ins and outs of the Titan transports. Jacob and his officers would have daily meetings by view screen. Once a week they would come out of hyper-space and have a face to face meeting while Demock recharged himself. Demock would attach himself to one transport and shuttle the officers to the other transport to discuss the main strategy.

After a month of discussing their options they all agreed with Jacob's plan. Jacob paced back and forth scratching his chin in a conference room on Leo's transport.

"We land on Earth and split up. We meet near the landing sight once a month. If we send a messenger, we use code name 'Jim' with the response 'Kelly'."

Phil looked at Mike with a sense of bewilderment. Phil reached up and put his hand on Jacob's arm stopping him from pacing.

"You all right, man? You don't seem yourself."

Jacob looked at Phil like his father use to look at him before he would punish him. "Hey I got the weight of the world on my shoulders and all our lives at stake. I'm likely to twitch now and again. You'll have to cover me when I do."

Jacob relaxed his arms at his side and looked at the ceiling. "I want you guys to start thinking about something. You are in a position now where you can't always be your fun loving selves. You will be giving orders that will be putting people in harms way. You might have to sacrifice the few to save the many. Figure out how you will handle it because you are going to have to tell your officers how to handle it." Jacob smiled at his officers. "Then you can let me know."

Jacob looked around the room. Cathy stood in the corner biting her lip, concerned over Jacob's tenseness. Matt and Doug sat across from Phil and Mike at a clear glass Titan table. They were all staring at Jacob.

Jacob walked around the room and put his hands on Phil and Mike's shoulders. "Listen, we have to know we will take back Earth as a fact. To the survivors of the Titan invasion we are going to look like heroes, Gods. We are going to be symbols of human freedom. We have to act like movie stars with all the confidence we can muster. They have to feel that we know we are going to win. We can never show to them that we are scared and unsure. They will need our confidence."

Jacob resumed his pacing again. "We will organize the survivors and search for the jamming station. Once we know where it is we will form an attack plan on the station."

Jacob stopped pacing and turned to the group. "Any thoughts?"

Cathy pushed off the wall. "No questions Jacob. The plan is good. It's been through both ships and all have agreed on it."

Doug stood up. "Yeah if you screw up it's more likely any one of us would probably have done worse in your place." They all chuckled, even Jacob worked another smile onto his face.

Jacob walked back to the head of the table. "We'll talk before we jump back to our solar system in one hour. We'll keep our daily meetings over the video for the week until we arrive back on Earth."

They all stood up shook hands, hugged each other and left the room. Cathy and Mike and four of their captains boarded Demock with Jacob and left for their transport.

An hour and ten minutes later they jumped back into hyperspace. By the end of the week they were at the edge of Earth's solar system.

Jacob spoke to both transports at the same time from Demock's bridge. "Thank you Cathy for volunteering to go to Europe." Cathy's smile lit Jacob's view screen, "No problem Jake, I want to see what's in style in France these days."

Mike Paquette stood next to Cathy and shook his head. "I don't think you'll like what they are wearing this year Cathy."

Cathy blew a kiss to Jacob and whispered: "Be careful and good luck. I'll see you soon."

Demock formed his stargate. He shot through the gate leaving the two transports on their own. With in the hour Demock was on the opposite side of the solar system than the transports.

Jacob looked at a holographic map of the solar system in one of the sections of the transparent wall. "I want Earth directly between us and the two Titan transport ships Demock. Can you navigate a path that brings us into Earth at the opposite angle as the transports? I want to draw as many Titan fighters to my side of the planet as possible."

Demock mapped out a path in red on the holograph. "No problem Jacob, we'll have to wait several hours before our Titan transports are in position."

Jacob sat back in his chair again and the map of the solar system changed back to a transparent wall. "Demock, it will give me time to think. Proceed when it's time."

The lights on the bridge change to blue then back to a cool white. Jacob looked around for a problem. "What was that, Demock?"

The lights change blue then back to white. "I sensed that you were going to a mood change. I scanned you to confirm. Is there anything wrong Jacob Skyler?"

Jacob held his breath then let out slowly. "I feel a lot of pressure Demock. My world is counting on me. It seems I was just getting used to my baseball team counting on me. What happens if I fail this time?"

Demock brought up a small picture of Earth. "They'll be no one around to blame you."

Jacob smiled softly and sat up in his seat. "Well I got that going for me."

Demock reported in an Earthier accent, "Jacob Skyler it is time we jumped to Earth."

Jacob sat up in his chair, "By all means Demock, jump."

As soon as the Aderain fighter appeared one AU outside of Earth Demock reported contacts. "Jacob I have detected three Titan fighters two minutes away."

A small holograph of the fighters appeared on the left of Jacob.

Jacob rubbed his hands together. "Demock, I want to avoid the Titans until we get to Earth's atmosphere if possible."

Demock picked up speed. "No problem Jacob Skyler. I can show you some of the fighting maneuvers I am capable of doing on the way."

Demock swam through space like a dolphin playing in the ocean. Always staying ahead of the Titan fighters. The closer he got to Earth the more Titan fighters started joining the pursuit. Demock soon had eight fighters behind him.

When Demock approached the Earth's moon a large swarm of Titan fighters strung out in front of him. Demock approached in a cork screw type manner while Jacob sprayed the Titans with small laser fire.

The Titan fighters scattered. Jacob pointed to a hole in the Titan line of defense. "Bee line it to Earth."Jacob turned the gun sights around at the pursuing Titan fighters. Jacob paused his finger over the fire button as he lined up his targets.

"You bastards aren't stopping me now."

A hail of red laser blasts shot out of Demock's laser cannon. Three Titan fighters burst into large fireballs. The rest of the Titan fighters broke off the attack and scattered again.

Demock cut through Earth's atmosphere. "Jacob I have our first transport over Europe on the horizon. I am closing in on it."

Demock hugged the landscape most of the way then shot up high. "Jacob, Cathy Michella's transport is right below us."

Jacob put his thumb over Demock's missile launcher. "I've set detonation for a hundred feet above the transport. Taking aim... fire."

The missile exploded just above the transport ship. The transport adjusted it's coarse like it was hit and nose dived safely into a heavy forest in France.

Demock shot across the sea heading towards the North American coastline. Jacob spotted the other transport and Demock headed right for it. Before they could get above it a blue ball of electricity smashed Demock from above. He dipped and started to zigzag into position.

Jacob shook off the hit and asked Demock, "What was that?" Demock reported, "That was a blast from the main gun of a Titan cruiser."

Jacob grabbed the joy stick to aim the missile. "Missile away, get us out of here Demock."

The missile exploded a hundred feet above the transport. After the explosion the transport darted towards Earth and made a rough landing in Harriman state park in New York.

"Demock, I want you to form a stargate but don't go through it. Turn away from it at the last possible moment then hug the planet and fly to where our transport landed in New York. We'll meet up with our comrades and you can rest for awhile."

Demock skimmed across the planet when he hit the coastline he shot up into space. "To tell you the truth Jacob Skyler, I haven't been so surprised by fighting tactics like yours in a millennium. I don't want to rest."

Pride made Jacob smile. "Sorry Demock, I've got to keep you under wraps until the big finish. You're my ace in the hole."

Demock formed the stargate; when it blasted shut, he flew back towards Earth. He brushed the tree tops curving around the mountains. He came upon Leo's transport within moments. The transport had landed close to the foot of a mountain.

Demock landed on a small ledge just above the transport. Jacob pushed up out of his chair. And walked out of the back of Demock. "We'll cover up the transport with brush and tree limbs. I suppose we have to do the same with you."

"That's all right, Jacob Skyler. I come with my own camouflage." Demock's outer shell slowly change color blending in with the rock around him. Jacob had trouble making out the edges of the fighter standing just a few feet away from it.

"Nice trick, Demock. I wish I could do that. I have to go say my farewells, and then start looking for that Titan jamming station. Is there anything I can do for you?"

"Yes Jacob, hurry back and don't get killed."

Chapter 8

It was late September and an early frost had started the Fall process in southern New York. The crisp smell of the falling leaves was refreshing. A thin layer of red and orange leaves blanketed the ground. Jacob hung onto the trees to keep himself from slipping down the mountain on the leaves.

When Jacob reached the transport it was already covered by cut down trees and brush. With the help of their Debarrian friends, Doug and Matt landed the stolen Titan transport close to the tree line near the foot of a mountain. The surrounding hills and valleys provided good cover for the transport from the air and ground.

Doug, Leo, Phil and Matt walked up to Jacob. Leo spoke up, "We're just about done here Jacob. I guess we can start to go our separate ways?"

Doug threw a light jab at Leo's arm, "Don't forget your pipes. You might need them." Jacob added, "Yeah you might have to burn them for heat."

They all laughed for a minute than came the quiet awkward moment of silence. They felt like brothers, and if they were they would give each other a hug goodbye.

Leo walked up to Doug and put both arms around Doug's shoulders giving him a great big bear hug. "I'm safe enough in my manhood to give my friends a hug good-bye. "Doug smiled embarrassingly and pushed Leo away.

Jacob cleared his throat. "Don't forget to come back or send someone back for a report of our search once every two weeks."

Phil looked over at Kerri, a tall confident young woman with short black hair. "Kerri, Caesar and the two Debarrians will stay close to the ship and gather the reports to pass to the others."

Jacob smiled at Phil and looked at all his friends. "Well my comrades, we have a mountain to move. Let's get to it."

Each of them carried a nap-sack of small explosives and hand lasers that were donated by the Galactic Community with the two stolen transports. Leo picked up the only laser bazooka instead of a hand laser. He slung the five foot piece of hardware over his shoulder like a big game hunter. As they moved away from each other they said their goodbyes.

Jacob headed towards the Hudson River. He noticed large white towers around the town where he used to live when he flew over the area. He had promised those who lived in the area that he would look for their families and friends.

Jacob walked through the woods for hours. He didn't feel any fatigue at all. The deep smell of the pines filled his nose with old childhood Christmas memories. He gained strength with each step he took. It felt good to him to be back home on Earth. It was like he was getting his energy from the ground under his feet, a feeling of one with the planet. How special Earth had become to him since it had become in jeopardy of being lost.

He left the planet as a kid. Now he played a major roll in saving it from being stripped of all its resources from an alien race and, saving the human race from extinction. Jacob thought to himself: "I wonder if dad would think I'm taking on enough responsibility yet?"

The day was unseasonably warm. The temperature was no higher than seventy and no lower than sixty. The fall breeze felt fresh and clean and full of old memories.

Now the sun was getting close to the western horizon, turning the clouds in the sky a warm rusty glow. The breeze became more of a chill and a reminder of past school days.

Jacob stopped to absorb the last rays of the setting sun on his face. It was something he hasn't felt or seen in a year.

As he watched the beauty of nature he felt eyes on him. "Well make up your mind." Jacob shouted.

There was complete silence then a small figure, which was

shaded by the shadow of trees, appeared twenty yards in front of Jacob. In a demanding tone a young man barked back at Jacob, "And who the hell do you think you are?"

Jacob walked up to the shadowed figure and stopped in his tracks when two more figures jumped out from behind trees on either side of the shadowed figure. "I'm Jacob Skyler, I use to live around here before the invasion."

The tone in the shadowed figure's voice became irritated and confused. "Jacob Skyler is dead. He died when the flatheads invaded."

Jacob walked up closer ignoring the two men on either side of him. "Terry McGuire, Doug Marcoux and myself were abducted the night of the invasion by another alien race: the Flarconeans."

A young blond-haired man walked out of the shadows, his clothes worn and ripped. His face was dirty and weather beaten. His eyes were starting to water. "Doug Marcoux is alive. My brother Doug is alive."

Jacob stared hard and his eyes opened in amazement. Gram, Gram is that you? It's Jacob, Jacob Skyler."

The two childhood friends ran up to each other and hugged. Gram whispered into Jacob's ear. "It's been horrible, Jacob. They kill without care. They kill humans like we were annoying bugs."

Jacob held Gram at arm's length. "My family, is my family alive?"

Gram bowed his head ashamed, "I don't know Jacob. They're not in that slave camp over the mountain I can tell you that."

He turned away from Jacob. "You don't understand it was crazy here. Bombs constantly dropping from the sky for what seem like an eternity. Then they hunted us down for months. There was no giving up, if you got caught you were killed." Gram reached up to his eye and wiped away a tear. "Then they started capturing us and using us as slaves to mine and farm."

Gram looked back at Jacob with the innocent eyes of a child. "People were in shock Jacob. Ian and I were together when it started, that's the only reason why I know he's alive."

Jacob dropped his head and released Gram from his hold. "I'm sorry man I had no idea. I didn't mean to push. I just hoped that's all."

Gram turned back to Jacob. "Where's Doug?" Noticing Jacob's height and girth he continued, "How did you get so big in a year. Where have you been? What aliens?"

Jacob looked at Gram and leaned up against a tree. "Doug has headed west." Gram huffed and through his arms up in the air. "Why west? His family is here."

Jacob put a hand on Gram's shoulder to calm him down. "Gram, your brother and I and hundreds of others have been living on a planet named Flarconea for over a year. We've been training to fight the Titans. Living and training on the planet has made us grow bigger and stronger than normal."

Gram paced around in a five foot circle. "Another planet training? Why did Doug go west? Isn't he curious to see if his family is still alive?"

Now Jacob was annoyed. "Don't be stupid Gram. It took all the persuading I could muster to get him to go west. He's heading west looking for a Titan radio jamming station. We've got to find it and destroy it."

Doug turned to face Jacob. "Why, what the hell would that do?"

Jacob looked at Gram's two companions and they moved closer. "If we're going to take back Earth we got to be able to organize and communicate with the rest of the world. The Titan jamming station prevents us from communicating with each other."

Jacob punched his hand. "If we destroy that station we can organize world wide and cut Titan communication at the same time."

Gram turned away in disgust. "You don't get it. You haven't been around this last year. You can't beat these blue flatheads, I don't care how big you got."

Jacob stepped forward and pointed down at Gram. "I'm fighting back. I've learned things and know ways to beat the Titans."

Gram shook his head with disbelief. "You and what army?"

Jacob folded his arms with confidence. "Well there are some of us in Europe and almost two hundred here on the east coast. I'm hoping I just found three more volunteers."

"We'll see Jacob, we'll see." Gram walked away from Jacob.

One of the other men traveling with Gram leaned over and whispered in his ear. Gram smiled and motioned to Jacob. "I might be able to find you some volunteers if you can convince them. We'll take you back to our main camp sight in the caves near West Point."

Jacob was disturbed by Gram giving him such a hard time. "Fine, then let's go."

Gram barked right back at Jacob. "No problem, let's go."

Jacob followed Gram through the woods heading north parallel with the Hudson River. Neither one talked to the other. Their emotions in turmoil not knowing if they were mad at each other, jealous or just feeling guilty about some missed responsibility.

They walked through the woods for the rest of the day. It was night fall when they arrived at the caves. The night sky was clear but the woods were hidden in blackness. The mouth of the camp's cave was small. Jacob had to crawl on his hands and knees to get inside.

Jacob crawled down a tunnel twenty feet deep inside the mountain. Then a small enclosure opened up to a room thirty feet in diameter. The ceiling coned up to a small opening to the night sky, a few feet in diameter, where smoke from a fire drifted out. A small group of twenty-five people in well-worn clothes huddled close to a decent size fire for heat.

Gram waved an arm out to show the cold hungry people to Jacob. "Here are your warriors. You'll have to get them some uniforms."

Jacob bit his lip. He wanted to crack Gram over the head for making fun of these people's misfortune.

Jacob introduced himself calmly and gently. He shook everyone's hand making sure he made eye contact with each person. As Jacob walked further into the cave he could stand straight up. The poor souls around the fire were frightened by his great size and good health.

Jacob scanned the room and spoke boisterous enough for all to hear. "I want to tell you a story. A story of galactic war and hope."

All eyes glare at him with excitement. Jacob looked around and took out his hand laser he got from the Galactic Community. "But first let's warm this place up a bit more." Jacob pointed the laser to one wall of the cave and adjusted his weapon. With a low intensity beam he heated some of the rocks in the wall. The rocks glowed red and the cave got warmer and brighter.

"That's better, now let me tell you what's been happening to me this last year."

Jacob told the absorbing crowd about the abductions and the year of hard training on Flarconea. He left out the part about Demock. He thought that the knowledge that an Aderain fighter was on the planet was too much danger to put these people in. He did tell the group of the plan to take back Earth by the abductees. How the Galactic Community was backing the humans.

He ended his story with one question. "I'm not going to lie to you. We could all die, but I have to do more than just survive. This is our planet."

Jacob stared up out of the small opening in the ceiling. He scratched his chin reminiscing. "I've killed some Titans already out in space. I know I shouldn't feel this way," Jacob punched his opened hand hard with his fist echoing a sharp smack down the cave, " but it felt good."

Looking at the group around him he could see tears welling up in their eyes. "Maybe it's because of the mass destruction the Titans did to the human race. Maybe it's because I feel I'm doing something to keep the human race alive."

Jacob looked at Gram through his eyes right to his soul. "I'm ready to admit it felt good because I needed to take revenge for my friends and families who didn't survive the invasion. I'm human, that's how I feel."

Jacob stepped back away from the group. "So I'm asking you all. Will you help us take back Earth?"

Some of the raggedy crowd couldn't hold back their emotional sigh. They sucked in a quick gasp when they saw the hope in Jacob's face. They stood up and yelled yes all together.

Jacob smiled at them. He saw Gram's shock and disappointment from the far side of the cave. Jacob walked into the crowd and congratulated them on their decision.

Jacob nodded his head at Gram. "Do you have somebody on watch for the night?"

The crowd turned towards Gram. Gram was caught off guard and muttered softly, "The Flatheads never come up here. There's no reason to post a guard."

Jacob Skyler played the diplomat. "Your probably right Gram but now we are a military force now. Although this is a secure place, we must get in the habit of posting guards around the camp at all times."

Gram nodded his head in agreement. The group was eating up Jacob's charisma and confidence. He quickly and easily was becoming the leader.

Jacob raised his hands up to calm down the group. "Everybody get some rest. Gram and I will take the first watch. Who will volunteer to take the second watch?"

Every body's hand shot up quickly. They wanted to be part of a force that was going to take back Earth.

Chapter 9

Early the next morning Jacob walked through the area around the cave. He pick out a strategic guard post around the camp. He organized a rotating guard duty with Gram. Before breakfast he took a small hunting party out and came back with a big buck with a ten-point rack. The camp took on a whole new positive feeling.

Through out the following day he kept Gram by his side asking for his opinion on things. He didn't want Gram to feel non-important. In the days that followed Jacob took time every morning to walk down a path to a spot where he could stare at the sun rising over the Hudson River. He would stay in the cover of the pines and watch the deep red and orange trees light up the hillside.

The younger kids would gather around him for a story about Flarconea or space. Jacob would tell them stories about Flarconea and what he has learned about the Galactic Community.

At the end of the first week he slipped in the story of King Arthur and the Knights of the Round Table. How honor, courage and especially truth were the most important virtues of lords and ladies of King Arthur's time. He told the story of the Quest for the Holy Grail, comparing it to his mission. He explained why he had to go look for the jamming station. He didn't want them to think he was abandoning them.

The next morning, the youths started calling him Lord Skyler. He would respond by bowing and saying, my lord or my lady. By the end of the day everyone was calling Jacob Skyler, Lord Skyler.

Another week had passed and the camp grew more organized. At the end of every day they would gather around the fire in the cave. Jacob would take this time to speak to the whole camp. "It's time we started sending out small survey teams to look for the jamming station." The group listened intently. "We'll start off with three day searches. At the end of the first day you make camp. The next day you head out in one direction for half a day then turn around and come back to your camp. The third day you head back home."

Jacob waited for questions but the group trusted his judgment. "Once we know what routes are safe we'll set up permanent post so we can venture out farther."

Jacob walked around the open part of the cave. "Since there are only about thirty of us, we'll send out three patrols made up of three soldiers each. One solider heading north, the other west and the third south."

The group all mumbled their agreement of being called soldiers. Jacob smiled and continued, "You must remember you are not an attack force but a reconnaissance patrol. You will help any human you can but no direct assaults on Titans. The lower the profile we have the easier the mission will be."

Jacob took a moment to look into some of the eyes of his listeners. He wanted the idea to sink in. They nodded to each other and then focused back on Jacob. "Any one we find we'll send back here with the pass word, "Jim" answered with "Kelly". Then we'll know that the survey crew has sent them to us."

Everybody started speaking at once volunteering for the first patrol to go out. Jacob put up his hands to quiet them down. "I've already talked to Gram about it. We've picked out the three teams that will go first. If your not picked this time you'll get picked next time."

Everybody protested how unfair it was. Everybody wanted to go. Jacob put up his hand again to calm them down. "We leave tomorrow morning."

The group mumbled to themselves knowing he was right but didn't want to risk not being chosen.

The next morning Jacob woke up to the sweet smell of ham, eggs and coffee. Gram was waiting outside Jacob's nook in the cave. A small room dug out by Gram when he first starting sleeping in the cave. He insisted Jacob take it. Gram looked in with a lantern when he heard Jacob stir. "They made you breakfast my Lord. They want to give you a big farewell. They're afraid you won't come back."

Jacob sat up in his bed and rubbed his eyes smiling. "They need a little reinsurance."

Jacob rolled his shoulders back and swung his arms back and forth in front of him to start his blood pumping a little faster.

"*Hoooo Raaaaaa.* Good moments should be enjoyed. Let's go."

Jacob walked just outside the cave and met everyone physically. He greeted them with a big smile and a friendly slap on the back, or he gave them a firm handshake or a gentle understanding placement of his hand on a shoulder.

The last morning in camp he said he wanted to hear more of their survival stories. So he listened to them ramble and followed every small detail of their tragic stories. The panic they felt during the first week of the invasion. How the government seemed to disappear the first day when all television and radio shows were cut off. Then being chased by Titan hunting parties who just wanted to kill everyone.

Jacob also heard their triumphs. How they escaped and survived by finding clothes, food and shelter. They told him of ideas on how to make the camp better. Some even told him they had dreams of a better future now that he was here.

Jacob thought to himself, "They have dreams again."

He gobbled up his breakfast with everyone looking on happy that he was enjoying it. The whole camp climbed down to a lower ledge to see Jacob off. Gram and Rick were already mounted on top of strong horses. They waited on the road along with the others picked to do the survey.

Two boys held the rains to a hardy gray stallion. Gram leaned over and said to Jacob, "We'll make better time and cover more ground on the back of these horses than our feet." Seeing Jacob's eyes light up with admiration for the horse Gram added, "His name is Stenson. He's yours to ride. "

Jacob smiled and hopped up on the horse's saddle. He took to the horse very naturally. He pulled the reins of the horse to turn him around and then he reeled the steed on his back legs. He held up his fist and yelled: "*Human!*"

He bolted down the path and the crowd cheered him. Gram and Rick chased after him with the rest of riders.

Once at the foot of the mountain the group split up into their patrols. Two men and a girl head south and three more men head north. Jacob, Gram and Rick headed dead west.

For the first six hours of their journey the only sign of the Titans was the lack of humans they saw. Two Titan transports passed over them just past noon. Taking food, minerals and wood to the moon to be re deployed to another Titan outpost.

The rest of the day they had no trouble. They enjoyed the good weather and shed some of their cloths off their back. Their heading remained due west towards the Pennsylvania, New Jersey and New York boarder.

At dusk they heard a train whistle blow three times. Jacob looked at Gram rubbing his chin. "What was that?"

Gram stood in his stirrups looking south just over a hill. "It's the slave train express. The Titans must be cutting down trees in the area again. They work humans until it gets dark and then bring them back to the slave camp."

Jacob started heading towards the whistle. "Are they from the slave camp from our old town?"

Gram shook his head no, "They're from further north of here. The people in our old town our mining Hi-Tor mountain."

The men dismounted from their horses and tied them to trees. They walked up to the top of the small hill. They could see a quarter mile away, humans being loaded onto a freight train like cattle. Jacob stared intensely at the scene. "Are those Titan tanks on either side of the train?"

Gram nodded yes, "They sure are. We can't blow through that armor. The Titan hover tank is heavily armored."

Jacob remembered learning about the Titan hover tank during one of Des Troyer's lectures. "A Titan laser tank is ten feet wide and thirty feet long. The angled octagon plates on the tank make it able to reflect most shots taken at it. The tank hovers five feet off the ground and can reach speeds up to two hundred miles an hour on long flat surfaces."

Jacob remembered the holo-image of the soulless machine and asking Des Toyer about its armament. "Good question Jacob. It's equipped with four small lasers, mounted at each corner of the tank, and one laser cannon. It's laser cannon, mounted on a revolving turret, is devastating. The laser cannon uses so much power that it takes ten seconds to recharge it's self.

Jacob put a hand above his eyes to block out the last rays of the sun for the day. Jacob glanced at Gram and nodded to the train. "Will they be back tomorrow?" Gram stared at Rick who stopped in his tracks, then he looked back at Jacob. "Why, what are you thinking?"

Jacob smiled at his two companions. "I'm thinking a little distraction at one end of the work area, killing a couple of guards at the other work area and poof, more freedom fighters."

Gram walked up to Jacob and grabbed the lower part of his arm. "Listen here Lord Skyler. Those people down there have lost all hope and wish they were dead. You can't save them."

Jacob smiled slowly at Gram.

"Yes I can. You want to help? I need to set some traps tonight to create a diversion in the morning. Besides they might have heard something about the Titan jamming station."

Gram looked at Rick in disbelief.

"What about the idea of keeping a low profile?"

Jacob's face went cold and his stare turned scary. "Human life is our priority. To the captives who don't escape, they will now have hope and that's all a human needs to change the world."

Jacob studied the area again, "Besides it's not their main headquarters I'm attacking. It's just a small work detail."

The train chugged off and the three riders rode to the tree cutting had stopped. Rick and Gram started carving messages into the trees that would tell the prisoners where to run when it was time. Jacob walked up to the tracks where the train had stopped and planted some explosives he got from the Galactic Community.

They rode back over the hill and made camp. Jacob went over the plan four times before they went to sleep.

The next morning the train arrived before the sun broke the horizon. Jacob, Gram and Rick stayed in the shadows of the trees waiting for the work crews to deploy into the woods. The train rested on the same small hill again. The Titans barked and pushed the humans down the hill to where they had left off the day before. Two Titan tanks took positions at the front and the back of the train.

There were thirty Titan guards where spread out among the humans. The large blue aliens looked like over sized humans with hound dog jowls and flat heads. Some stood over eight feet tall.

The human slaves walked tiredly into the woods and started to cut down trees with axes and chainsaws. Some of them saw the messages left carved in the trees. They searched the forest, out of the corner of their eyes. They didn't want to attract attention to themselves. Gram and Rick caught a few of the worker's eyes and signaled them by putting their fingers to their lips, to stay quiet.

As the humans started working, the Titans gathered in small groups of four and five away from the humans. The work area covered two football fields and the trees being cut were along an open field.

Jacob caught Gram's eyes through the woods and nodded his head. Jacob squeezed the trigger to the explosives and whispered to himself, "This ones for you Jim."

The first explosion cut the peaceful quiet like a nightmarish scream in church. It caught the side of the Titan hover tank, by the front of the train, and flipped the tank upside down.

The train's engine rolled over on it's side and slid down the hill at a group of Titan guards. Three Titans couldn't get out of the way quick enough and were run over and crushed by the sliding engine.

Three more explosions followed one after the other. The Earth shook knocking humans and Titans to the ground. The explosions worked their way back from the front of the train to the caboose, twisting and shredding the whole train.

The second Titan hover tank at the back end of the train headed down the hill and spun around to face the train. Two more explosions tore up the ground where the Titan hover tank was.

The Titan guard, near the top of the hill, signaled to half the guards to stay with the humans. The rest of the guards ran up the hill towards the train thinking the attack was coming from the other side of the tracks.

Jacob charged out from behind a tree with his Aderain sword above his head. He rushed towards the closest Titan to him. Like a panther he leaped twenty yards in three giant strides. He was on top of the alien before he could comprehend what was going on.

Jacob split his scull with a crunching blow to the top of the Titan's head down to his shoulders. A laser blast skimmed over Jacob's shoulder from behind.

As if he had rehearsed the move a dozen times Jacob took out his hand laser, turned to the Titan, and charged him firing repeatedly at him.

The Titan let another shot go and Jacob dove out of the way and rolled back up on his feet right next to the Titan. He swung his sword like a baseball legend screaming, "Get off my planet!" cutting through the neck of the surprised guard.

The Titan's head toppled through the air landing upside down on the flat side of it's skull. A pair of infrared binoculars fell next to Jacob's feet. He grabbed the piece of hardware and slung it around his neck.

The humans started running scared screaming and waving their arms. Gram and Rick yelled at them.

"Hurry, hurry, this is the way to freedom."

They herded the humans away from the train and deeper into the woods. They jumped down into a ravine five feet deep and thirty feet wide. The group ran keeping their heads low.

The other guards that ran to the top of the hill now started firing into the woods at the escaping humans. Jacob fired his laser at the Titans. With three shots he picked off the three other guards that were suppose to be watching the humans.

The surviving Titan hover tank turned its attention on him. A blast from the Titan laser cannon took out thirty feet in diameter of thick forest. Jacob was knocked to the ground barely escaping the concussion and large splintered pieces of a maple tree.

He looked up and saw Gram fifty yards away at the top of the ravine in the woods with a wide eyed worried look. Jacob smiled and waved his arm signaling Gram to head out. Jacob jumped to his feet and sprinted quickly towards the ravine as the tank moved towards him. The guards up the hill spotted him and started firing at him. Trees exploded all around Jacob as he zigzagged to the ravine and dove into it avoiding the Titan Tank's blast.

The Titan tank followed Jacob clearing itself a path into the woods. It maneuvered into the ravine with careful skill. It took off down the ravine sloshing side to side up and down the walls of the ravine chasing after the humans.

Jacob passed a bend and stopped, peeking carefully around the corner. "Human slaves? Not in my neighborhood." He pushed his transmitter and set off his last explosion in the ravine directly underneath the hover tank. The blast knocked out the tank's hovering capabilities and it dropped like a stone.

The explosion from the last Titan tank started a fire slowly filling the woods with smoke. It gave the escaping humans cover from the space fighters now swarming over head. They fired randomly into the woods starting more fires. They stopped when they realize they were burning their own resources.

Gram and Rick kept the group moving in the ravine for a quarter mile. Then they climbed out into a clump of trees and some heavy brush. Jacob caught up to them and scanned the rag-tagged group. "Is everybody all right?"

The freed humans cautiously nodded their heads. Jacob smiled and offered a hand to a thin young man with worn torn clothes and dark bags under his eyes.

"I'm Jacob Skyler," he said, motioning to his friends. "We're part of the Earth Defense Force. Would you like to join us?"

The group was slow to respond but then they began to smile to each other. The young man shook Jacob's hand, "We're human, aren't we?"

The rest of the day was a constant stop and go movement. Titan fighters would swoop down from over head and everyone would hug a tree and pray. It took the group a day and a half to make it back to the caves at West Point. The feeling of freedom kept the weak group going.

Once they returned to the camp the ex-slaves were fed and given some warm places to sleep inside the cave. After they rested Jacob explain his adventure to the new recruits and his commitment in taking back Earth. The over worked and under fed survivors all volunteered to help in any way they could.

The next morning the patrol that headed south came back. Ed a fourteen year old boy with broken glasses ran into camp yelling, "Lord Skyler, Lord Skyler, I must talk to Lord Skyler."

Jacob heard the boy shouting from inside the cave and came running out. "What is it Ed? Have you found the jamming station?"

Ed bent over resting his hands on his knees catching his breath. "No, my Lord. I heard from an escaped slave that a lord, like you, had been captured. A Lord Ruzzi."

Jacob stared into the boy's eyes. "Where is he now?"

Still puffing Ed pointed south, "He's in the slave camp near the bend in the river, where you use to live."

Jacob Skyler dismounted from his tired gray stallion, Stenson, and patted him gently on his head. He took to Stenson like an old family dog and the feeling was mutual. He appreciated the unconditional love the strong beast had for him.

They paused on a small rocky ridge that was part of an old fire road running up the mountain. A chilled breeze blew swiftly down from the Canadian north across the New York, Hudson valley. It carried a cold air that made goose bumps scatter up and down Gram's back twice until his shoulders involuntarily shook it out of his body. Gram turned to Jacob and Michael pulling his worn out jacket closer to his body. "Man, it got cold."

The young men were all dressed in dull-colored pants and shirts, which had enough rips in them to remind them that the nip of winter was starting to fill the air. They wrapped any old rags they could find around the tares in their clothes, and wore dark oversized hooded cloaks, trying to keep the pinch of cold off their skins. The chill and dampness always seem to have a way to find you.

It was an hour past dusk. They had ridden south of West Point for a day and a half with little rest. The temperatures dropped the last couple of nights below the comfort zone. Recent harsh rains and the constant danger of being caught by the Titans kept the men tired and achy. They were nearly spotted by Titan fighters twice yesterday still searching for the humans Jacob liberated.

The men learned to conserve their energy and relax whenever they could. These short-lived moments of peace and quiet were now considered the good times. Jacob's comrades Michael, Rick and Gram kept a very close eye on their new leader. They trusted his leadership but feared his recklessness to put himself in danger.

Jacob stared at the valley lying between him and the Hudson River. "The Hi-Tor mountain area was used in colonial times by the Americans to fight for their independence from England."

Gram shook his head and mumbled. "These guys aren't from England."

An over tired Michael took the reins of all the horses. "I'll take them to that small patch of grass back down the path to feed."

Gram stood next to Jacob and looked across the valley. "Tell me about this jamming station?"

Jacob smiled and remembered that Gram wanted nothing to do with his ideas when he first arrived.

Jacob chewed on his lip then looked at Gram. "Before the invasion the Titans landed on Earth to set up the jamming station. When the invasion started all communication was jammed around the planet. Humans were cut off from each other and everybody panicked.

With no communication and the unrelenting bombardment, the world went into chaos. The Governments disappeared over night."

Jacob turned away from Gram. Talking about the invasion made Jacob feel uneasy. He felt guilty about it. He was safe while others suffered.

He remembered the first Friday night in March when he and his friends were all abducted. It was the last night of a normal life he had. Leo, Doug and Jacob, met Leo after his bagpipe practice for the St. Patrick's Day parade. The last thing Jacob recalled on Earth was driving with the guys towards the movie theater when, what looked like a low flying helicopter, started shining it's lights on them. A couple of days later they all woke up on a Flarconean ship in a large cargo bay. They were taken away from the destruction and the pain everybody else had to endure. The Flarconeans told them they were the only hope the human race had to survive.

Jacob looked at his friends and said with his hands clenched behind his back, "The human race is running out of time. The longer we take, in kicking the Titans off the planet, the deeper they dig in."

Jacob looked at Gram: "Ed didn't say the name of the Titan prison guard that help the human to escape, did he?"

The men looked down at a small Titan slave camp forged in the valley between them and the Hudson River, just north of New York City. Jacob gripped his pair of Titan infrared binoculars and studied the slave village thoroughly.

Gram looked at Jacob in awe. The kid he knew as Jacob Skyler had changed into the man Lord Skyler. Gram hesitated a moment and looked Jacob up and down. "No Jacob he just said a Titan captain with one eye that works in this prison was bribed." Gram pointed towards the center of the town. "The flathead hangs out in the Titan bar in the center of the camp."

The middle class bi-level house neighborhood was ripped up. Some huge chunks of asphalt were standing ten feet straight up in the air like some post-apocalyptic Stonehenge. Telephone polls littered the ground like giant toothpicks. What were once manicured lawns are now overgrown with weeds and small shrubs.

The only remnants of what use to be, were several bi-level houses with rusting mailboxes, probably still filled with old bills. Most of the houses burnt to the ground, or lie in pieces from being blown apart. The town reminded Jacob of a picture his grandfather had, an old black and white photo of England during World War II, right after a German air raid.

Jacob talked softly to Gram. "The stories told by the survivors of the Titan warships firing on the planet for week upon weeks sounded frightening. A constant bombardment on all the major cities around the world."

Gram peered at Jacob not knowing why Jacob was bringing the subject up. "Yeah it sucked."

Jacob smiled at his wise-ass friend. "The Flarconeans sent in a probe to monitor the invasion. We were able to watch the destruction on a monitor. The Titans took out Washington D.C. and Moscow in the first strike. Soon all the major cities around the world were destroyed."

Feeling that uncomfortable feeling again Jacob looked out into the night sky. "Titan fighters finished the destruction of the cities and the small communities that surrounded the cities in the weeks that followed. Then the probe was discovered and destroyed."

Gram looked back down at the slave camp. "You know during the day the Titan white marble towers and buildings looked quite Romanesque in the surrounding orange and red fall foliage. The slave camp has a beauty that concealed its true ugliness."

Rick joined in on the conversation. "Yea their buildings are nice but the Flatheads themselves are freaking ugly. Some of them grow over ten feet tall and weighed over five hundred pounds. There large, over weight, blue, flat headed ogres with a thirst for killing." Rick let out a big sigh than turned around and headed back to where Michael was feeding the horses.

This was a typical Titan slave camp, filled with beaten and sometimes starving humans, forced by the Titans to harvest the resources of the Earth. The better camps harvested food from large farms. Human slaves worked long hard hours, but could steal food from the fields now and again with the risk of death if they were caught.

The dreadful camps like this one, mined for minerals. Human slaves remained black with grime and dirt, day in and day out, from the conditions of the mines. A mining slave had a short life span.

The thought of human slaves turned Jacob's stomach into a tight gut-wrenching knot. Friends, family, everybody he had ever known before, was subjected to the Titan's cruelty.

Jacob looked toward his companions. "This is the place. Look at all the extra security. There are a lot of Titan hover tanks here.

Look in the center of town, near the main building. There's a heavily armed shuttle."

Gram looked through the binoculars. "I haven't seen that Type of Titan shuttle before. It's not a fighter or a regular transport."

Jacob slapped Gram on the back. "That means someone important is here, and I think I know why."

Michael walked up behind Gram and Jacob and mumbled, "Lord Ruzzi is why. The question is who is that someone?"

The men all nodded in agreement. Jacob pointed down to an old bridge on the far side of the camp. It was close to a dense part of the forest. "We'll enter there at the south side of town near the bridge."

Jacob studied Gram for a minute. He was just over five and a half feet tall and had a ruff look about him. There was no fat on his bones. His skin had become tan and tough like leather, a feature every free human now had. He had long unkempt dirty blond hair, which sometimes looked like a lion's mane when he galloped on his horse. Surviving in the wild for more than a year made him as serious as a tribal king protecting his tribe.

Jacob had given him a Titan hand blaster he had gotten from the Galactic Community. Gram kept it strapped on his hip like a gunman in a western. He was itching to use it. He also carried a large baseball bat that he strapped to his back for close combat. He figured it would be easier to bash a Titan's skull in from on top of his horse with it.

Gram anxiously spoke up, "Lord Skyler, you should stay here. There's no need for you to risk your life over a small recon mission."

Being called Lord Skyler instead of Jacob was starting to taste funny to Jacob. It was starting to sound like it had a lot of responsibly to it. Jacob looked at Gram with a distasteful look on his face.

"Gram, enough with the lord thing already."

Gram leaned forward so his comrades couldn't hear him and whispered to Jacob.

"Our people need something big to look up to right now. The title *lord*, to those who trained on Flarconea and have come back to vanquish the human race, sounds bigger and better; more legendary."

Jacob smiled and almost blushed.

"Lord Leo and Lady Cathy are going to have a field day with that one. They're going to say I've become an ego maniac."

Jacob looked at the concern in Gram's face.

"Alright, alright, *lord* it is."

Jacob shook his head no. "As far as me staying back while you go in, Jacob put a hand on Gram's shoulder, "Gram it's important that I do this, trust me it's good for morale."

Gram rubbed the side of his face with his hand. He shrugged his shoulders and mumbled. He knew the Lords were the best chance humans had to overthrow the Titans. He didn't want to risk the life of one of them. He also knew it was hopeless to argue with Jacob once he's made up his mind.

Jacob grabbed the reins to his horse tightly and hoisted himself back onto his saddle. He turned the rejuvenated stallion down the path and gave him a quick kick in the ribs. They bolted down the trail in a full trot.

The other men immediately leaped on their horses and chased after Jacob, afraid to let him out of their sight. Over the last couple days they had taken on the roll of being his personal bodyguards. Jacob appreciated their concern for his safety but they were beginning to annoy him. Leaving quickly was his way of annoying them back.

Jacob's horse led the race descending down the over grown mountain trail with the others close behind. He leaned back in his saddle, trying keeping his body from tumbling forward.

Trees and rocks blurred by him with an occasional swipe at his head from a shadowed tree branch. Reaching the foot of the mountain the foursome darted through a small clearing, and bled back into the black forest. Chasing each other like a pack of wolves, each taking a slightly different path through the woods. Propelling their way through thick bushes, finally finding an old over grown road leading to the Titan slave camp.

Three hundred yards from the bridge the brush got thicker. The group slowed their steeds down to a slow trot. They dismounted quietly listening to the forest and walked the horses down through some bushes into an old dry streambed. The water had been rerouted by some laser blast that rearrange the stream's path.

The dry bed was no less than ten feet wide and five feet deep. All four men walked quietly in twos for fifty feet, then stopped when they reached a sharp bend.

Rick carefully peeked around the corner and saw the old bridge. The forest had swallowed up half the bridge with vine type bushes. The dead stream they were in used to flow right under it. They proceeded with caution until they were underneath the bridge. Michael again took the job of caring for the horses. He carefully tied them off to a rotting log.

Jacob turned to the group. "You guys stay here until I get back. If I don't find our one eyed prison guard in an hour, I'll come back."

Jacob looked sternly at Rick and Michael. "If I'm not back in an hour, you get the hell out of here. Head back to the caves and tell the camp what happen then go to the appointed point and tell Lady Keri what happened. You tell her I think Lord Ruzzi is here, and I think he knows where the Titan jamming station is."

The men shot wide open stares at each other with panic written all over their faces. Gram was annoyed. "One of our priority orders is to protect Lord Skyler at any cost. Letting you walk into a Titan slave camp alone isn't a good way to protect you."

Jacob just gave them a silly grin.

The three men dropped their jaws and gave weird shrugs to each other for a quiet moment, and then Michael and Rick glared at Gram.

Gram started pacing in a little circle again, his head down and his arms wailing about. "You look nothing like a human slave. Just about all human slaves are under six feet now, except for the lords and maybe my mutant brother, Ian. You're considered a giant at six foot ten. Let me go, I'll blend right in with the other slaves. They'll never know I was there."

Jacob stopped Gram right in his tracks, and grabbed him firmly by the shoulders. He looked deep into his brown, faithful puppy dog eyes.

"Look Gram, I'm not a piece of jewelry or something holy. I'm a human warrior with a built-in translator in my ear. He could divulge information on Lord Ruzzi's exact location."

Jacob said in a serious tone: "More than likely this one-eyed flathead will try a double cross. I'll pick it up with my translator. The rumor was he could be bribed to let humans escape into the woods. We were also told he couldn't be trusted."

Michael added, "Some humans were caught and killed before they reached the woods at the foot of the mountain."

Gram's head dropped in anguish. He threw his hands up with disappointment.

"But you'll need back up."

Jacob put a gentle hand on Gram's shoulder. "You're a great fighter Gram, but I think this meeting needs a little finesse." Gram looked right back into Jacob's eyes, as if he was looking inside himself for good reply. "If they find out who you are, you will be beyond dead."

Jacob bent over and slapped Gram playfully on his cheek. Then he slowly gave him another ear-to-ear grin. Straightening up he started walking towards town leaving his horse behind. A few feet away he looked back and smiled at his glum companions. "I just might tell them who I am. Maybe it'll shake them up a bit."

Their jaws dropped in horror again, then Jacob flashed them an even bigger smile. They turned away in anger and started mumbling something foul about Jacob under their breath.

Jacob climbed out of the dry riverbed and onto a deserted broken up paved road. It had started to give way to the local vegetation. The potholes were large enough to park a car in. The road led straight towards the slave camp.

The closer he got to the camp the more broken up the pavement was and the muddier the road got. Each step became orchestrated with a slight squish and a plop.

Titan security was loose around the slave camp. Since the

invasion there hasn't been much resistance. Most of the adults were killed in the beginning, leaving the children frightened and confused. A lot of humans had become dependent on the Titans for food and shelter.

Small food rations and beaten severely for anything or nothing was part of day-to-day living. These children have become a scared, frightened, people who never dare think of escape.

What security the Titans had wasn't setup to stop people from trying to get in. Titan guards were relaxed and over confidant. Fear kept the humans from escaping.

The Titans criss-crossed the slave camp with spotlights from on top of all four marble guard towers. The spotlights automatically ran down the streets, not really looking too hard for anybody. Not many humans were out after dark, unless they had permission. The streets were practically deserted, except for an occasional Titan taking a stroll.

Jacob Skyler made his way cautiously towards the center of the camp, jumping from shadow to shadow, his back sliding along the walls of abandoned houses and old grocery stores.

In the center of the Titan slave camp was a tavern, where any alien could go for a drink or a smoke. The Titans set up the place as a reward for good behavior. They also used it to listen, and know what the humans were up to.

Most of the Titans drank in the back room, away from the humans. Earthlings were like pets to the Titans. Humans were considered a savage race, uncivilized. That's where Jacob would find his one-eyed Titan.

The bar was in a Titan marble building. The door to the tavern looked oddly out of place. The dark oak wood door mounted on a three story white marble building, was a sharp contrast, even at night. The door was enormous and heavy. It was at least twice Jacob's height, and three times as wide as a normal door.

Jacob reached out and grabbed the iron door handle, and with little effort swung the door wide open. "Well balanced."

Without warning his nose was assaulted by a gruesome rotten egg smell. He threw an arm sleeve over his nose to no avail. The body odor of the Titans was incredibly offensive to the human nose. It plunged down Jacob's throat into his stomach grabbing his insides with an unforgiving grip. He turned his head in disgust, and tried to spit out as much of the vile taste as he could.

He slowly walked into the building, and the stench got worse. He felt nauseous. It was all he could do to keep what little food in his stomach from coming back up.

The *nanites* in his body kicked in and he started to regain his composure. He scanned the room slowly, looking for danger and trying to ease his stomach.

He was impressed by the fine craftsmanship of the woodwork. He learned on Flarconea that the wood quality on Earth was rare in this part of the galaxy. The Titans used it to accent the corners, and supports in their buildings even though they didn't need them. The high ceiling was decorated in thick wooden beams. For such a vicious race, their architectural designing was beautiful, and probably stolen.

Over all it was an immense room with high ceilings. In the center was a beautifully crafted round fireplace built out of stone, at least eight foot in diameter. The fire threw off heat in all directions. It was like some fancy ski resort would have without the fuzzy sweaters.

Jacob strolled further into the room. The parquet style hardwood floor reminded Jacob of his high school gymnasium. There was a bar at the far end, which ran the length of the back wall, a good forty feet. It was made of a thick oak base, with slabs of polished pine that laid on top of it. The top of the bar was clean except for several mismatched glasses of ale in different degrees of emptiness. The only things on the wall were two broken beer signs and a four foot cracked mirror.

The humans stood up to the bar because there were no chairs for them to sit on. The dozen raggedy-looking humans huddling together stopped drinking when they saw Jacob walk in.

Jacob saw no Titans so he walked up to the round fireplace that was halfway between the bar and the entrance. There was some good heat generating from it. He stopped to warm his hands, trying to get the night's chill out of his bones.

He noticed two more doors in the room. One was certainly the kitchen, the odor sneaking out from behind the door was incredibly nauseating. The Titans liked their meat fresh and uncooked. They ate anything and everything. They left little to no waste at all, including bones.

The other door was probably where the Titans drank their carbonation. They loved coca- cola, and could get inebriated on half a liter.

"May I help you, unusually large human?" The voice was harmonizing in a calm tone, talking slow like an old wise priest, or a brotherly monk. Jacob looked down to see a small hairless gray elf, with pointed ears. The alien dressed in a light blue tunic, starring back at Jacob with shy cat like eyes. He folded his hands together and blinked once or twice real slowly. Wearing a strange no lip grin on his narrow face, he tilted his head and studied Jacob's features.

Jacob stared back. The alien couldn't have been more than four feet tall. His body proportions were strange. He had a small torso with long lanky limbs, like thin twigs. Even his head seemed a little too big for his body.

"My name is Hitock, let me guide you to the other humans at the bar."

Jacob recognized the alien as a Drek. He learned about them while he was training. They were the last civilization conquered by the Titans. They were the so-called, peace loving geniuses of the galaxy. "Hitock, how did a smart guy like you, end up in a dump like this?"

Hitock responded in a slow boring tone. "Like humans, we were conquered by Titan numbers. We did endure longer in defending our planet than the humans, but that's only because our body of knowledge was superior to Earth's and the Titans. We just couldn't hold up against their suicide runs on our bases. Within two months we were also a conquered race."

"Conquered!" Jacob barked at him. His blood started to boil. Jacob grabbed the small skinny alien by the throat firmly ceasing its primary function of breathing.

He lifted the tiny alien off the ground, and brought him right up to his face. Jacob growled through his teeth at him like a wolf ready to rip out his throat. "Listen elf, don't ever say that the human race is conquered. Do I look conquered to you?"

Jacob looked around and saw the horror stricken faces on the thin slaves at the bar. He took a deep breath, and slowly loosened his grip around Hitock's neck and gently put him back on the ground.

The Drek's slightly pompous attitude quickly changed. He rubbed his neck trying to work the gray blood back into it. He now stuttered in fear of losing his life. "Mm my apologies sir. I, I, I didn't mean any insult."

Jacob patted him lightly on top of his head like a little puppy, trying to put his mind at rest. "Don't worry Hitock, my fight's not with you, as a matter of fact, I could use your help."

Jacob looked down at Hitock. "That is unless you are a dedicated slave to the flatheads."

It's not easy to read facial expressions of other alien life forms, but when a Drek's cat like eyes turn to slits, and his small pointing ears stand up straight, you just know he's pissed off. His monk like calmness disappeared, and he harmonized at Jacob in a sharper tone with more confidence. "My body is held by the Titans, human. My mind is not."

Jacob let a little grin sneak out of the corner of his mouth and nodded his head in agreement. "Good, your more human than I thought. I'm looking for a one-eyed Titan prison guard. Have you seen him?"

Hitock nervously looked over his shoulder at the bar, looking for prying ears. He gestured to Jacob to bend down. Covering his mouth with his thin hand, he whispered to Jacob softly. "You do live a dangerous life, human. You're looking for Tog. He's not come in yet this evening. You get a drink at the bar and I'll let you know when he gets in."

Jacob stood straight up and threw his shoulders back. "I'll tell you what Hitock, when Tog gets in, tell the flathead that I saved a table for him in the back."

Hitock shoved his way between the door to the Titan's back room and Jacob. He chattered at him anxiously. "Excuse me sir, no disrespect but the back room is for Titans only."

Jacob reached inside his cloak and pulled out a rolled up brown bag and handed it to Hitock and pushed him out of his way. "Here are some crystals. Get me some ale, and bring it to me in the back room."

Jacob knew there was a chance one-eye would double-cross him. He didn't want to give him the chance to trade his life for that of some poor human at the bar. Jacob thought he would take him down in the back room where there is no possibility for a human hostage to be taken.

Hitock walked away then stopped and turned around quickly. Jacob watched his eyes suddenly increased in size. Hitock figured out that Jacob was one of those who helped the humans escape from the train the other day.

Chapter 10

Looking up, Philip Ruzzi was blinded by a sharp light. It burned his eyes to tears when he tried to look past it. An intense white spotlight surrounded him like an illuminated white cone. The rest of his prison cell was pitch black.

Phil glanced around and saw no iron bars or a door, nothing but a solid wall of darkness. The air felt damp and cool against his skin as if he was under ground. His prison had a musty, stale smell, and a nasty rotten egg smell, the odor of Titans.

He knew they were just beyond the blackness waiting, watching, wanting to kill him, but they didn't.

The drug they injected into Phil made him light headed and nauseous. They injected him every couple of hours to subdue his special mind abilities that he used on some of the Titans who caught him. With the injection of small *nanites* into his body on Flarconea, he developed some telekinetic and telepathic powers.

Since his capture, a day ago, Phil Ruzzi was beaten, drugged and kept awake continuously. He lost all sense of time. Exhausted and drugged, he was starting to get a pale complexion. Most of the time he felt woozy and disoriented. His *nanites* were working over time keeping his body functioning.

Suddenly a desperate urge to escape came over him. A memory flashed inside his head. He remembered he had found the jamming station in a horseshoe valley in his sector. He had to find Jacob Skyler and inform the others of it's whereabouts. The more time that passed, the more humans were killed around the world.

Phil went to stand up and felt heavy chains holding him down. He realized he was chained to the floor like a beast. Heavy bulky manacles cut into his wrist, with three feet of thick chain anchored deep into the concrete floor. To the Titans he was nothing but a beast of burden, a slave. Phil coughed then yelled, "I am not a slave."

Phil felt desperate and frustrated. He looked into the light and roared his anger. He squatted down by one of the chain's anchors. He gripped the chain with both hands. He fixed his feet firmly on the floor.

He took a moment and paused. He stared straight out in front of him into the darkness. He focused his thoughts and he pulled the chains tight, straining with every muscle in his body. The chains clinked tight as he strained to free himself.

Chips of cement started to flake off the floor, but the anchor didn't budge. Phil battled with his chains for a long minute. Finally the drugs kicked in and he clasped to his knees from exhaustion. He wiped the sweat from his brow, with his forearm as if it weighed a hundred pounds.

Phil Ruzzi's short black curly hair dripped with sweat. His soft brown eyes were blood shot and hazy. Twenty years old, Phil Ruzzi still had the face of a young Italian boy, although he was the size of a professional football player. He grew five inches in the last year. The boy was now six-foot four, and weighed over two hundred and twenty pounds. He was molded like a Greek body builder and he was stronger than he looked. Titans rarely saw humans so big, and had never seen them with such strength.

Looking out into the darkness Phil Ruzzi saw two red eyes starring at him, the red glowing eyes of a Titan. He scanned the room and saw two more pairs of eyes on the opposite sides of the room.

One of the three Titans, on Phil's far left, spoke out in his native tongue.

"Commander Godon do you think he can pull those chains out?"

Phil Ruzzi hopped back to his feet into a low fighting position. He was off balance and staggered back and forth, but he was still willing to fight. He screamed at the Titans in frustration. "You blue flat headed idiots. I can't understand you. "

Grabbing his bloody ear he yelled out again,

"You ripped the translator out of my ear."

Another Titan spoke out in the Titan language.

"He is the biggest human I've ever seen, I heard that they all used to all grow this big before we invaded."

Commander Godon walked out of the darkness and under the spotlight in front of Phil. The large blue Titan dwarfed Phil by three feet. The over weight alien commander weighed at least five hundred pounds. He was as tall as a polar bear standing on its hind legs. His massive arms were as big as tree trunks.

Phil Ruzzi looked helpless, covered in ripped rags, next to this giant killing machine. Godon was dressed in dull black metallic armor head to toe. His battle armor surrounded his body as if it was an extra layer of skin. It covered every extra roll of fat the Titan's body produced.

The Titan commander reached out and grabbed Phil's arm with a grip that would have shattered any enslaved human's bones. Godon's oversized, four fingered hand covered most of Phil Ruzzi's bicep. Phil grimaced in pain.

Commander Godon yelled over to his comrade. "He didn't get these muscles on Earth, not with the stuff we been feeding them."

Phil Ruzzi looked right into the commander's eyes for a long second, then he thrashed his body forward then back, pulling Godon off balance, and breaking the strong grip the Titan once had on his arm.

The Commander instantly spun with the momentum. He completely turned around facing Phil Ruzzi. He stopped and grabbed Phil by the neck. He moved quickly for such a large beast.

A Titan Commander is a top killing machine. You became a Titan Commander by killing your superiors in one on one combat and political sabotage.

No one has attempted to challenge Commander Godon in years. The fear of being struck down with a single blow scared most of his young officers. He dismembered his last challenger and hung parts of him for public display.

Now Phil Ruzzi hung at the end of this monster's arm a couple of pounds of pressure away from a broken neck.

Commander Godon spoke to Phil in English, through his harmonizing translator. Most Titans had one implanted just inside their throat. "Tell me why you are here, human?"

Godon grabbed Phil by each bicep now and shook him like a rag doll. "I know you are a human warrior. The Flarconeans trained you to be a fighter didn't they?"

Godon turned and smiled with his sharp teeth at his comrades and whispered with a little sarcasm, "Some of the slaves, with a little persuasion, have said there is a new rebel force starting up. Who is the leader of this so-called Earth Defense Force? Rumor has it he's in this region."

Godon started shaking Phil again, yelling at him. "Who is your leader? Tell me where I can find him and I'll let you die quickly or are you their leader."

Phil had to escape, too much depended on him. He lunged his hands up for the Commander's throat. The chains clinked tight, and his hands fell short of their target. He stared hard into the Commander's red eyes. "Screw you, flathead. You're going to lose your head."

Commander Godon snarled like a bear and swung a crunching backhand at Phil's jaw, knocking him to the ground. Godon followed through with a frustrated kick in the stomach. Godon wanted to make sure the human was just unconscious and not dead. Phil replied with a low groan.

A large welt started puffing up on Phil's lip. A little blood trickled from the corner of his mouth. The Commander reached down and grabbed Phil by each bicep. Lifting him off the ground as far as the chains allowed. The commander lowered his head, bringing him inches from the Phil's face.

At the top of his lungs, commander Godon started screaming. "Why do you resist, human? You gain nothing except a long, painful death. I don't understand you. We should have killed you all when we invaded."

Phil starred straight back into the commander's blood red eyes.

"We got the Titans all figured out. Not understanding the meaning of human revenge will be the Titans end."

Phil spit blood from his cracked, puffy lip, into the Titans face. The commander dropped Phil and wiped the blood off his cheek. He hesitated a moment to let the anger in him build. He thrived on the rush of power it brought him.

He drew back his oversized hand with a snapping snarl in the back of his throat. He let go a devastating blow to Phil's jaw, letting up at the very last second. The impact was hard and would of broke several bricks. It almost snapped Phil's neck. His body went limp and he crumbled to the floor.

The Titan commander went ballistic. "That's not the answer I wanted, human." The commander shook his head and turned to one of the guards. "Throw water on him and wake him up! When he wakes don't let him go back to sleep."

The commander paced back and forth. "Beat him every time he closes his eyes, but don't knock him out or kill him and remember to keep him drugged at all times or he'll get back his telekinetic powers and crush your throats."

Godon stared at the two prison guards and pointed a finger at them. "Remember this, he escapes or dies, you die."

The commander took one last puzzling look at the unconscious human. He himself wouldn't take this type of painful death. Why would the human take it? It made no sense to him.

Godon turned and stormed out of the jail cell. He walked down the narrow hallway shaking his head.

"Stupid humans."

The fluorescent lights flickered with each step he took. The basement steps creaked from the pressure the large Titan put on them.

Outside a well-guarded armored Titan hover tank waited. The craft was thirty feet long, ten feet wide and fifteen feet high of gliding death. It was made of smoothed angled green steel that could redefine the surrounding scenery in a matter of minutes.

The hover tank's extensive laser barrel was scanning the area. Fully charged, it cast doom anywhere it pointed. The war machine was perfectly balanced, hovering five feet above the ground. It barely made a noise. Commander Godon appeared outside the jail. Instantly the whole back of the tank split in half. The door lowered quickly with a swish, as the colder air inside rushed out to meet the warmer air.

A dozen of the commander's personal guards lined up in two lines, leading into the war machine. The commander never risked the possibility of an assassination.

The commander stomped inside the tank and yelled. "Get this piece of crap moving! I want to be off this burning planet in five minutes!"

The driver grunted a positive reply and started hitting switches. The tank tilted slightly down and to the right as it turned around and headed to the center of town. The sounds of twigs snapping from the electrostatic power could be heard a hundred feet away as the tank made it's quick maneuver. The burnt smell was all that was left behind. The tank hurried through the streets of town stopping at the Titan headquarters.

The door of the tank swished back open. The commander rushed out and headed straight to his shuttle. The heavily armed shuttle was already warmed up for take off. The commander marched inside and sat in his seat with a huff, then screamed again. "Get me to the moon base, now!"

Chapter 11

All the humans at the bar froze in terror. They watched Jacob go where only their worse nightmares would take them. All their fears and horrors lurked behind the door to the Titan's back room. There, sadistic Titans were drunk and rowdy, looking for a human to torture for their pleasure.

Jacob glanced over his shoulder at them with pity. Remorse sat in his stomach like a lead weight. The human spirit is already dead. The pressure of living in hell made them barely human anymore. They dredge through a life of sorrow with no hope of freedom. There is no sparkle of life in their eyes anymore. The humans at the bar felt Jacob's stare and turned away in shame.

Jacob could feel his anger start to wind up inside him. Grinding his teeth was the only way he could remember not to scream out. He wanted to tell the humans at the bar to fight back, that they weren't dead yet, but he knew it wouldn't do any good. These people were scared to stand up and fight. Most of them physically looked like the walking dead.

Jacob stared at the forbidden door and mumbled under his breath, "What these people need is a taste of freedom, to get their desire to live back.

Jacob didn't hesitate, he strutted up to the door that led to the Titans back room, and swung it open like he owned the place. He didn't let the attacking stench slow his pace. He wanted to give these slaves a memory, a story of hope to tell others. The human race is not dead yet, the human spirit lives on.

Jacob strolled into the room calmly and confident, closing the door behind him. His mood was slightly side tracked when he saw the care in which the room was decorated. It was detailed in different kinds of beautiful woodwork. The Titans covered the marble walls and ceiling in hand carved pine. The wood's swirling grain lines were brought out more by dark staining. The hardwood floor was done in oak, also stained in a dark color. The large tables and chairs were made of mahogany. Nicely crafted and made by human hands, Jacob thought. The flickering stone fireplace gave the whole room a gloomy feeling of a castle during the Dark ages.

The room was practically empty of Titans. The three that were there were too busy to notice the arrival of the big human. They were caught up in a test of brute strength, on the far side of the smoky room. There hands clinched together struggling intensely in an arm wrestling match.

The smallest of the three watched the two bigger beasts with admiring blood in his eyes. His two comrades were superior warriors compared to him. They both struggled against each other, grunting and snarling, constantly shifting their massive weight back and forth. The smaller private watching envied their power.

Liters of coca cola bottles littered the area around them. They were intoxicated, and never noticed Jacob walk across the room. He silently strolled over to the opposite corner of the place, and took a seat with his back to the wall.

Jacob noticed Hitock's large cat like eye peeking in by the door, blinking slowly two or three times. Jacob thought it would be like walking into the lion's den for him, to serve a human in the Titans' room. He's risking a severe beating, showing his defiance in public to the Titans. Jacob didn't want to put him in danger, but he had to see if he was willing to defy the Titans.

The Titans were still struggling furiously grunting and growling at each other. They never noticed Hitock start across the room. Jacob could feel the two Titan's battle was coming to a climax, as their swearing was getting worse and loader.

Suddenly the larger corporal quickly cocked back his fist, and let go a crunching blow to the center of his comrade's forehead.

The Private's head snapped back like a whip. His skull seemed to hover off his shoulders for a moment, while his dark red eyes crossed together slowly.

In the next moment all the muscles in his body relaxed, as if someone hit a switch and turned him off, but before the unconscious Titan slapped against the floor, the back of his wrist was pinned to the table.

The corporal dropped his grip on the private's hand. The private finished collapsing to the floor.

The corporal held his arms up in victory. He looked down on the unconscious private with his sharpened teeth showing a sadistic smirk across his face. "If you want to win pup! You have to know when to change the rules."

The corporal burst into uncontrollable hard laughter, the shorter private joined in with him. They snorted hysterically through their nose, slapping each other on the back. It took them a good minute to slow down to a chuckle.

They were ready to take another swig of soda, when they spotted Hitock handing a mug of ale to Jacob Skyler. "Hitock!" The victorious corporal growled like a bear.

"Hitock, what the hell do you think you're doing? Serving a human back here? You know he will die and you will be severely beaten for this."

Jacob stood up and grabbed his ale from Hitock. He looked into the small alien's eyes with respect, ignoring the drunken pompous aliens. "Thanks for showing me that the Drek race still has courage." Jacob held his mug up in the air and saluted the Drek. In one big gulp he downed the ale and wiped his mouth slowly with his sleeve.

Hitock took a deep breath nodding his head in thanks. He looked up at Jacob and smiled.

"I know who you are; you are the human leader. You're one of those humans the Titans are talking about; maybe the one who slaughtered those Titans in hand-to-hand combat. To think that I have given you hope gives me honor."

Then Hitock lower his voice even more. "I believe I can help you some more. I have some information I think you might want."

Hitock was about to say something else when the corporal

yelled out again. "Human is life so tuff in the wilderness that you would come in here and commit suicide."

Jacob Skyler put his hand on Hitock's shoulder and thanked him once again with a nod and a smile. "Excuse me my friend I have to take care of something."He gazed over his shoulder sizing up the Titans for the fight to come.

Jacob turned to the two drunken Titans and took a step in front of Hitock. Both Titans took a step closer to the brash young human. The smaller Titan shook a half-full Coca-Cola bottle at Jacob, yelling in a harmonized voice.

"If you thought life was tough before, slave. Wait till we get through with you."

Both Titans started laughing again, not expecting a reply. Jacob looked for Hitock, but he had left the room, a positive strategic move on his part. He did notice some humans crowding at the door peeking through, waiting to see what was going to happen next.

Jacob calmly looked back at the two Titans. "There are only three of you and none of you are over the rank of a sergeant. You might want to go get some more of your friends to help you, don't you think."

As the Titans blood began to sizzle, the smaller Titan crushed his plastic soda bottle in his hand.

Jacob's mood changed. The wild beast in him started to come out. His heart started beating faster. He could feel the rush of adrenaline pumping into his veins. Jacob peered at the Titans as if they were his prey. "Well flatheads, if you think your human enough to try me. You can give it your best shot, but I promise, you will lose your heads in the process."

One corner of the corporal's upper lip rose up like an attack dog, showing off his jagged teeth. They had been sharpened to piercing little daggers.

"A brave human, this is rare. You must be new to Coal Fifteen."

The shorter Titan took a step closer, tensing the shrinking atmosphere between them even more. "Such disrespect, you must be taught humility slave. The question is will you live through the whole lesson."

Both Titans started to walk across the room throwing chairs out of their path, wiggling their fingers eager to lunge at the human fool. Jacob reached behind his neck, and gripped his sword, that he kept concealed, strapped to his back, under his cloak.

Jacob felt the madness taking him over. It was time for revenge. Jacob's knuckles turned white as he gripped the chair in front of him. His fury built more and more. Jacob was flooded with thoughts of his parents being taken away and tortured by the Titans. The Earth was being endlessly bombed from space. People panicked in the streets. He was ready to explode.

Thoughts of possible strategies for the fight that was about to happen flashed into his head. Jacob was ready to go crazy. A long tense silence was burning down, like a fuse on a stick of dynamite. The Titans could feel it too.

Everybody was ready to spring at each other, when a baritone Titan voice cut in from the bar. "Corporal we don't kill informants until after we get information out of them."

Jacob turned around to see a ten-foot, one eyed, Titan captain filling the doorway. He blocked the exit completely, obstructing any view out to the bar. He strolled slowly into the back room between the two Titans and Jacob.

The captain never bothered to cover his ripped out eye socket with a patch. It was a scar from a battle, and he wore it like a medal of honor. He was the perfect example of Titan obesity. Layers of fat seemed to be slipping off his body. The Titans were obsessed in getting as large as they could, no matter how out of shape it got them. Large meant power to a Titan.

The Captain stomped over to Jacob's table, staring curiously at him with his one good red eye.

The corporal and private were sloppy drunk, but still able to manage to stand at attention. Fear of their superior officer was enough to sober them up a little. This ten-foot beast had killed his way up to the rank of captain. He was not to be under estimated.

The corporal slurred off a report to the captain in the Titan native language, but Jacob Skyler's implanted translator picked up the translation. "Didn't know he was a squealer sir. We were just about to question him."

The captain's hairy brow wrinkled up in disbelief. A sly evil grin emerged on his face. "Sure you were corporal, after I'm finished with him you can have him to play with. "

Both drunken Titans started laughing and walked back to their table. Tripping over their passed out comrade, who was still hugging the floor, mumbling in his sleep.

The giant one-eyed captain gestured politely to Jacob to sit back down. He sat quite peaceably across from Jacob in one of the large wooden chairs. "You are a brave human to try and sit back here without an escort. You must have something big in mind to risk your life so easily. Tell me something good human and I might let you leave here alive."

Jacob knew the flathead was lying through his sharp pointy teeth. He understood the captain's promise to give him to the Titans soldiers as soon as he finished talking to him.

Jacob's first reaction was to slice off his head with a quick clean cut. He even started to reach for his sword again. It was all he could do to restrain from taking it out and do justice to this alien.

Jacob thought about his priorities. This flathead knew where Phil Ruzzi was. He has to get the information from him before he can kill him. Phil had to know where the jamming station is. It's the only reason he would come back this way. "Let's get down to business one-eye, I have crystals, you have information I want."

The Titan captain was unusually civil with a smile. It was quite patronizing for a Titan to do, which made Jacob even madder with each passing second. Jacob turned away from him in disbelief and said under his breath, "Who the hell did this flathead think he's kidding? Does he actually think I'm stupid enough to trust him?"

The captain replied with a broader, faker, smile and a bit of a chuckle in his voice. It was a pitiful attempt at deception. "So you want to trade, human. You want your life and information? You better have some very big crystals on you."

Jacob leaned over the table slowly, and whispered back to him.

"Bigger than you can ever imagine, One-Eye. Just tell me where the new captive, Phil Ruzzi, is being held."

The captain's attitude changed at the mention of Phil's name. He had been ordered not to kill the new prisoner. He pushed himself back in his chair, wrinkled his nose and while grinding his teeth. A look of hatred came over his ugly blue mug.

Jacob didn't realize that Phil had killed five of the captain's loyal guards resisting his capture. Two Titans had even lost their heads from the sharp edge of Phil's Flarconean sword, a bad thing in the Titan religion. Titans believed if you were beheaded you would wander through eternity without purpose, a Titan hell.

The captain's feelings started to shift again. He relaxed himself, and resumed his fake smile. "Phil Ruzzi? Mm, let me see, Phil Ruzzi, yes I remember. The human is already dead. The fool spilled his guts about everything he knew, about the so-called human rebellion. So, as a reward, I killed him quickly."

Jacob knew no matter how much they tortured Phil he would never talk. Pain would not be a problem when it came to keeping a secret from the Titans. Phil's passion for humans retaking Earth was too strong to break.

Jacob knew the flathead was lying to him again. This game was starting to get frustrating to Jacob. He stood up gripping the edges of the table, and growled back at the Titan. "Where are they keeping him, flathead?"

The insult infuriated the captain. He grabbed the table like he was going to charge. The Titans were a flat headed race, but they took the description as an insult.

The captain slowly regained his composure again and relaxed his grip on the table. He spoke to Jacob calmly but firmly. "Sit down slave I have a question for you. Tell me the identity of the human who attacked the Titan train and I might let you live."

In a lighting move, Jacob reached across the table and grabbed One-Eye by his chest.

With ease, he dragged the obese alien across the table, holding him nose to nose. The captain's eye widened with surprise at the humans speed and strength.

Jacob growled at him again in a harsh whisper. "I'll give you a gift one-eye. The most wanted man on the planet, Lord Jacob

Skyler the great train robber, stands before you ready to chop off your head and send you to an eternal damnation!"

Jacob shoved the captain back into his seat and reach behind his back. He slid his Aderain sword out of its sheath and swung it like he was going for the fences.

Jacob's speed was no match for the Titans. His blade sliced right through the Titan's neck as if it was made of butter. Jacob barely felt any resistance until his blade shot out of the Titan's neck, and buried itself three inches deep into a near by thick wooden beam.

The captain's head tumbled through the air across the room, rolling right in front of the other three Titans. The captain's head stopped and stared in shock upside down at the warriors.

Their laughing and drinking came to an abrupt stop. They stared at the head with disbelief and confusion. The captain's head stared right back at them, with a similar look of surprise on it.

In the soldier's drunken state they had to take a moment to decide, whether the terror was real or not.

Jacob seized the opportunity to charge them. Screaming at the top of his lungs he lunged across the room in two great strides, waving his sword above his head.

He brought the edge of his blade down in the middle of the corporal's flat skull, cracking it wide open. The Titan dropped to his knees, and fell forward. A flood of blue blood started oozing from his head, surrounding his corpse.

Jacob looked up to see the shorter private start to pull out his laser pistol, strapped to his belt.

Jacob spun around reaching his sword out just long enough to smack the weapon out of his hand. Going with his momentum he spun around again with a back kick to the private's chest. The kick staggered the Titan back knocking him off balance.

Jacob took another full swing with his sword, and sliced right through the private's neck. The Titan's body went stiff with fright, and then collapsed backwards to the floor. His head bounced right into the fireplace.

The Titan that was passed out on the floor lifted his head up. In a daze he was still able to draw an accurate bead on Jacob with his laser pistol. "I'll receive a medal for killing you, human."

A flash of red light came from across the room and bored a hole right through the Titan's forehead. His eyes crossed for the last time. He started shaking uncontrollably, squeezing off half a dozen rounds.

Jacob dove to the ground and the shots went crashing through the window of the bar.

There was stillness for two deep breaths, a moment of calm and relief. The next moment the camp's alarms started going off. Everybody in the place started screaming and scrambling for the door.

Jacob looked to see who fired the shot that saved his life. He saw Hitock waving a laser pistol from the bar room door. He started screaming at Jacob. "This way Lord Jacob Skyler, follow me."

The Drek dashed behind a huge barrel near the back wall of the room.

Sword in hand, Jacob chased after him and found a small hidden door heading into the side alley. Jacob could barely hear the Drek whispering to him from the alley outside. "Hurry, Lord Skyler, the Titans are about to burst in."

Jacob peaked around the barrel behind him to see Titans pushing their way through a wave of fleeing humans trying to get out of the tavern.

Jacob looked back down at the small door leading into the alley. It was almost half his width, but the motivation was there to get out. He squeezed through the small hole with no room to spare. He scrambled to his feet and scanned up and down the dark alley, but Hitock was gone. "Man, those Dreks are fast."

A tiny calm voice at the end of the ally whispered back. "When properly motivated, Dreks can be very nimble."

Jacob headed towards the small voice at the end of the alley, towards the back of the building.

Hitock met him halfway. "Lord Jacob Skyler I have the information you seek. I know the whereabouts of another human as big as you. The one that was recently captured in this area."

Out of the darkness of the night a wooden club swung out of nowhere and hit Hitock in the back of the shoulder. Hitock flew through the air like a light tumbleweed, slamming hard against the wall of the alley. He slid to the ground like a heap of wet laundry.

Chapter 12

Commander Godon stared quizzically out of his space shuttle's porthole. Captain Chuckton, who was in charge of the moon base, stood by his side. Godon was focused on his Earth production problem. "Humans trained by Flarconeans?"

The colossal moon crater, Archimedes, filled his view. The Titans sank their military base directly in the center of the massive crater at the far end of Mare Imbrium, (the sea of rains). From space the base looked like a gigantic silver fishing bobber in an immense black sea of the moon.

It was a typical Titan base. A cylinder shaped structure with a point at one end. A complete military base that burrowed half a mile deep into the crust of the moon, like an unrelenting deer tick. The main portion of the base housed Titan warriors and electronic sensing devices. The other half of the base held five squads of Titan fighters and a dozen troop transports. The two Titan cruisers that patrolled around Earth and the Titan moon base was enough of a fighting force to defend Earth from conventional Flarconean weapons.

Captain Chuckton was a few inches shorter than Godon and nearly as heavy. He cleared his throat and stepped up to the captain. "Excuse me sir the daily report."

Godon showed his razor sharp teeth and snarled at the captain. "Chuckton, you border on dismemberment." Godon quickly snatched at Captain Chuckton's throat with a fierce grip.

Captain Chuckton never wavered in his demeanor. He whispered as loud as he could. "Better killed doing my job than not doing my job."

Godon almost cracked a smile. "Your getting there Chuckton, continue."

Captain Chuckton rubbed his neck and adjusted his shoulders shaking off Godon's strength. "The space fighters are completely stored on the top three levels of the base. The robotic laser cannons are on line and have been tested. They are sporadically placed to ward off any type of low fighter or ground troop attacks."

Godon looked back out the window. "Seeing that Aderain fighter last month was not a good sign. If the Aderain fighters have interest here we have to be prepared to defend."

Captain Chuckton nodded in agreement and continued. "The electro magnetic force field is at full power around the dome. The structure of the base is impossible to destroy with laser fire. The ground would give way before the structure would. The base would just sink deeper into the ground."

Commander Godon shook his head with satisfaction. "The Aderain fighter sighting has motivated the workers to finish ahead of schedule."

Godon waved his hand for Captain Chuckton to continue. "There are two fighter patrols out to help control Earth. There are five more patrolling the rest of the solar system."

Captain Chuckton cleared his throat again. "Now for the bad news. Earth is the closest port to the front lines. We are four weeks away flying in hyper space, to be in Flarconean territory, thirty light years away."

Captain Chuckton adjusted his shoulders again. "The Dillbanians are a non space fairing race but the Flarconeans have established a small base on one of the Dillbanians five moons. From the moon base they are defending the planet with ten Flarconean cruisers and two Flarconean destroyers that carry the "C" type conventional Flarconean space fighter. There has been no sign of an Aderain space fighters."

Godon shook his head no. "So the stargate production hasn't started there yet. It's a one-way trip."

Captain Chuckton shrugged his shoulders. "The Flarconeans are fighting us daily near Dillbane space. We haven't been able to land on the planet yet, although our forces gain ground everyday. Command has mentioned that this last year Earth has been the main supplier to Dillbane. It turns out Earth is the richest planet, with food, water, and minerals in the quadrant. It has become the oasis for the front lines."

Commander Godon rubbed his forehead roughly. "Great nothing like having a little more pressure to help run things smoothly."

Captain Chuckton fought back the smile of his commander's discomfort. "The maintenance on our stargate is complete. The main laser that shoots into the warped space to make the tackyon tunnel has been adjusted."

As the shuttle slowly descended towards the moon, Commander Godon sat down in his seat and started scratching his flat head. "What are these damn humans up to? If food production slows down anymore, my superiors will send a hit squad after me."

Godon sat down and tried to relax. "I've got to find the leader of these trained humans and kill him as soon as possible. I have to crush the hopes of the human slaves before they get rebellious and slow down production. What an annoying species."

The Titan space shuttle hovered quietly in the vacuum of space, high over the silver dome. A quarter mile in circumference, the thick metal dome split at the top when it opened. A static flash of white lighting signaled that the force field was down around the perimeter of the base, and the large shield started to slide open.

The Commander's shuttle gently descended onto the landing pad. The enormous metal doors of the dome slowly sealed themselves again. Breathable atmosphere howled through the landing area, in a strong gust of wind, almost instantaneously.

The shuttle's door opened, and Commander Godon rushed out, still totally absorbed in his human problem. Figuring out the possible strategy of irrational humans was not an easy task.

Humans are savages, but the Flarconeans have trained them to battle Titans, Commander Godon thought to himself. *They know our different strategies and military tactics. An intelligent savage is dangerous, especially one defending his home planet.*

A short Titan private ran up to Godon with a metal pad in his hands. He bowed his head, and held out the pad to commander Godon. With a grunt, Godon slapped it away with the back of his hand.

"Don't make me read it, pup! Tell me what it says."

Message relay was the worse duty a Titan solider could get, especially if the message was bad news. The private snapped to attention, and started to squeak out his report. The commander turned and started to walk away. He had better things to do then listen to another routine, mundane planet report. The short private scurried after him, laboring to keep up with the commander's quick long strides. "Commander Godon there was some trouble at the mining camp you just left."

Commander Godon came to an abrupt stop, reached out with one hand, and grabbed the small private by his throat. "What! If those lousy pitiful prison guards let that human escape, I'll cut off their heads myself! The human is the key to finding the other human rebels."

The private was pulled to the tip of his toes, and he struggled desperately to free himself from the unrelenting hold of his commander. He pleaded with him, barely able to get the words passed the commander's grip. "No sir, no sir, Phil Ruzzi is stilled locked up, and under heavy guard."

Godon dropped his grip, and proceeded to head for his quarters. "Then what is it pup?"

Rubbing his short neck working his blue blood back through his veins and trying to regain his composure, the private started to struggle after commander Godon's great strides again.

When he caught up to the commander the private replied more calmly. Making sure of course he was out of the commander's grasp. "It seems another over sized human has walked into town, and sliced up four of our soldiers again, including chopping off the heads of two of our soldiers, a private and Captain Cootow."

Godon stopped again, wiggled his nose and scratched his chin, thinking about the loss of Captain Cootow. He shrugged his shoulders carelessly. "Cootow was corrupt anyway. "

Then the commander scratched his flat head vigorously. "So there's another human warrior in the area."

Flashing a deadly stare at the private, like everything was his fault, the commander barked out. "Was the human killed?"

The private hesitated in fear of the response to his question, so he spit it out quickly, to get it over with. "No sir, but patrols are hot on his trail."

Godon snarled in disbelief at the private and raised his hand as if to clobber the private. The private cowered in fear, and Godon decided not to bother with the little pup. "They'll never find him, and you know it. He'll disappear into the mountains like they always seem to do. Double the patrols, and if they don't find a large human in one Earth rotation, someone will die for it."

Godon marched off to his quarters mumbling in frustration. The private quickly headed in the other direction as far away from the commander as possible. "Yes sir, double the patrols."

Chapter 13

Jacob Skyler raised his sword above his head ready to attack.

Gram suddenly strolled out of the shadows, a bit of a hop in his step. He carried his club over his shoulder and a smug look of satisfaction on his face.

"Got them, my Lord. Did you see him fly when I cracked him? I bet you I could have been a baseball star, if we still had a baseball league that is."

Jacob buried his chin into his chest trying to hold back his anger rising in his throat. Jacob kept repeating over and over in his head, he meant well, he meant well. "Gram what are you doing here? You might have blown my first real lead to Phil Ruzzi. That Drek might know where he's being held."

Gram walked over to Hitock and shoved him with his foot. "He's still breathing my Lord. Don't worry, I'll get the information out of him when he wakes up. If not sooner."

Jacob ran his fingers through his hair intensely, almost pulling his hair out in frustration. He took a deep breath and tried again. "Listen Gram, that Drek, is on our side. He wants to help us. He was just about to tell me something important, when you turned out his lights with that Louisville slugger of yours."

Gram shrugged his shoulders. "How was I supposed to know? He's an alien and doesn't belong here. You can't trust him Jacob. He's nothing but trouble."

Jacob stood up straight and stared at Gram quizzically. For the first time he realized that the hate was towards all aliens, not just the Titan invaders. Making friends with the Flarconeans gave Jacob a different perspective on aliens than the survivors of the Titan's invasion. "Gram this Drek's world was conquered and his people were enslaved by the Titans. The Dreks hate Titans just as much as we do."

Gram tilted his head as if he didn't understand what Jacob was saying. Jacob realized he wasn't reaching Gram on this point. He decided to bring it up later after Hitock helped them.

Lowering his voice a little Jacob changed the subject. "What are you doing here anyway? You were supposed to head back to camp within an hour."

Gram stared at the stars for a moment avoiding eye contact with Jacob. "True my Lord, but there are five more minutes before that hour is up."

Jacob looked at Gram out of the corner of his eye. He couldn't quite hold back the small grin that kept on appearing on his face. He knew all along Gram wouldn't leave the area without him. "Watch yourself Gram. I need to know you'll follow my orders when it counts."

Jacob pointed at Hitock. "Now pick up your new friend and let's head for the horses."

Gram picked up Hitock easily and tossed him onto his shoulder like a bag of potatoes. He hated the idea of carrying an alien. He truly despised the Drek just because it wasn't from his planet.

The camp's alarms hadn't stopped, and Jacob knew they would be bringing out the hover tanks soon enough. They made their way through the street's shadows, hugging dark walls keeping an eye on the searchlight. They avoided small groups of stampeding Titans rushing through the camp.

They reached the outside of town quickly, where the other two men had kept the horses. Jacob greeted them both with a bit of a snarl. "I see you two listen just as well as Gram does."

They both pointed their fingers at one another then at Gram, mumbling the whole time under their breath. Mike walked over to Gram and asked about Hitock, "Who's the elf?"

Jacob put a hand on Mike's shoulder and answered for Gram. "He's a friend that Gram mistook as an enemy and he clubbed him. Don't you guys make the same mistake."

The two men looked at Gram with baffled looks on their faces. They had the same hate towards all aliens that Gram had.

Gram shrugged his shoulders back at them.

Jacob shook his head in disbelief. He grabbed his horse's bridle and swung himself onto the saddle. "Come on, lets get out of here before the Titan tanks make their way out of camp."

A large bulky Titan hover tank couldn't maneuver over the tough terrain that Jacob chose as an escape route. Jacob studied the Titan's hover tank on Flarconea. It is a decisive weapon on flat lands. It's massive laser cannon and it's arsenal of small laser weapons, could turn a town into rubble. Its only problem is it hovers off the land. The narrow valleys and hilly terrain surrounding the slave camp made it almost impossible for a hover tank to maneuver. It would have to stick to the old roads and highways.

The men climbed on their horses and galloped away. The ride back to camp was back crunching. Titan fighters skimmed across the treetops looking for them. The group traveled all night. The trail they took was narrow and very mountainous but the thick pine trees covered them from the Titan fighters heat sensors.

Gram, Michael and Rick wondered about their captured alien while Jacob wondered what his next move would be.

Chapter 14

Jacob walked into camp holding the reins of his hoarse. Hitock regained consciousness more than an hour after being clubbed. He walked wearily by Jacob's side with a lump on his head. Gram, Michael and Rick approached the camp with their heads flopping from a night with no sleep. Their eyelids tried to close over their eyes but their will kept them half open. The human rebels were almost asleep on top of the horses.

The guards guarding the camp had become experts at concealing themselves in the woods. Carefully hidden behind the rocks and the shadows of trees like the clever forest creatures they had become. Jacob knew they had spotted them. He had his suspicions where they were.

The group walked up to the outside of the caves where the camp was concealed. A handful of men and women came scurrying up to aid them into camp. They led the tired men and weary horses to food than rest.

Jacob looked at his small band of young loyal warriors before he went to bed. Perfect soldiers, young, experienced with a passion to kill the enemy.

There was a diluted feeling of relief for Jacob coming back to this all too portable camp. The camp was barbaric but secure from Titan eyes and that made it comfortable.

Jacob's mind needed to unwind for a few hours with some deep sleep and meditation, maybe even a little beneficial news to help be himself again. The whole human race needed a long vacation.

Jacob made arrangements for Hitock to get some rest than walked into the cave himself. Light bulbs strung through out the cave, like old worn Christmas lights. The cave was lit with just enough light to get you to the next dimly lit glow.

It was the perfect place to meditate for Jacob. It seems easier for him to reach a state of calmness surrounded by the comforts of mother Earth. A reaction from being off planet for the past year he guessed. In this cave he could rest without worrying about being seen by the Titans, protected by mother Earth.

Jacob thought if Phil found the jamming station he would have left word with Kerri and Caesar at the transport site. He could relax his aching bones until the other Lords arrived. They would all be returning soon once the word got out that Phil had found the jamming station, if he has found it.

Hitock had given Jacob some hope in finding Phil Ruzzi. Right now Jacob had to focus and think how tonight's actions affected his over all plan. What will the Titans think? Will rescuing Phil jeopardize the attack on the jamming station?

Jacob Skyler's body poured into his canvas cot, as if he was a cool piece of butter melting on a hot serving of mash potatoes. His aches evened out to dull sensation as his body fell into relaxation and his mind began to unwind. He was floating in the universe.

Thoughts leaped into his head, "If the Drek isn't too mad at Gram, to lead us into a trap, we could plan Phil's rescue for tomorrow. "

Jacob could see the feeling of distrust in every human he met. Even in himself. He felt to judge an alien race on a couple of encounters was stupid but vengeance is a good motivator for a rebellion.

Demock would help some humans lose some of their distrust for aliens. It will take time and sacrifice, Jacob thought. *For right now though going into battle with the probability of getting killed is not the time for thinking straight. Seeing your family killed can leave a lot of hate and craziness inside you.*

An epiphany flashed in Jacob's mind.

How could humans ever recover? They will always be emotionally scared from the Titans. It's best to focus their hatred towards the Titans and hope the next generation of humans can recover from the horror and the prejudice of aliens.

Jacob had no idea what happened to his family, and it ate at his nerves. He used his intense rage inside him to fuel his fights with the Titans. He can only hope his parents had escaped to the forest, and are still alive. Human survivors tell him most of the elders were taken and slaughtered right in the beginning.

Jacob got a cold shiver down his back. "I can't think of these things now. I must relax and clear my mind again."

Jacob concentrated relaxing all his muscles in his body. He reached out past his outer shell. He felt himself floating above himself with his inner eye. He studied his dim surroundings in the cave.

The night he was kidnapped by the Flarconeans popped into his head. Flashes of the space flight to Flarconea rushed into his mind. His Flarconean teacher, Dez Royer once told him, in his solemn monk tone, the choice the human race had.

"Our race, Jacob, was thrown into galactic war four thousand years ago just like yours is now. We were taught by the Alderainians how to fight. We later took the burden from them of protecting the universe from those who would take goodness and peace from worlds they encountered.

The human race must choose to take the role of protecting this sector from us. If they don't the Titans will and that would mean doom for Earth and a lot of other worlds. What I am now, you will become."

Jacob was brought back by a small noise out of place in the cave. In Jacob's mind's eye he could see a shadow moving ten feet from his cot. Someone was hiding behind some crates.

Jacob then heard Gram running towards his section of the cave. He thought to himself, something's up he has to return to his body.

Gram, out of breath and nervous, stumbled into Jacob's small section of the cave. "Excuse me Lord are you awake? The Drek has escaped. Don't worry we will capture him before he gets to far."

Jacob slowly rolled over in his cot to face Gram. He looked at him very calmly. "Gram my friend, don't you ever listen to me? Hitock, the Drek, saved my life. He knows where Phil Ruzzi is. He is free to do what he pleases. He can not escape, because he was never a prisoner, understand."

Jacob stretched out his arms and yawned. "Gram when you see Hitock ask him if he would please speak with me. It would be nice if you apologize to him for knocking him out too. He's to be treated as a special guest."

Gram turned away embarrassed and mad about the good treatment the alien was receiving. He stomped off out of the cave.

As soon as Gram was out of ear shot Jacob look towards Hitock's hiding place. "Hitock I'm sorry that my friend clobbered you. He reacted before he thought. Humans are not perfect, but please remember we are not the bad guys on this planet. I hope you are feeling better."

Out of the shadows Hitock's small voice sounded unsure. "I don't trust that human. He hates all aliens."

Jacob watched the small elf looking alien come out from behind a box of supplies, rubbing his over sized baldhead. Jacob said with sympathy, "Can you blame him Hitock. The first time he met an alien his parents were killed and his youngest brother was taken away. Kind of leaves a bad taste in your mouth."

Hitock grimaced as he felt the bump swelling on his head and got defensive. "I did not kill his parents. I may not be human but I hate the Titans just like you do, just like everybody does."

The Drek shook his head in bewildered, "I can help you battle them."

Jacob scratched his chin and wondered for a moment. "Why must you assist the humans against the Titans? Maybe you're a Titan spy."

Jacob saw the frustration in the Drek's face, then a look of disbelief. "I am one of the leaders of a Drek underground against the beasts. I give you this information as a sign of trust. It can kill me if you want it to."

He put his thin hands on his hips and tilted his head to the left. He seemed to strain to look deep into Jacob's eyes. "Dreks don't give up easily either. Don't you remember?"

He walked around Jacob and studied him. "I have information

that you want. I know where the other Lord is."

Jacob's cheeks couldn't hold back his smile anymore. It burst on his face like a light of hope. It was exactly what he wanted to hear. "I had hoped the information you had was about his whereabouts. I noticed your voice isn't harmonizing now. You picked up English quickly."

"Thank you, Lord Skyler. We Dreks are told that we are apt to figure things out."

Still trying to feel him out Jacob criticized him. "Except for the Titan's battle tactics."

With a sharp glance, Hitock looked at Jacob Skyler with astonishment. He took a deep breath and looked around the room until his first reaction subsided. "Yes maybe your right. Maybe it took a little more time than we thought to figured them out."

Jacob wondered about their strategy against the Titans and turned to question the Drek's last remark.

Suddenly a commotion rose from the people outside the cave. Jacob poked his head out of his little cove towards the entrance of the cave. "Excuse me Hitock, I'll be right back."

Out side the cave people stood with torches around Terry McGuire. He was perched on top of his horse laughing at nothing in particular. He reared his horse on its back feet and waved his hand in the air laughing his contagious laugh, playing out some old western character.

Jacob was happy, confused and a little relieved to see his old friend.

He yelled to his seemingly insane friend. "Hey get off of that horse before you break it."

Leo stopped and focused his stare at Jacob. His ear-to-ear grin slowly grew even larger. Leo's innocent smile brought back warm thoughts of childhood games that they played together as kids. After their abduction they were more like brothers than just friends. A stronger relationship developed between the two of them.

Leo steadied his horse and dismounted. He hurried over to Jacob with his arms open, giving him a big bear hug.

"Buddy, how have you been? Nice beard, I like the long hair

too." Leo held his hands out like a movie director with his thumbs touching and the rest of his fingers pointing straight up, like framing a shot.

"It's very Viking like."

Jacob returned the hug and patted his husky friend with enthusiasm on the back. "Leo, you dog. How have you been? Where's your Irish brigade you've promise to rise?"

Leo put his arms up above his head and slowly let them down as if he was making an invisible circle. "They have the place surrounded. I wanted them to get use to this area."

Jacob leaned down and put his hand around Hitock, who timidly came out of the cave and took shelter behind Jacob. "I have a nice surprise for you my friend. Our new ally has some information that we could really use. Come into my office and we will talk some treason."

The two friends proceeded to walk into the cave laughing out loud. Hitock followed quickly behind them lost in their shadow.

Jacob shouted to one of the camp guards. "Greet Lord Leo's people and get them some food."

Leo asked Jacob: "What's all this *lord* business?"

Jacob turned back to his old friend and smiled. "I'll explain later. Were you able to teach the bag pipes to anyone?"

He rubbed his two big fists together excitedly, like a kid in a candy store. "Oh yeah, I came across someone who already knew how to play the flute. They picked up the pipes no problem. It really scares the Hell out of the Titans."

Leo looked at Hitock with a little doubt in his eye. "Why, does your little friend play? So what's your name Drek, and where did you meet my ugly friend Jacob Skyler?"

Jacob spoke up seeing the uneasiness in Hitock's hesitation. "My friend's name is Hitock. He helped me out of a little jam at a slave camp in Rockland. He knows where Phil Ruzzi is."

"Phil got caught?" Leo studied the Drek carefully. "A very useful individual. So where is Lord Ruzzi? I haven't seen him since we landed. Kerri told me Phil had found the Titan's jamming station?"

Jacob looked at Hitock and punched his open hand. "Yes! I knew he had good news."

Hitock stood next to Jacob obviously feeling a little intimidated by Leo's rambunctious way of expressing himself. Hitock never saw such happiness from a human before. Leo was full of life.

Leo wasn't as tall as Jacob, but he had grown wider and was very physical in his movements.

Hitock answered him slowly. "I saw Lord Ruzzi in prison two days ago, in what the humans call the old school. I was being punished for insubordination. I saw your Lord Ruzzi from a distance while they were taking him down stairs to the interrogation room."

Leo scratched his new beard like it was infested with bugs and looked at Jacob. "What's this Lord stuff?"

Jacob raised a hand to Leo: "I told you, I'll explain later."

Leo looked back down at Hitock. "How did you know it was Lord Ruzzi and not just another good-looking human? I figure we all look alike to aliens."

Hitock responded with more confidence. He would not be called a liar.

"I'm sure it was him. I never saw a human slave spit in a Titan's eye before. He swore and threatened them constantly. I also haven't seen to many humans who are as tall as a lord."

Leo leaned up against the cave wall, folded his arms and relaxed. "Ah yes the benefits of living off world. Living on Flarconea while you're still in your growing years, has its benefits."

Jacob moved to sit back down on his cot. He looked at Hitock. "This man you saw was probably Lord Ruzzi or at least another lord. We can't take the chance that it wasn't."

Leo's voice got a little more serious. "So Jacob, what's your plan to get our captured friend out of jail."

Jacob looked up at Leo with an impish grin, he knew Jacob all to well. "I guess bail is out of the question."

Jacob walked around Leo slowly. "What I need is a diversion to get some of the prison guards away from the school. If you could make it look like there's a major assault on the slave camp's headquarters. It should draw some of the prison guards there for reinforcement."

Leo slapped his hands together hard grabbing every one's attention. "Well my friends if you need a diversion you got one. Jacob if you believe that we can get Lord Phil Ruzzi out before they kill him, I believe it too. Just one question. When do we leave?"

Hitock looked at Jacob with his cat like eyes opened wide with fright. "You can't be serious. You're going to attack a Titan slave camp?

Jacob gave a soft reassuring smile to Hitock. "Don't worry my friend. We're a lot better off then the Titans lead you to believe."

Jacob looked around the room. "We leave tomorrow just after night fall. They will be looking for us tonight, after our little disagreement earlier this evening. I'm sure by now that they have doubled the guards and have sent in extra air support. We'll have to let them calm down a little before we can get close enough."

Jacob threw his arm around his friend. "Terry McGuire we have to catch up on the last couple of weeks."

Leo smiled and put his hand on Jacob's shoulder. "Buddy you don't know the half of it. I can project my feelings without saying a word. I'm guessing it's a side affect from living on Flarconea or the *nanites* working in my brain. I just got to think, "sleep", and people will get tired around me."

Leo looked at Jacob, "Have you had any strange things happen to you?"

Jacob shook his head no. "I can sense things around me but nothing like you're mentioning."

Leo added, "I heard from Keri that Phil has telekinetic powers now."

Jacob smiled and slapped Leo on the back. "It sounds like we got more than we bargained for."

Jacob looked out of the cave and called for Gram. He arrived spitting out a report giving the Drek a nasty look.

Jacob put up his hand and interrupted him. "Gram give our friend, Hitock some food and water, and go relieve Lord

Leo's people around the camp."

Leo looked at Gram and smiled. "Man you look ugly."

He then proceeded to hug the air out of Gram. "You're alive, thank God."

Leo took a moment and just smiled at him. "Look for Ginger she's in charge. Tell her I found my brother and to come into camp. I warn you though, treat her with respect, she might kill you if you don't."

Gram gave a sharp salute with a smile and gestured Hitock to follow him out of the cave.

Chapter 15

Leo and Jacob talked half way through the night and, most of the next day, reminiscing about their training on Flarconea and their last month back on Earth. In the last month, Jacob had recruited over a hundred humans, mostly escaped slaves. Word got out of his boldness in fighting the Titans. Leo had gathered up to fifty fighters during his ride south into Jersey. Most of them were girls from an all-girl school that had been invaded by the Titans.

An hour after dark, three quarters of the troop headed out in an indirect route towards their attack positions. There were two groups: Jacob, Gram and Hitock led thirty fighters to the old high school; while Leo and Ginger took a hundred humans in two groups of fifty to the southern end of the slave camp.

Each fighting force walked most of the night. The night carried a slight chill in the breeze when the wind decided to blow, but no one seemed to feel it. No one complain about anything. They were doing something to free their planet and it felt good. Morale was high.

They weren't in position until late in the evening, closer to morning. They each had a half hour to rest an absorb their targets.

Jacob lay down on his back in a field of tall grass resting, a hundred yards north of the Titan's new prison. His old High School had turned into a tanned brick fortress. He couldn't help chuckling to himself at the irony that Leo had pointed out. "You thought it was a jail before the invasion."

The school stretched a football field and a half long with a three-story annex at one end. Two enclosed tunnels extended across an open courtyard to connect the annex and the main part of the school.

Hitock and Gram lay beside Jacob studying the old brick building. Out of the darkness of the night a ten-year-old girl with milk chocolate skin appeared out of nowhere like a sudden breeze. Wearing black pants and a worn out black jacket, she had become part of the night.

She looked at Jacob and gave him a sweet little smile. "Excuse me Lord Skyler. Everybody is in position."

Jacob smiled and whispered back, "Thank you, Shelly. You can go back to your position and wait for the signal and keep your head down."

The young girl turned and jumped back into the darkness of the night, just as quickly and quietly as she appeared. The kid was a good soldier. Jacob mumbled to himself, "She'll be fighting the rest of her life."

As if the Drek was reading Jacob's mind, he said: "I wondered what kind of human society would rise out of this war, children fighting savagely for survival and revenge. What kind of government would rise out of this rebirth of human warriors?"

Jacob propped himself up on his elbows and listened to Hitock, who turned to look Jacob Skyler right in the eye. "The ones who fight now, what kind of knowledge and prejudice would they pass on to their children? They have nothing to offer but hate and revenge channeled into fighting skills."

Jacob looked to the stars. "The future of the human race is in the unborn children of tomorrow. Children who will learn how to survive day to day, with peace as a motivation to live."

Gram turned his head and added, "It must be the kids of those who fight now that learn about peace. Peace to us now is like a promised holiday that never comes. These kids of today will never understand peace. They will be a generation of warriors."

Hitock nodded his head in agreement with Gram, which caught Gram off guard. Gram slowly sat up on his elbow and rested his head in his palms. He started going over the conversation in his head again trying to figure out how the Drek was agreeing with him.

Hitock tilted his head and put his ear up towards the wind. He looked at Jacob Skyler questionably. "All we have to do is wait for Lord Leo's strange music to start? Lord Skyler, what does bagpipe music sound like?"

Jacob was staring at the stars. He was strangely relaxed and very conformable. The moment almost felt like an old dream. Something like the calm before the storm he guessed.

The cool Fall breeze was now whistling steadily through the top of the trees. The night sky was a dark rich black, nearly blue. It made the stars seem that much brighter. With no real pollution in the last year to haze the sky, the stars seem a lot closer, almost too close.

Jacob started to think about Leo playing his bagpipe music on Flarconea. When Leo was abducted by the Flarconeans he had his bagpipes with him. He was practicing for the St. Patrick's Day parade.

Jacob remembered Leo practicing one Sunday morning. He stood by himself in the center of the football field. "Leo is someone who believes in the tradition, honor and the magic of the Bag Pipes."

Jacob rolled on his side to face the Drek and grabbed his shoulder firmly, "It's the music that has pumped the blood of warriors for thousands of years."

Jacob quickly sat up and moved his hands around like a magician. "The incantation that flows in the tune can make your hair stand on end, if you had any. It can push butterflies from your stomach and turn it into pride when it finally reaches your chest with one moving melody."

Jacob rolled over on his back again. He turned his focus back towards the stars. "The music does have a human magic to it. They say those who march behind the songs of the bag piper will enter into battle shielded from fear."

Placing his hands behind his head for a pillow Jacob continued, "To your enemies, it becomes an unnatural and very terrifying death song. It will strike fear into the hearts of all your enemies."

Hitock looked like a kid daydreaming, sitting in the grass with curious looks of puzzlement and amazement on his face. Then he smiled knowingly at Jacob. "Sounds like the Lords have a little knowledge about magic of the spirit."

Jacob turned his head and looked Hitock straight in the eye. "Yeah you could say we learned how to tap back into human magic. Something we picked up from the Flarconeans. Something we always had, but forgot it was there."

Jacob and thirty other armed Earthlings hid behind shadows of trees and over grown bushes waiting for the music to play. They were starting to get on edge.

They listened to every noise in the night carefully.

They waited and watched the moon slowly crossed the night sky. Trying to remember the way it was before the invasion. The breeze picked up and quickly died back down again like a sigh. Quiet filled the air and it felt as if the Earth had stopped breathing. Even the insects stopped clicking waiting to see what was going to happen next.

Silence slipped out of the air and a steady rising, haunting hum of the bagpipes took its place. The music flowed through the valley, echoing off the mountain walls. Leo had somehow amplified the music. When the pipes reached their peak of intensity, a set of drums started pounding out an unrelenting military march. It made Jacob's heart take up the beat.

The tune changed to a quicker up lifting melody. It created a building force that felt as if it was going to burst wide open. Some of the girls Leo recruited started howling. They could be heard on the other side of the slave camp. Howling and screaming like wild animals ready to attack. Their screams had no fear in them.

Jacob let the screams fill his soul. He felt the need to battle fill his veins but had to wait for the guards to be called away to help reinforce the human attack on the headquarters.

Gram felt Jacob's anger build. He could feel the atmosphere around Jacob intensify. He shifted a couple of steps away from Jacob.

Hitock noticed Jacob's body stiffen too. The Drek reached out to touch Jacob on the shoulder from behind.

Gram's hand shot out and grabbed Hitock's wrist and

whispered, "Touch him now and you may lose your head. I don't know how Dreks fight, but humans fight with alot of intense emotion."

Hitock tilted his head in a quizzical fashion. "I have heard that. Titans are fierce but they don't want to die. I had heard how difficult the humans were when they were first caught. I also remember Lord Skyler slaughtering those three Titans at the Tavern. The human seemed to be insane when he fought."

Hitock looked Gram up and down.

"All the adult humans resisted after the Titans invaded. That's why the Titans killed most of the adults in the first year of the invasion."

Hitock folded his arms over his chest. "My race is more logical and, rarely gets emotionally upset like most enlightened species. Life is too precious to throw away. Dreks think their way out of their problems."

A large explosion suddenly accompanied the music. Part of the town lit up then was quickly eating back up by the darkness.

Titan alarms started screaming from the slave camp. Two squads of Titan guards appeared out of nowhere in front of the Titan jail. They gathered into a small circle in front of the prison.

A large Titan officer stepped out side and barked out orders. Half of the guards started stampeding south toward the center of the slave camp.

More flashing lights from explosions reached high into the night sky on the far side of town. It made the Titans guards around the prison flinch towards cover.

Then a series of small explosions started going off. Jacob focused on the school with his eyes. "Lord Leo's attack is in full swing."

A deep booming explosion shook the entire slave camp. It could have been lightening except that there wasn't a cloud in the sky. A Titan guard ran out of the jail and started screaming and yelling for the rest of the guards to follow him. Another herd of Titan guards began running towards town, leaving just two guards to guard the front door of the school.

Jacob Skyler never took his eyes off the two bulky guards. "All right Leo. The man knows how to start a party."

Never taking his eyes off the guards, Jacob whispered to Gram.

"Gram, you take the guard on the right. I'll take the one on the left. On the count of three."

Gram, in a kneeling position, raised his crossbow to his shoulder and placed the Titan's throat right in the middle of his crosshairs. Jacob took a similar stance a few feet away. He stood with his crossbow as still as a stone.

Jacob counted in a calm tone, taking a small breath between counting. "One,... two..., three."

Gram squeezed his cold trigger finger and in a low whisper blew out of his mouth: "See you."

Without warning, a moment of calm for the two Titan guards turned into terror. Both arrows hit their marks. The two guards feverishly grabbed the arrows embedded deep in their throats.

They look to each other for help and saw nothing but a look of bewilderment and horror on their comrade's face. They slowly dropped to their knees and their struggle began to lose its momentum. The two flatheads dropped on their faces. All was silent in front of the old school.

The rest of the human soldiers quickly moved in and took positions closer to and on top of the old high school. Three young soldiers made their way to the roof of the school by climbing on the back drain pipe. The two guards that use to watch the back of the school now lay on the ground, with their heads stuffed with arrows like a pin cushion.

Once the human soldiers reached the top they took some plastic explosives and placed them on the Titan generators mounted on the roof. The Titan generators now ran the power to the whole school.

The soldiers planted the explosives and took safety behind the entrance to the roof. The brick structure stuck out of the roof like an old tool shed.

Just as the human soldiers took cover, the door to the school roof swung open. Two Titan guards had ran up the steps and squeezed out of the door onto the roof. They took no more than two steps before the plastic explosives blew.

Thousands of small pieces of generator shrapnel punctured the Titans in hundreds of different places. The human soldiers were knocked down by the concussion even though they were behind cover.

The power went out in the whole building. You could only see by the light of the moon.

Gram and Jacob scurried up a wide but short concrete staircase to the front of the building. They held their ground next to the dead guards with Hitock right behind them. There was one small emergency light by the double doors that Gram quickly knocked out with the butt of his crossbow.

Jacob nodded to Gram and Hitock, and they started to open the door. A laser blast hit the top half of the door ripping it right off its hinges.

Two more shots exploded above Jacob's head, and he rolled forward into the dark prison, scrambling to his feet, then dove behind a wall.

The entryway to the school had a thirty-foot ceiling. Four long halls that connected to the corners of the entry way ran the width of the school.

Two more blasts came out of one of the dark hallways at the far end of the room. Blowing off chunks of the wall Jacob was using for cover.

With incredible speed Hitock swiftly ran inside the prison behind a desk, without being shot at.

Gram came through the door dodging a shot above his head. Another shot smacked him square in the shoulder, ripping through his flesh. The blast knocked him back off his feet into the open doorway.

Jacob turned back towards the door and dove on top of Gram, grabbing him by his clothes and, rolled him back outside in one swift move. A blast flew out the door followed by another blast from Hitock, who zeroed in on the Titan guard firing at Jacob. Hitock's shot hit its mark and the Titan roared out in pain.

A blast hit the desk Hitock was using for cover, splitting the wood and knocking it on its side.

Peeking around the front door Jacob traced the shot back to its origin and, let off three quick shots. Two of the shots ripped through the Titan's body. The only noise the Titan guard was able to make was the slap of what was left of his face hitting the floor.

Hitock moved further into the dark room and two more humans scrambled in the school supporting his position. Jacob turned around and knelt over Gram. Instinctively he started packing Gram's wound with some torn cloth from his shirt. "You're always looking for attention Gram."

Jacob looked at Gram's wound and saw that most of Gram's shoulder was blown away. Blood was flowing steadily, quickly soaking up the piece of cloth.

Gram coughed and whispered back: "Don't worry, my Lord, I stopped the shot with my shoulder. I didn't want them to hit any trees, save the Earth and all."

Jacob bit his lip and scanned the outside area. He raised his hand and signaled into the woods. Two young boys ran out of the brush and rolled Gram into a blanket.

Jacob looked back down at Gram with concern. "You'll be all right Gram. Craig and Tommy will bring you back to camp. Just stay cool. They'll fix you up there."

Gram smiled and relaxed. He closed his eyes slowly. His chest rose one more time then stopped.

Jacob put his hand on Gram's chest and his ear to Gram's mouth. There was nothing. Jacob suddenly felt alone and abandoned. He just lost one of his childhood best friends.

Those emotions didn't last long. Jacob's feelings turned to fury. His whole body started shaking from the pure hate that was rising up from his heart and soul. He had a sudden surge of power and energy, a feeling of being invincible.

Jacob Skyler looked back into the dark old school. The other soldiers had taken up positions to secure the lobby. Jacob rushed back into the doorway, wanting to destroy more Titans and to find Phil Ruzzi. He was done fooling around. He wanted Titan blood.

Jacob put his back against the wall next to Hitock.

"Hitock, where do you think they're keeping him?"

Hitock scanned the area getting his bearings. He pointed to the other side of the room with his little hand. "Lord Skyler behind that door there are a set of steps down to the place of torture. That's where Lord Ruzzi probably is."

Without hesitation Jacob ran to the other side of the room and put his ear up to the wooden door. Two shots followed his steps. Hitock and another human picked off the Titan remaining in the lobby.

Turning to the other soldiers Jacob waved his arm for them to follow him.

Jacob slowly opened the door and disappeared down the steps. Three humans followed him down.

Hitock froze and stayed by the door at the top of the steps. Memories of long severe beatings came to his head.

Jacob made his way through the school's cellar. The badly wrapped steam pipes were now cold and dribbled water from the joints. The dampness was thick in the air. Half lit emergency lights barely showed the way down the corridor.

Fueled with anger, Jacob had already taken out his sword and was ready to punish any Titan that got in his way. He made his way down a long hallway. He spotted bits of light coming from under a door at the far end of the hall.

He approached the door quietly and could hear two Titan guards arguing on the other side. "Kill him now before they come for him." One guard yelled out. The other replied in a deeper and more confident voice, "Don't panic pup. Just because the lights go off doesn't mean where being over run. Do you think that humans would ever attack a Titan mining camp? It's probably just a drill"

Jacob took half a dozen steps back and lowered his shoulder. He charged the door with everything he had. He crashed into the door hard knocking it off its hinges. Jacob and what was left of the door landed on one of the Titans, knocking him to the floor.

The other Titan instantly gripped his laser on his hip.

Jacob recovered from his collision and had his sword in motion. He swung hard with both hands roaring like a beast in a frenzy. The standing Titan's head separated from his shoulders cleanly. It rolled on the floor to the feet of Phil, who was still chained down.

Kneeling on one knee Phil raised his head up slowly exposing deep colored bruises in his face. He saw it was Jacob Skyler and he squeezed out a smirk.

Phil looked back down at the head of the Titan and whispered in a tired scratchy voice, "I told you I would see your head at my feet one day Flathead."

Jacob raised his sword straight above his head and came down on Phil's chains. They broke away easily. Phil staggered forward from dizziness. He almost hit the ground before Jacob caught him.

Jacob cradled his head in his arms. "Phil it's me, Jacob, can you hear me?"

His reply was typical. "Sure I can. Those *nanites* are working on over time though."

The other soldiers came through the door with their lasers in hand. They quickly pulverized the Titan that was moaning from under the door. Jacob sheathed his sword and carried Phil back up the stairs on his shoulder.

Chapter 16

A dark, human silhouette stood on top of a small hill against the dark blue evening sky just outside the Titan slave camp. Leo unsheathed his sword with care and grace. In one smooth movement, he thrust it high above his head to signal his piper to start playing.

A weather-beaten young man stood hidden by bushes and the cover of night. Leo had hooked up a microphone powered by car batteries near the pipes. He had several speakers carefully spread out through the woods around the south end of the mining camp.

Leo told stories to his troops of how brave the piper had to be back in the olden days. These men were known to be the most courageous of warriors. The pipers will summon the courage that dwells deep within any person's soul. Thoughts of honor and pride of their forefathers would enter their head.

The piper licked his lips and adjusted his mouth on his bagpipe. A slow but steady majestic, haunting sound started rising with the breeze as if it was the voice of the planet.

It flowed down and out of the forest and into the slave camp. A mysterious melody of the Bag Pipes slowly filtered through the valley. The full Moon threw a strange white magic glow of light over the top of the forest. Enchantment flowed around every gnarly tree branch carried by the force of the music. The atmosphere was bewitching and had become thick with tense blood lust anticipation.

All that made a human proud started rushing into Leo's mind. His heart was pounding with excitement. With both hands on his sword, he spun around and thrust it towards the slave camp. His feelings rushed out of him like tons of water exploding through a hole in a dam. His emotions rushed through the bushes and touched the very roots of the trees.

When the strong sturdiness of the drums started the marching military beat the mood changed within Leo. His knuckles turned white as his fist tightened tighter and tighter on his sword handle. A strong sense of anger started swooping over his thoughts. Wondering if his family had survived the invasion. If they were slaves or maybe even tortured to death. A year of not knowing was boiling his blood into a state of pure fury and revenge.

The young soldiers hidden in the forest felt his passion pour out of him and into their souls carried by the Bagpipes. Any fear of the coming battle slowly disappeared from their minds and were replaced with anger and revenge.

There was one thing that humans had in their culture that no other species had. Not one civilization in the galaxy had a word that meant revenge. The Titans would kill for profit or survival but not for emotional reasons. They invaded Earth to rape it of its resources, to feed the Titan Empire's advance. The Titans said revenge was what made all humans savages. Leo's hatred and feelings of revenge now leaped out of his body and into the souls of his human soldiers.

The Titans on guard duty heard the haunting bagpipe music. The melody had put fear into the Titan's eyes. They had heard wild stories of large herds of crazed humans, who fought with malevolence and a constant fire in their eyes. Killing with extreme violence was their way. They became wild beasts with a lust for blood.

The intensity of the battle music expanded. The Titans ruled with violent persuasion, but these Earthlings were not intimidated. The music incited a madness of revenge in the humans.

The mood was quickly taking over Leo completely and his raging troops. The soldiers in Leo's brigade could not hold back their spiteful cries and curses any more. They started yelling and screaming anxiously waiting for the clash. They wanted retribution. They wanted more than their pound of Titan flesh and they wanted it now.

Leo raised his sword over his head once again and as loud as he could he shouted out a chilling war cry. The night became illuminated with loud explosions, bursts of light and crazed howling. Preset explosives started filling the air with loud continual booms in and around the slave camp.

The camp's loud ear piercing alarms added to the night's mad confusion. The Titans started scrambling, and firing aimlessly into the woods. The searchlights looked feverishly for the unseen enemy.

Leo's archers took aim and started shooting flaming arrows through the windows of the Titan's main building. For one long minute the Titan headquarters was swarmed with balls of fire like bees around a hive.

The majority of Titan soldiers were in their quarters sleeping. They jumped out of their beds when the alarms started going off. The few Titans on duty started a skirmish line into the village. They scattered through the town and into the edges of the forest not knowing where the enemy was exactly. Shooting anything that moved or thought about moving.

Leo watched the battle from the southwest flank of the town with anticipation. His position was secure on a high point on a hill. From the cover of the trees and bushes he could watch the whole battle develop.

Leo turned to Susan, one of his runners. "This is the worst part of the battle for me. Watching others risk their lives for my battle plan."

Leo knew he had to wait for the right moment to attack with the secret weapon. To use it to early would bring instant air support.

The Titan searchlights were one of the first things to blow up with the use of homemade hand grenade launchers. The Titans were taken by surprise. Humans had never attacked a Titan slave camp before. Leo could hear Titans screaming as deadly booby traps went off along the edge of the woods. Total confusion swarmed over the entire camp. Human slaves woke up in panic. They peeked out of the windows and doors. They flagged down some of Leo's soldiers.

The soldiers guided them to safety outside the camp.

Leo saw what he was waiting for. A Titan tank crawled around from behind the main Titan building. This huge war machine hovered five feet above the ground. It's heavily armored turret with its large laser cannon, started turning towards the trees where some of Leo's people were evacuating the slaves.

It was time for the secret weapon. Conventional lasers couldn't do any real damage to a Titan tank. Leo redesigned a laser cannon he salvaged from a Titan tank he helped destroy. They mounted the cannon on an old pick-up truck. The only problem was it took ten minutes to recharge.

Leo lowered his goggles over his eyes and firmly gripped the controls of this destructive weapon. He stared through the sights and locked on to the target. As loud as he could, he yelled, "Fire in the hole!"

A brilliant flash of blinding red light shot through the night, lighting up the whole village for an instant. The explosion reached high into the air. The loud rumble of the explosion filled the valley for seconds that seemed to stretch on. Everybody in the town could feel the Earth shake.

The air smelled of burnt lightning. Guards fifty feet away from the tank were knocked to the ground from the force of the explosion. When the smoke cleared half of the Titan hover tank had melted away. What was left of the tank lay on the ground broken open like a cracked egg with flames reaching out of it.

A grin of satisfaction slowly came to Leo's face. "That should make them think twice." Looking up to the night's sky Leo added, "That should also bring some Titan space fighters down from the moon."

A girl named Michele turned to Leo and smiled.

"We've got them now, Lord Leo."

Leo shook his head up and down.

"But the Titans are known for their combat skills in the heat of a battle. They will recover quickly from the surprise attack."

Leo smiled at Michele. "We created a diversion. It's time to get our people out of the area."

Leo raised his sword and looked to his piper. The music stopped and everything seemed to stand still.

Leo waved his sword three times, and the piper started playing again. This time the music was slightly different. The melody was quick and happy. The music laughed in the Titans face. Leo's troops knew the song was a signal to fall back. They knew that Titan space fighters would be here any moment. The Titans would incinerate the woods with their lasers, wiping out an area a couple of miles around the whole town so they had to move quickly.

Leo's people started to leave east and west of the village. They spread out in wide groups through the woods, running as fast as they could. A couple of miles away from the town, they would head north back to camp hidden deep in the Appallation Mountains of New York.

A small squad of Leo's people started a fire south of the village to lure the attention away from the retreating rebels. The smoke and fire would also cover the rebels from the glow of the full Moon and block the Titan's heat sensors.

Leo had no way to know if the plan had completely worked. Whether Jacob and Phil had gotten free of the jail. He would find out back at the caves.

Chapter 17

Jacob carried Phil on his shoulder and ran back out of the cell and, bolted up the stairs. Hitock was guarding the top of the stairs. He was waving his arms in a circular motion like a windmill in a hurricane for Jacob to hurry up. "Quickly Lord Skyler, I hear Titan space fighters overhead."

The sounds of small arm lasers still hummed back and forth in the school's lobby. The humans still held the lobby but Titan reinforcements would be arriving soon. Hitock tilted his head to listen. "Lord Skyler, I can hear laser fire on the roof. It would'nt be long before we started losing ground."

Jacob gave the signal for everybody to follow him out. They took advantage of the night and the Titan confusion. They ran into the woods in different directions.

The troops started regrouping outside the town. The fires were set for the escape and smoke dominated the air over most of the town.

Two Titan fighters swooped out of the clouds. The high pitch sounds of six laser bolts were heard as they peppered half a dozen shots into the woods south of the town.

Jacob talked to Phil on his shoulder even though he was unconscious. "The Titans are going after the small fires Leo's people had set to the south of the camp. I hope they got out in time."

Jacob broke into a light run heading west, over a small hill, where the horses where tied up. The team was already hitched up to an old wagon when they arrived.

Jacob gently laid Phil in the back of the wagon. Gram's body was covered with a blanket in the back of the wagon. A man with a leg wound helped Jacob lay Phil down in the wagon.

Jacob took a long stare at the unmoving blanket that covered his old friend. He bowed his head and he whispered to himself, "Now isn't the time to mourn. We have to get to safety."

He turned away and went for his horse. The small group galloped to the top of the hill and started down heading back to camp. Jacob paused at the top of the hill and looked back at the school. There was a small fire in the lobby. Most of the school was still dark with random flickers of laser blast shot at humans that weren't there.

Jacob could see the Titan slave camp was burning beyond the school. Titans were rushing around putting out the fires. They were gaining control and regrouping quickly.

Jacob looked back at the covered body of his friend and whispered to himself, "Gram you did not die in vain. You will be remembered as a hero in the first battle to save Earth. The Earth Defense Force will get revenge on the Titans for you. I know that's what you would want."

The wagon jerked forward and moved out. What was left of the small raiding party surrounded the wagon, some doubled up on their horses. Their heads hung low with the lost of Gram. They moved slowly through the darkness of the wood, with the threat of Titan fighters flying above their heads.

Victory kept every body's spirit from getting too low on the ride back to camp, except for Jacob. It was a bitter victory for him. He loss an old friend in this new world. He felt guilty, angry, remorse. He would not forget Gram or this night.

Chapter 18

Twelve of the Lords had got the news of Phil Ruzzi finding the jamming station when they checked in with Kerri and Caesar at the stolen Titan transport. The Earth Defense Force had grown to five hundred soldiers. Free humans have become scarce on Earth. The new soldiers camped out in squads of ten for miles along the Appallaction trail in southern New York. They were scared and unsure but they knew they had to do something about the Titans.

The new named Lords and some of the human survivor leaders gathered around deep inside one of the caves in Jacob's camp. A large bon-fire was gobbling up a six-foot tree trunk like it was a delicious meal. Its smoke drifted quietly up and out an old airshaft blending in with the night.

Jacob waved his arms to quiet every one down so that Phil could speak more easily. Phil was well fatigued. His wounds were cleaned and bandaged and he started gaining some strength back after eating some soup and bread. The *nanites* were making his recovery quicker than that of a normal human.

Phil spoke with pride and confidence. "The jamming station is hidden in my sector, in Pennsylvania. It's a week west from here by foot, hidden in a horseshoe valley. It's a large white marble fortress with several large satellite dishes pointing up into our sky."

The crowd cheered and Jacob had to quiet them down again. Phil looked into the crowd with a worried frown pressing on his eyebrow. "It will be to much for just infantry to destroy it. We'll need heavy artillery to take out their big guns and Hover tanks. Not to mention penetrating those thick walls that surrounded the base."

Ginger was one of the leaders before Leo had found her and her group of girls. Now she was Lord Leo's second in command. She pushed her way forward closer to the fire, raising both hands up to break into the discussion.

"You can't just attack the jamming station with one laser bazooka. It may be powerful enough to destroy one hover tank, but after the first couple of shots they'll zoom right in on it with their big guns."

Another voice shouted out: "What about Titan air support? As soon as the jamming station is under attack, the Titans will call to the moon base for help. We'll have Titan space fighters swarming all around us."

Everybody started grumbling and arguing over the grim insight. They were out manned and out gunned by the Titans. Then Leo stepped forward closer to the fire. His bulky size moved people away from the fire quieting them down. When he spoke, he voice was deeper and louder then the rest, grabbing every one's attention. "Ginger is right, without air support we will be at the Titan's mercy. We need to attack the moon base at the same time as the jamming station."

The band of humans broke into louder arguments of disapproval and disbelief. They started turning back into scared children. Ginger pushed her way next to Leo. "How are we supposed to get to the Titan moon base?"

Jacob stepped forward towards the fire quieting the disrupted group down again. He had been silent most of the night because of the loss of Gram. He could barely face Doug when he arrived but Doug had said he didn't hold Jacob responsible. No one wanted to bother Jacob.

They all turned their heads and quieted down to let Jacob speak. "I have a plan. Lord Ruzzi has told me that another slave camp is located half a day's walk west of the jamming station. That's where we'll get our artillery."

Jacob started barking out his plan as if he was going to do it with them or without them. "They have a couple dozen Titan tanks there. When the Titans are fast asleep, Lord Leo and Lord Ruzzi will attack the camp with the majority of our forces. We will get our artillery and password codes for the moon base there. We'll steal all the hover tanks we can get our hands on."

Ginger flailed her arms about. "How the hell are you going to get to the moon base? What about Titan fighters? Won't they help the slave camp under attack?"

Jacob stared at Ginger and was tempted to smack her for being so smart. He was trying to keep Demock out of the conversation. He was still hidden in the forest.

Everybody started mumbling again and Jacob was getting tired of their petty bickering. He let out a ferocious roar to get their attention. "I will be distracting the Titan fighters when we attack the slave camp and the moon base. Doug and Matt will bring an attack force to the moon base the same way the lords arrived back on Earth."

Jacob lowered his voice. "We'll tie the Titan's hands on the moon. Once we get control of the moon base we'll control the skies again. Then we will turn our complete attention to the jamming station."

Ginger yelled out, "How will you tie the hands of the Titans on the moon base?"

Jacob stared at the group and never blinked an eye. "You'll have to trust me. It must remain a secret. If one of you are captured by the Titans our ace in the hole will be revealed."

Ginger kept quiet. She folded her arms and stared skeptically at Jacob.

Jacob held his fist up and shouted, "We can and will win this battle! The timing has to be right and it will be right. Remember at all times, when you fight, this is your planet. You are no longer black, white or yellow. There are no more nationalities. Earth is now our country. We were all born on Earth. We fight to save the human species."

Confidence was returning to their faces. Jacob couldn't tell if Leo was influencing them or not. Either way he was grateful to see it.

He started shouting at them. "We are all humans! The Titans are the invaders!" The group roared with pride.

Jacob went on, "We will take back what is ours and free our people. Then we will seek revenge."

The crowd all stood close to the fire and raised their fists in the air and started shouting. Their adrenaline was pumping. They started chanting at the top of their lungs: "*Humans! Humans! Humans!*"

All except Ginger.

Jacob turned to Leo and whispered under the crowd's chanting.

"You and Phil and the rest of the Lords will leave first thing in the morning. It will take you about a day and a half to get there. Saturday at two a.m. the Titan transport will land a mile east of the slave camp to get the moon base codes from you."

Jacob put a hand on Leo's shoulder. "Take the slave camp's headquarters as quickly as possible. Use your fastest rider to get the moon codes back to the transport."

Leo nodded his head in agreement and smiled. "What about Cathy and Michael in Europe?"

Jacob looked at the rest of the group. "I'm going to drop her a letter."

Both men turned to the crowd and joined in with the chanting. The group of leaders walked to the front of the cave, encouraging everybody else to join in with them. Now it was time to celebrate the successful rescue of Phil and the great devastation they inflicted on Mining Station eighty-one.

Chapter 19

Jacob left an hour before sunrise for his Aderain fighter. He asked Ginger and her squad to act as bodyguards. They stayed close to the trees and off any paths. Titan fighters were swarming over their heads most of the time.

Not all the lords had made it back to the stolen transport before Jacob left. The thirty lords who had heard about the plan from Kerri and Caesar had only ten or twenty recruits with each of them. Most of them volunteered to go to the moon base with Matt and Doug.

The first half hour of the ride Ginger was staring down the trail biting her lip. Finally she spoke to Jacob. "I hope you're not mad at me for disagreeing with you last night."

Jacob was half listening to her. He was preoccupied with Gram's death. "No I'm not mad at you."

Ginger lowered her eyebrows in anger. She felt like she was being ignored. "You know I have a right to my opinion."

Jacob looked at her and smiled. "As a matter of fact it's because you disagreed with me that I will always ask for your opinion in the future."

Jacob observed Ginger for the first time closely in the early morning light. She had long, straight, dark brown hair that had a slight reddish tint when the rays of the sun shined on it. It was hard to tell with the layered clothing she wore but Jacob guessed she had a more athletic shape then a seductive one. Leo said she had a powerful body. She was an athlete in school. It went with her confidence.

Jacob took his eyes off her and stared down the path. "I'll know you won't hesitate to give it."

Ginger shot Jacob a glance then kicked her horse in the ribs to gallop to the front of the group. "You got that right buster."

The four other women around them giggled in chorus. Jacob looked at the young women nodding his head up and down. "She's a leader all right."

A tall blond girl, covered in a long navy blue coat, rode up along side Jacob. "She'll keep you on your toes, Lord Skyler. She has been our leader since the Titans invaded. She was a military brat or something."

The ride took most of the day. The area was crawling with Titans. Jacob and his group had spotted two Titan hover tanks off in the distance. They had Titan soldiers riding on each one traveling up and down the main roads. Most of the patrols wouldn't travel to far into the mountains, except on the roads that crossed over them. The Titan hover tank couldn't handle the mountainous terrain and the Titan soldiers were too hot to hike too far.

Jacob and his escort arrived at the stolen Titan transport just after the camps breakfast. Kerri and Caesar greeted them eager for the latest news.

Kerri asked Jacob about Phil Ruzzi before even greeting him. "Jacob did you see Phil Ruzzi? He found the jamming station. I see from your entourage that you ran into Terry McGuire."

Caesar smiled a greeting and Jacob gave Kerri the update. Having to go over every detail two or three times Jacob pawned the job of story telling to the four girls.

Jacob put a gentle hand on Ginger's shoulder. "Come on, I want to show you something."

Ginger walked away from the group only to stop out of earshot of them and put her hands on her hips. "Excuse me, almighty Lord Skyler. What is it you got to show me that you don't want to show anyone else?"

Jacob leaned over and whispered in Ginger's ear. "It's our ace in the hole but you can't tell anyone. The less people that know about it the better."

Ginger looked at Jacob and smiled then turned to the girls. "We'll be right back."

All the girls smiled at Ginger and the tall blond shouted out, "Be easy on him Ginger he's only a man even if he is a Lord." They all laughed then went on jabbering with Lady Kerri.

It was turning into a beautiful day. The sun was warm on Jacob's face yet, the cool northern breeze never gave his skin a chance to get hot. His mood changed, as he got closer to Demock. He got a sense of security and comfort.

Scanning the area Jacob could see no signs of trouble. The Titan fighter patrols had slowed down towards the end of the day. The sunshine fell across the top part of the mountain where Demock was hidden. The tall pines held the sun light from hitting the rocks at the foot of the mountain, keeping it cool and shady. It was quite and peaceful.

Jacob and Ginger startled a deer when they first came upon the clearing near the rock base of the mountain. The young doe picked up its head. It looked in three different ways real quick and then bolted gracefully in the opposite direction Jacob and Ginger were coming from.

Jacob and Ginger dismounted from their horses and unloaded duffel bags of leaflets. Ginger swung one over her shoulder. "Ugh, these sacks are heavy. What does the note say anyway?"

Jacob carried one under each arm and walked closer to the foot of the mountain. "I'm going to drop them over Paris to the other Lords. The leaflets tell them to start listening to their radios on All Saints Day."

Ginger looked at Jacob and smiled. "You have another space ship hidden don't you?"

They walked another twenty steps when Jacob looked back at Ginger. "If a Titan captures someone who has seen this Aderain space fighter they would be drugged and made to tell where it was. That's why I'm only showing it to you."

Ginger looked back up at Jacob with fear in her eyes. "What about Lord Ruzzi? He had to have told the Titans about it."

Jacob shook his head no. "Phil was able to resist the drugs. Living on Flarconea for a year has changed our bodies slightly. We have medical *nanites* in our blood stream. Our stamina is higher now."

Jacob grabbed Ginger's arm and stopped her in her tracks. "You must keep this a secret and don't get caught alive by any Titans."

Ginger smiled at Jacob and started walking closer to the base of the mountain. "I understand, Lord Skyler, but I won't get caught."

She stopped after a few more steps. "Well, where the hell is it?"

Jacob smiled at Ginger then looked to the base of the sheer rock wall. "Show yourself, Demock."

Ginger took a step back and looked quizzically at what she saw, a haze seem to appear in front of the rocks. It was like a mirage. "I can't make out the edges."

Jacob nodded his head with a smile. "When Demock decides to blend in, he virtually disappears. Go a head and touch him."

Ginger walked closer and reached out her hand. "Oh its shell is so smooth."

Jacob walked up to the space ship just behind Ginger. "The on board computer's name is Demock. He is an Aderain space fighter that has chosen me to be his captain. He's a just over a thousand years old and he's had eight other captains." Jacob patted the wall of the space fighter. "They died of natural causes. A credit to Demock's skills as a space fighter."

Jacob rubbed his chin. "He can be quite cocky but there isn't another space fighter close to its superiority in battle."

Jacob cleared his throat and gestured politely towards Ginger. "Demock show yourself completely to my friend Ginger."

The color of the ship turned to a rich black color. Ginger took two more steps back. "It's shape like an egg. The surface looks three dimensional."

Jacob touched the craft again. "Open up Demock"

With a deep mechanical cha chung, Demock unlocked the back hatch. Where there was no crack before, now one appeared with a sharp white light defining the edges of the door. The large rounded back end of the craft began to crack open. The door lowered like a drawbridge.

Without warning Demock spoke low, in a holy monk's monotone voice. "Jacob I'm picking up another human in the immediate area. I am also picking up some other type of four legged creatures. I believe them to be horses."

Jacob turned around to see Ginger's amazed face as she took a couple more steps back. Jacob turned back to Demock. "Ginger and the horses are our allies."

Demock responded in an English accent. "Greetings Ginger, it is a pleasure to meet you."

Ginger smiled and looked at Jacob. "What's with the English accent?"

Jacob patted the space fighter affectingly. "He thinks he's amusing."

Demock barked out like an English sergeant talking to a superior officer. "Sir how goes the war effort, sir."

Jacob and Ginger walked up the ramp into the craft. Ginger touched the inside walls in admiration and wonder. They placed the sacks down as soon as they walked in. The room was a sterile white, with rounded walls. Jacob patted the walls proudly. "This is Demock's cargo bay."

Jacob paused and realized what an extraordinary life long companion Demock was going to make. "This way to the bridge."

Jacob made his way towards the front of the ship with Ginger sticking close to his heals. The space ship was as long as a small yacht. They passed through a short narrow hallway and walked onto the bridge of the ship. The Ancient Aderain fighter had only two rooms.

Jacob sighed as he stood on the bridge. "Demock, the war effort moves forward. Phil Ruzzi found the jamming station. Our mission now is to deviate the Titan space fighters from the human troop movements towards the jamming station. In other words, we are a diversion."

Looking at the bridge of the ship Jacob felt the power of undeniable victory again. He felt a renewed confidence in the outcome of the coming battles. A feeling he hadn't felt since he started his crusade.

Demock started talking in an American northeast accent. "Is Ginger going for the ride Jacob?"

Jacob looked at Ginger and put a hand on her shoulder. "No Demock, she doesn't think we can deviate the Titan fighters away from the camp. I just wanted her to meet you to renew her confidence."

Demock chuckled: "Sssheezze, you've got to be kidding? Ginger, I am over a thousand years old. I've been fighting battles most of that time. I would say I'm an authority on the subject of war. Don't worry about the Titan fighters we can distract them. Once an Aderain fighter has made an appearance, the Titans will focus all their attention on me."

Ginger frowned than gave a smirk little smile. "If your so great old man, why don't you wipe out the Titans yourself?"

Demock's voice was serious. "Because I would lose a direct frontal assault on the Titans. They would take heavy losses but I would be destroyed in the end. I'm afraid they would still rule over Earth. Good question though."

Ginger crossed her arms in a huff. "Why doesn't Demock destroy the jamming station?"

Jacob smiled at her. "Another good question. Demock can't be in two places at once. We have to take the Titans out in one good shot. We can't endure a long confrontation with them. After Demock destroyed the jamming station the Titans would send its entire fleet after him. He would escape or be destroyed. Either way the Titans would still control Earth and build a new jamming station. They have the upper hand. We have to split and confuse their forces."

Jacob rubbed his hands together. "We get everybody in position to strike where they can do the best, like chess. Demock's best position in battle is in space against Titan warships."

Ginger nodded her head in agreement. "I understand that makes sense."

Jacob smiled at Ginger and took another good look around the bridge. "The moon base is the real key to our attack."

Ginger jumped in, "Cutting off the head of the snake, right?"

Jacob smiled at Ginger and nodded his head yes. He walked around the catwalk that encircled the outside of the bridge. He placed his hand on the smooth holy white walls affectionately then looked over his shoulder at Ginger. "Army brat huh."

Jacob walked to his chair in the center of the bridge. He felt the soft, comfortable material of the chair and smiled. "It's good to be back Demock. I've missed you these last few weeks. I have to brief you on our present situation."

Jacob plopped down in the cockpit seat like it was an old recliner chair in the family living room. He gripped the arms tightly and wiggled his body deep into the absorbing cushions and smiled at Ginger. "You know this seat fits to my body. This is the most comfortable chair. I really miss it."

Demock spoke up in a sly, sexy, French women's accent. "Thanks for the complement handsome. Remember though I'm not just a great body with soft cushions. I got a great brain and a wonderful personality."

Ginger and Jacob laughed. Demock continued, "Well Jacob Skyler what's our situation? What have you been doing all this time with out me?"

Jacob swung around the control console attached to the chair's left arm. He started flipping switches doing a systems check like Demock had taught him. "Well my friend the Lords have been very busy."

Demock interrupted him "The who? Excuse me Jacob did you say, the Lords?"

Jacob hesitated in his systems check and shrugged his shoulders. Ginger stepped up and put a hand on Jacob's shoulder, "Yeah that's right the Lords. My civilization has gone back to the Middle Ages Demock. The children were the only survivors of the Titan invasion. They make sense of reality with the old stories that they heard from their parents, before the invasion."

Demock's voice was humble, "I'm sorry to hear your civilization has gone back to the middle ages Ginger."

Ginger was ashamed of her tone and calmed herself down. "I'm sorry too Demock. You see in our eyes those who trained on Flarconea, are Lords, something like King Arthur and the Knights of the Round Table. Do you know that story?"

"I'm afraid not Ginger? I have only been scanning Earth's transmissions since the Flarconeans rescued the Lords. I have picked up a lot of earth's transmissions in space, very entertaining."

Ginger looked at Jacob studying his face hard. "It's about a guy who fights for the good of all." She broke her gaze at Jacob and looked at the interior of the fighter. "I think you might be a Lord too Demock."

"Thank you Ginger."

Ginger smacked the back of Jacob's seat. "I believe you guys can handle it. I better get going now. I got a long ride ahead of me."

Jacob stood up as Ginger left the ship. "Thanks Ginger, good luck and keep low."

Jacob sat back down. "Demock I want you to do a quick systems check now on the engines. Then let me know how we stand on how fast we can take off and go into battle."

Demock replied in a soldier's response, "Yes sir! What is the plan, sir?"

"We have to drop some leaflets over Europe, and then distract the Titans from the human's movements. We'll spend a week flying around in space keeping the Titans focused on our whereabouts, then come back to give air support to Phil and Leo's attack on the jamming station.

Jacob continued: "Matt and Doug will attack the moon base with the stolen Titan transport."

Demock replied with enthusiasm, "Yes sir, I've had lots of rest. I'm ready to keep busy. Systems check is done sir. The main laser cannon is ready. We can leave at your command."

Jacob called for a visual. "Turn on the radar Demock and close the door."

The screen in front of Jacob came to life. It lit the small cockpit with the rock face starring back at him. There were also four more screens in the corners of the big screen. One of the screens had Ginger riding away from the Aderain space fighter.

"Demock, are you ready to start this new adventure. Let's give Ginger an inspiring exit. I want her to have something to think about on the way back to camp. I'll fly us out."

"Aye, aye captain."

Jacob gripped the joystick that extended from beneath the console. The spacecraft started a low deep humming and Jacob could feel his heart start to pump faster. He squeezed the handle a little more and pulled it straight up. The Aderain space fighter floated softly five feet off the ground. Jacob backed out and away from the face of the cliff, nice and easy. He floated gracefully with precision and coordination, rotating around and facing north, rising just above tree top level.

Jacob got a pleasant view of the beautiful Hudson valley. The Hudson River curved in between the mountainous landscape like an enormous python. Jacob smiled to himself. "Going up!"

Jacob pushed the joystick forward. In a blink of an eye Demock climbed straight up into the sky, shattering the sound barrier.

The quick rise and booming thunder took the breath away from Ginger as she strained her neck watching the Aderain fighter with awed amazement.

Ten thousand feet off the ground Jacob released the joystick and Demock stopped dead. He bobbed for just a second then Jacob turned him in another direction.

The fighter bolted south, and was out of Ginger's sight in less than half a heartbeat. Halfway down America's east coast Jacob headed Demock east towards France.

Before letting go Jacob cleared his throat. "Demock could you navigate me to Paris France? That's where the other stolen Titan transport landed?"

"No problem Lord Jacob Skyler but remember my long range radar is being jammed."

Jacob got up and walked to the back of the Aderain fighter. He loosened the tie around the bags of leaflets he and Ginger brought into the spacecraft.

Demock's curiosity couldn't be denied. "Jacob what's the leaflet say?"

Jacob dumped the leaflets out onto the floor next to the back hatch. "Jim Kelly salutes you. We have a good bingo. Put your walkmans on the day after All Saints Day for further instructions."

"What's it mean Jacob?"

Jacob drew in a deep sorrowful breath. "Jim Kelly is the password to let Cathy and Mike and the rest of the Lords know it's me."

Jacob finished spreading out the leaflets on the floor and walked back to the bridge. "We have a good bingo means that we found the Titan jamming station. Walkmans are another name for radio and a day after All Saints day is the second of November."

Jacob sat back down in his chair. "Demock could you make yourself transparent?"

The walls seem to disappear and Jacob could see right through them. Jacob stared mystified at the ocean Demock was skimming across. "I know the chance of Cathy getting the message is slim but it's something and if the Titans get it they won't understand it."

Demock reported to Jacob, "The coast line is coming up."

Jacob studied the view screens. "Head straight for Paris. When we get over the city open the back door."

The Aderain space fighter rolled over the landscape. As Demock approached Paris he gained altitude.

Jacob pushed a button and closed the door to the cargo bay from the bridge, "Demock, open your back hatch."

Demock cracked open the back door and a rush of air swept all the leaflets out over the skies of Paris.

Several red laser shots bounced off Demock's hard shell. "Jacob a Titan installation to the south is firing on us."

Jacob gripped the joystick. "Give me laser cannon control."

He targeted the slave camp and put his finger over the trigger button of the laser cannon. "Let's return fire."

Demock banked right and took a direct path towards the Titan guns. There where four white marbled towers each standing a hundred feet high. They where laid out in a square, a quarter mile apart. Jacob targeted the Titan white marble buildings that stood within the towers perimeters.

A wave of red laser fire passed over Demock. Jacob pressed his thumb on the button and shot a blue laser ball directly through the front door of the Titan building.

As they soared over the Titan slave camp Jacob blew up parts of the four Titan towers before ordering Demock to head north. After a minute of low flying over the Earth, Demock shot straight up and disappeared from the Earth's sky.

Jacob felt a sense of relaxation as space engulfed around him once again. He loved space travel. Some moments of beauty he'll never forget. Green and red gas clouds in beautiful shapes and endless sizes. The perspective he got on life from being in the vastness of space. Jacob spoke to himself out loud. "The back yard sure has gotten bigger."

"Demock let's hit the Moon Base first, quick and hard. Let them know were here and we are looking for trouble. I know we've probably already been picked up on their scanners. Who knows, maybe we'll get lucky and squeeze that oversized tick of a base, out of the Moon."

Demock replied in teacher type fashion. "Remember Jacob, the Titans fortify their bases with a heavy force field. It is highly unlikely we will do any major damage to the base. It is possible we could overload the shield and knock out some base functions. This however will not be of any real military significance."

Jacob rubbed his back side to side in his comfortable chair. "That's all right. We're just trying to draw their attention, for now."

Demock darted to the Moon base. They streaked across space away from Earth, keeping Earth between them and the Moon base. Demock turned around in a large quick arch. Realizing the Titan fighters had already picked them up on radar.

Jacob brushed his hair back with his hand. "We'll get one good swoop of the base before we have to go on the defensive. We have to make it a good first strike."

The Titan base was like an upside down bowling pin. Three quarters of it buried under ground. The dome shaped landing pad was the only part of the base that was on the Moon's surface. A force field was around the whole base, even under the ground. It was as if a splinter wedged itself firmly under the skin of the Moon.

Demock made his final banking maneuver and was now approaching the moon at a high velocity. Jacob leaned forward in his chair and studied the landscape.

Demock reported, "Jacob I'm picking up a Titan cruiser closing in on us from sector forty three, point eighty-five. Breaking away from Earth's orbit."

Jacob bit his lip. "Demock, I want to blast the surface of the moon just before the force field. We'll kick up some dirt and make it look worse than it really is and just maybe we'll be able to shift the base a little. You know, dig up the ground around the base."

Demock sailed smoothly over the moon's surface without a sound. He moved effortlessly gliding slightly up and down, adjusting subtly over the hills and craters of the moon.

The scenery was a blur to Jacob, except for the moon base directly in front of the Aderain space fighter. Jacob paused his finger over the firing button. "I'll target fifty feet just outside the base walls."

Demock picked up speed as he approached.

Jacob pushed the button at the last possible moment. "Pull up! Pull up!"

A white laser blast kicked up two tons of moon rock and a high dust cloud. Demock blasted right through it barely missing the top of the base's force field.

Demock turned the ship sharply ninety degrees straight up from the base. Jacob gripped his chair until his knuckles turned white waiting for the "G" force that never came.

Black space flooded Jacob's view and it took a second for his eyes to adjust. Hundreds of red laser fire streaked past them into the big empty.

Jacob barked out, "Rear view center screen." A flowing gray cloud of dust had covered the station completely. Jacob stared intently at the station trying to see if they shifted it.

Demock broke the silence. "Sir, I have picked up four Titan fighters and a Titan cruiser heading right toward us from Earth. Should we take them out now?"

Jacob turned in his chair and rubbed his beard and thought about it for a moment. "Avoid the cruiser. Leave one Titan fighter to report and get reinforcements. Then we'll head towards Jupiter.

If we wipe them all out now they have reinforcements here within the week. "

Demock immediately banked right and turned down in a large arch, heading back to attack the Titan fighter's bellies. The Titan fighters rolled and fanned out.

Before the Titans could get an attack vector Jacob fired off two red streaks of laser. Two fighters close to the center of the splitting group flashed in a great explosion from direct hits from the Demock's lasers.

Demock flew through the flaming debris.

Jacob spun the cannon around to lock on to a third fighter. The slaughter lasted only half a second as Jacob fired one more shot.

Demock shifted trajectory with a heading towards Jupiter. A blue ball of light from the Titan cruiser hit the Aderain fighter broad side.

Demock tumbled through space out of control. Jacob yelled, "Systems check."

The Aderain fighter regain control of it self and continued its course. "Jacob we've loss thirty percent power. The main laser cannon is down to blue power. We won't have white for another minute."

Jacob checked the view screens. The cruiser was still heading for the wounded Aderain fighter. "Fire small arm lasers at the cruiser and get us away from Earth and the moon base."

Five red laser bolts shot across space towards the Titan cruiser. The skilled Titan captain dipped the front of his cruiser down and took the shot on the thickest part of its shields.

Two shots streaked passed the cruiser. The other three were absorbed into the Titan's shields, weakening them.

Demock reported, "They've slowed down their pursuit but they're stilled following."

Jacob asked, "Demock anymore Titan fighters in the area?"

Demock responded quickly. "Yes Jacob. It seems that the base is sending all its fighters our way."

Jacob smacked his fist into the chair. "All right, they took the bait. Demock keep ahead of them so they can track us but not fire on us for at least twelve hours."

Demock didn't respond right away. "To keep their attention for twelve Earth hours we'll have to engage them at least a dozen times."

Jacob nodded his head yes. "Good, that's fine. Then we'll hyper out of the area and come back the following day."

At high speed the ancient Aderain fighter zigzagged away from Earth through the solar system.

Chapter 20

Phil and Leo stood on the edge of a small rocky ridge, hidden by dusk and half dozen trees that blanketed the mountain side. The reddish orange glow of the setting sun added new shades of color to the Fall foliage.

Leo grimaced at the town. He had seen similar scenes in Jersey. Sections of the town were burned down to the ground. "The camp looks like a typical slave camp to me. Burned and scarred by Titan laser fire."

Phil shook his head. "It's like a modern day industrial ghost town." He pointed to the far end of town. "My scouts tell me all those buildings are abandon. The center of the town is the only place that's occupied."

In the center of the modest suburban town was a bright white marble building. It stood out like a Greek temple in Africa. The two-story building glowed like a holy monument. The building was built large to house the invading giants.

Leo sat back on a log and looked at Phil. "Tell me again how we're going to get in that building. It's a massive, solid, square stone structure."

Phil stared down at the town. "My scouts also tell me that the Titans have set up a barb-wire fence that's spread out a square mile, around the outside perimeter of the camp."

Leo smiled, "They must have heard of the girls attack on our old high school. Security has been stepped up."

The soldiers traveled all night in small groups to reach the slave camp. They took cover in the underbrush and tried to sleep all day. Leo leaned forward and rested his head in his palms. "The troops are worn out from the quick hike. I wish we could give them more time to rest."

Phil stood up straight and looked at Leo. "Don't worry about them, they're running on adrenaline. Besides, they'll be in better shape then the poor humans stuck in the slave camp. They're probably no better than walking skeletons."

Leo stared hard at the Titan camp. "There are ten tanks sitting around the Titan headquarters like guard dogs. None of them seamed to be occupied, but they are guarded by a handful of hot lazy Titans."

Phil smiled and put a hand on Leo's back. "Human soldiers aren't a reality to these Titans. The Titan guards are serene."

Phil Ruzzi was recovering quickly from his incarceration by the Titans with the help from the *nanites*. He looked Leo in the eye.

"Well, we made it here in good time, my friend."

He held his arm straight out towards the setting sun.

"I'd say it's around six o'clock. The sun is just touching the horizon. By the lack of activity in the camp, I'd say they haven't brought the slaves back into the camp yet."

Phil's face cringed like he ate something bad.

"Look at this hell hole." Phil stared at the camp scratching his head. "How are we going to get by all those tanks and guards quietly?"

Leo turned and gave his warm smile to Phil. "We only have to get in quietly, correct. We'll do what we have to, to get out. No matter how unnecessary the destruction may seem."

Phil nodded his head in agreement. Leo was always joking even in the toughest times he could make his friends laugh. When the Lords were first picked up by the Flarconeans he cracked jokes constantly. It was his way of breaking the tension.

Phil turned to Leo. "I take it my jolly friend that you have an idea, a scheme, a plan. Or is this one of those, play it by ear type of deals"

"Who me?" Leo said, with a devilish grin spreading out across his face. "The way I see it, all we have to do is have a small group take out the communications before they know we're here. After that I'd say it would be within the rules to hit them with everything we've got after that."

Phil scratched his head. "I'd say your right. Remember though if it doesn't work. I'll blame it all on you."

Leo smiled back. "I thought you would say that. Thanks for the support my friend"

Phil slapped his comrade on the back laughing. "No problem pal. That's why I'm here."

Both men walked away from the edge of the ridge to a small gathering of soldiers. Five of Leo's captains stood and talked among themselves, including Ian Marcoux, Gram's older brother.

Leo approached them and called for their attention. "Listen people. We got to start this one off quietly. Myself, Ginger and Ian will sneak into the camp first. If all goes well, we'll give the usual signal to my pipers. Loud explosions and all sorts of havoc."

All the captains laughed. Leo continued, "At the signal you are to begin your attack. Phil will deploy you to secure the compound and disarm the Titan tanks."

Leo looked up to the sky. "If there is any Titan air support we will break off the attack and meet at the jamming station. Are their any questions?"

Leo paused for a long second studying his men's reactions. "No.? Good, we leave in one hour."

Leo turned to Phil with his impish grin. "Now, don't forget to come and rescue me."

Phil threw his arms up in the air. "Rescue who?" He smiled and patted Leo on the back. "Don't worry, the cavalry will be there."

The friends patted each other on the back feeling the kinship that had grown between all the lords. Their companionship gave hope and courage to all the human rebels.

Leo and Phil walked away from the crowd talking of good times back on Flarconea. Ginger scurried up to Leo with a look of disgust on her face. "Are you crazy? Why Ian? We're supposed to sneak in. Ian's as big as any Lord. How are we supposed to hide him? It's going to be hard enough on me sneaking you in there. Is it because he's the eldest brother of Lord Marcoux? Is the Earth Defense

Force already getting political?"

Leo turned and gave Ginger a hard cold stare, uncharacteristic to his nature.

Ginger had ridden hard all day to reach the slave camp but she was tough. She never took any body's word unless they had already proved it, and even that didn't always do.

She didn't like the lords at first until, she saw them organize the people, and give them hope against the Titans. She was a pain in the ass sometimes to Leo, but she had saved many lives with that attitude before the Lords had arrived.

Leo grinned trying to lighten the moment. "Ginger haven't I proven my skill as a military genius to you yet. We don't want to use our laser pistols right away, they would draw to much attention."

Leo turned and continued to walk with Phil as he talked to Ginger. "I have seen Ian tangle with Titans in hand to hand combat. He was taught since he was a kid how to defend himself using an old martial art. He's not intimidated by their size or ugly looks."

Leo put his hand on Ginger's shoulder. "If he doesn't get some revenge soon for the death of his brother Gram, he might take it out on some of us. I have a feeling he will come in handy."

Ginger bit her lip in disappointment. She looked around to see the other captains watching the discussion. She didn't want to argue in front of the rest of the soldiers. She realized the importance of harmony in the command structure.

In frustration she shook her head up and down in agreement with the lord. She whispered at Leo. "Fine then, it's on your head if he screws up."

Leo nodded his head with approval. "Thank you Ginger. I appreciate it."

The hour passed quickly and the sky was getting dark. Leo, Ian and Ginger walked down the end of the slope. They made their way down the steep part of the mountain into the trees close to the slave camp. Keeping as far away from the guard towers that cornered the camp. They reached the foot of the slope and crawled on their stomachs through the brush and underneath the barbed wire fence.

They scurried across a small grassy clearing until they got behind the slave's sleeping quarters.

Leo studied the guards directly in their path into the camp. He reached out with his thoughts. "Confidence, security, no worries."

Leo went first. Crouched down, he quickly scurried across the clearing behind a small shack. He braced his back up against the slowly rotting wood wall. He edged his neck out and carefully peeked around the corner of the building. Looking towards the center of camp, he saw four bored Titan guards, looking into the air talking and day dreaming.

Leo turned back to Ian and Ginger and waved at them to follow. They ran across the clearing one at a time to the small shack.

Leo looked back around the corner and started projecting his thoughts. He put his thumb and forefinger to his head. "Thirst, thirst, dry throat, hot, so hot"

Within a couple of moments the Titan guards started licking their dark gray pimply lips and scratching at their stubby necks. One by one they started dragging their forearms across their brows wiping their imaginary sweat off.

They all gathered along side one of the tanks they were guarding and started talking to each other. They nodded to each other in agreement. A moment past and all but one Titan walked around the corner into the Headquarters building.

As soon as the guards were out of sight, Leo started projecting his thoughts again. "Sleepy, tired, eye lids are heavy, can't stay awake"

Immediately the guard yawned and reached for the sky in a long stretch. He scratched his stomach and made himself comfortable, sitting on the ground, leaning on one of the tanks. He gave his body another huge stretch and closed his eyes.

Ian whispered to Leo: "Why don't you have him shoot himself?"

Leo whispered back: "It would be against his nature and he would brush the thought off."

Leo ran to the tank farthest from the sleeping guard. A tank that was close to the main headquarters building. Ginger and Ian followed in the same manner.

Leo climbed aboard the tank quietly. He slid over the smooth metal and opened one of its hatches. Ginger jumped up on the tank. She quickly lifted a hatch and slipped inside.

Leo whispered down to her. "Remember what I taught you. It's just like an old video game." Then he said with a little sarcasm, "Don't wipe out all the tanks. Remember we're suppose to be stealing them."

Ginger didn't answer him. She gave him a quick dirty look and started studying the controls.

Leo closed the hatch to the tank and quickly scanned the area. Seeing no one he started climbing to the top of the tank. Standing on top of the tank close to the Titan building, he jumped to a window. He was able to grab the bottom of a windowsill. He pulled himself up and through the window on the second floor.

Ian quickly followed him with a little trouble. Leo had to pull him through the window as he was hanging on to the windowsill.

The room they entered was empty of Titans, but the smell of eggs lingered. There was one large bed. On the wall above the bed was a full range of weapons. There were three small daggers and two five foot long laser riffles.

Leo touched the blade of a nicely crafted dagger.

"We'll be back for those after we take the camp."

The ceiling was fourteen feet high and gave the feeling of being out in the open. Leo turned the door knob slowly and quietly opened the door. He looked up and down a long hallway.

He turned to Ian and whispered, "No one's around. The coast is clear."

Both men hugged the walls with their back and slid down the hallway. Putting their ear to each door they came to, listening for sounds of a radio.

Halfway down the hall, Leo froze in his tracks. He raised his head higher and tilted it slightly to the right. He could hear a Titan guard calling the moon base. He heard the conversation in English through his ear interpreter.

Leo pointed to one of the doors, telling Ian that the radio was behind this door. He waved Ian to come stand next to him and he whispered. "Once the Titan shuts up, we'll break in and break whose ever neck is in there."

Ian shook his head yes with an evil grin growing on his face. Leo put his ear back up to the door. The moon base gave the Titan the new codes for the week. Then the Titan signed off the radio.

Leo grinned and looked at Ian, who grinned right back because he thought Leo had revenge on his mind too. He couldn't understand a word the Titan was saying. Ian was very hard to control when it came to the Titans, unlike his brothers, Gram and Doug, Ian didn't have any sense of humor: he was all hate and destroy.

Leo heard the Titan's chair shudder across the wooden floor as he stood up. He turned to Ian and counted on his fingers silently, "One, two, three.

Leo lunged at the door with his shoulder. The door burst open and splintered off its hinges, slamming on the floor. Leo laid face down right on top of it.

With his hand on his hips, the Titan guard looked down on him with astonishment. Then he began to smile.

"Bad move, stupid human. You're going to pay for that. Ha, Ha, Ha, Ha."

Ian jumped through the doorway with a flying sidekick. Sinking his heel into the Titan's nose. The Titan's head whipped back and his massive bulk crashed hard into the wall. Dazed he slid down the wall and onto his butt.

Ian jumped right next to the Titan, grabbing the Titan's arm and putting his foot up against his head. With a quick jerk Ian snapped the Titan's short neck with a loud crack.

Leo rolled over and looked up at Ian. "Glad I could help Ian." Ian seemed to always be in the same dark mood. Even Leo couldn't persuade him by projecting good feelings. Ian's dark cloud was too heavy and hate became his nature.

Ian looked at Leo with nothing but business in his eyes. "Thanks. You think we should destroy the radio now?"

Leo shook his head at the thought of how focused this man had become on revenge. "Ian, I'll take care of it. You cover the door until I'm done."

Just as Leo had finished his last word, Ian jumped back over him, out the door, landing another side kick to the face of a Titan who was walking down the hall. The Titan flew back into another Titan and they both bounced off the walls and crumpled to the floor.

Leo snapped to his feet and headed straight to the radio. He grabbed it with both hands and ripped it off the table. He ran over to the window and threw it out towards the tank Ginger was in.

He stuck his head out the window and yelled. "Ginger! now!"

Ginger was scanning the area with the tank's equipment when she heard the radio smash on the ground. She had no problem hearing Leo telling her to signal the troops.

She pushed a button and started the motor of the tank. Shifting the levers in the tank she turned the turret towards a guard tower. A target screen popped up in "3D" right in front of her. She put the cross hairs on the tower. A slight push of a button and she let a blast of red light go.

The burst of energy streaked across the compound. A large explosion at the base of the tower shattered the marble type of stone. The Titan tower crumbled over. She let another shot go, putting a large opening in the perimeter barb-wire fence.

Loud piercing alarms that sounded like a European police car started going off filling the camp with panic. Titans half dressed were running out of their barracks.

Ginger backed up the tank and took aim at another Titan building. She focused in on the front door when a Titan ran out with his laser in his hand. He saw the large tank turn its turret and take aim right at him.

Without thinking, he dove back in through the door.

With a grin of satisfaction and another push of a button Ginger devastated the front of the building. This started a chain reaction that blew the rest of the building up. Ginger thought it must have been the armory and not the barracks.

She looked at her radar and scanned the rest of the area for

Titans. She grabbed a set of headphones and listened more intently. She heard through the tanks microphones the slow but steady haunting sound of the bag pipes. When the marching drums started, the music slowly grew louder than the volume of the alarms. Some Titans even stopped to listen as they were running for cover.

There was a steady stream of human soldiers flowing into the Titan camp. They overwhelmed Titan soldiers by five to one. Titan soldiers were taken by surprise and blown away point blank by gangs of humans.

Ginger turned the tank around to go behind the building to investigate the other Titan tanks.

She turned the corner of the main building to catch sight of a Titan tank, blasting a shot at the humans coming through the hole in the fence.

She targeted the tank and let a shot go, blasting the neck of the turret. The Titan tank was shoved sideways about ten feet. Smoke engulfed the Titan tank instantly hiding it from Ginger. She couldn't tell how much damage the enemy tank had suffered.

The cloud seemed to hang in the same spot forever. Ginger noticed that the smoke didn't dissipate or float with the wind. Then out of the smoke Ginger saw the tank starting to turn towards her.

Before it could fully turn around, Ginger squeezed off two quick shots in a row. The first shot blasted the tank's lower body. The second shot burned through the turret. The top of the tank turned red and exploded. The rest of the Titan hover tank dropped like a rock and blew up in a beautiful display of burning metal and sparkling Fourth of July type of fireworks.

Ginger scanned the area again and saw some humans taking positions around the rest of the unoccupied Titan Tanks.

Phil ran right for her tank. He jumped right on and started waving humans to take over the main headquarters.

Phil bent over and looked into the tank's camera. "Ginger if you don't mind, could you blow up the rest of the other guard towers? I'm sure we all would appreciate it."

Ginger gritted her teeth at the thought of how pompous this lord was. Then she smiled at the humor he was able to keep in this time of panic. Much like Leo. She replied to Phil in a lady-like manner, "I wouldn't mind at all, Lord Ruzzi. I'll be happy to bail you out."

Phil smiled and bowed politely towards the camera and then pointed towards a guard tower. "Please Ginger, would you mind blowing that guard tower over there into another time zone."

The tank's turret turned a dozen degrees to the right and the barrel raised a couple more degrees up. There was a clap of thunder, a bolt of red laser fire crashed midway into the guard tower. The tower exploded then collapsed in on itself in a white cloud of smoke.

The whole battle was over in a matter of minutes. The humans secured the camp. Phil Ruzzi met Leo on the roof with a great big bear hug. "Your alive my friend. Did you get the codes?"

Leo smiled and nodded yes. "How did the battle go out there?"

"The guards were taken totally by surprise. There are no Titan survivors. We have secured the camp."

Phil walked to the edge of the roof of the main Titan headquarters and started yelling to his warriors. "Victory is ours."

All of the humans looked up and cheered together. Leo looked at Phil and smiled. They'll shout at anything you yell now. He walked to the edge of the roof and shouted, "Long live rock and roll!" Another cheer went up by the human army.

Phil patted Leo on the back smiling. "Now is the time to act in the enemies confusion. A day from now Earth will be ruled by humans once again." All the humans broke out in cheers. Leo's piper started playing a victory song. The moment of triumph was theirs to glorify in.

Leo looked up just over the top of the trees and saw the stolen Titan transport coming in to land behind the Titan headquarters. He would meet with Doug and Matt and give them the moon base codes.

Chapter 21

The Aderain fighter skimmed over the cracked surface of one of Saturn's moons. Jacob sat comfortably in his seat searching the radar for a stable place to land. He picked out a nice quiet plateau on the side of a mountain that was facing Saturn. He touched the spot on the radar screen with his finger.

"There's a good spot to land, Demock."

Jacob took a deep relaxing breath as they landed. "Life is ironic. Hiding from the Titans on Titan."

Demock replied in his arrogant way.

"Of course, the Titans wouldn't look here, Jacob. They don't know what humans would call Saturn's moons or any other moon. Humans never even named their own moon. Why would humans name a moon or planet they can't even live on?"

Jacob smiled to himself.

"I know that, and you know that; let's hope the Titans never find out."

Demock filled the view screen in front of Jacob with an X-ray picture of the ship. "Jacob, before we go you should make a visual on that hair line crack on the outer shell of my starboard side. Sensors say it's nothing much but you should have a look. It will take two days before I can completely repair it myself. We'll be going into battle again soon. I'll need to know what shape I'm in with you at the helm."

Jacob shook his head and ran his hand through his hair. "Thanks for the vote of confidence pal."

Jacob mumbled under his breath, "Go Check my starboard side, go check my starboard side."

Jacob jump out of his seat. "I think you forget who's in charge of things around here Demock."

Demock turned off all the lights in the ship for a few seconds then turned them back on. "I say it's more a partnership. Jacob it only makes sense to check now while we have the time."

Jacob walked to the back cargo bay. "Very well, I'm going. For a great war machine you sure are a nag."

Jacob put on a space suit Demock had in a hidden closet in the cargo bay. As he put the space suit on it adjusted itself to fit to Jacob's body.

Jacob nodded to one of Demock's electric eyes and the back door slowly opened. He pushed off the ship and glided slowly through the thin atmosphere. He hopped around the outside of the craft in slow motion movements. He made his way around the ship in a few giant leaps.

"Demock what are my chances that I'll leap too far and float away?"

"Don't worry Lord Skyler, the suit has a small electronic device attached to its belt that link's it to me. I could pull you back to the ship in case you floated away. I only have two space suits. I'd hate to lose one."

Jacob ran his glove along the smooth surface of the beautiful craft. He reached up and touched a button on his helmet as Demock instructed. The helmet shield changed color and Jacob could see an x-ray picture of Demock's shell.

The line Jacob saw was so small he laughed out loud. It was as if Demock chipped a fingernail. "You got to be kidding Demock? I'll Kiss it and make it better."

"Jacob grabbed the small hand laser attached to your belt. You have to shoot the crack with the laser with short burst.

Jacob smiled at how tuff but yet sensitive Demock was. "There, now you don't have to wait a couple of days."

After Jacob was done welding Demock's wound he took a moment to scan the horizon. "The strange exotic views I have seen this last year, like the red sun of Flarconea, and its three large colorful moons. The overwhelming feeling you can get from the vastness of the big empty."

Jacob stepped away from the ship and stared at the planet. "Seeing how enormous Saturn is, gives me a whole new perspective on the size of a planet and how orange things could really be. Seeing color in the night sky use to seem strange to me."

Jacob relaxed his shoulders and let out a sigh as he stared towards Saturn. He could barely see the blackness of space behind the massive planet. The view was hypnotic and inspiring.

Demock's voice snapped him out of it. "Excuse me Jacob. The sun is breaking the horizon on the east coast of your continent. It's time we started attracting attention again."

Jacob dropped his head and remembered the reality back on Earth. He floated back through the rear door of the craft. The door closed behind him and the lights changed from red to white, to signify the return of atmosphere.

Jacob started taking off his headgear and the rest of his suit in the cargo bay. "Demock, do you have the delay on the fusion rocket set?"

"Yes Jacob, it's armed and ready to launch."

Jacob made his way to the chair and started pushing buttons, checking power levels through out the ship. "What are our chances of the Titans seeing us?"

Demock displayed five different view screens. The large screen in front of Jacob showed the Titan landscape around the ship. The four other screens were in the corners of the large screen. They showed Titan surveillance satellites that orbited around Earth and the solar system. "I estimate that the Titans seeing the explosion is ninety percent. Their scanners are very sensitive within this solar system. They are probably looking for us now. I'm sure we will attract their attention."

Jacob relaxed in his chair again and started watching different gauges and the radar screens. He took a deep breath then blew it out slowly. "Demock, let's get off this rock. It's time we go to work."

The hum of the craft revved up. The sleek ship lifted and slowly turned. Demock rose off the surface of the moon like a magician's assistant in a levitation act. The Aderain space fighter darted across the surface of the moon almost as close as its shadow then sprung out into space.

The Aderain fighter picked up speed as it got further away from Saturn and its moons. A thousand miles from the moon Jacob fired the prepared rocket towards Earth. "How long until it explodes Demock?"

A view of the asteroid belt appeared on the lower left screen. "Two hours from now, five astronomical units away from Saturn the rocket will detonated into a large explosion."

Demock shut down the Aderain ship except for the life support and radar. The momentum of the ship kept them slowly drifting away from Saturn. Jacob flipped three more circuits off and studied the monitors. "Demock, let me know when you see any Titan ships heading our way."

Jacob closed his eyes and fell asleep. He dreamed of his early childhood, playing football with his father. As he caught a pass from his father a tidal wave of fire engulfed his dad. He screamed himself awake.

Demock's senses told him Jacob was awake and illuminated the ship's lights twenty percent brighter. "Jacob our bomb has just detonated."

Not a minute had passed when Demock caught a blip on the screen. "I have three intruders coming toward us head on. They must have been patrols close by. Shall I power up?"

Jacob was awake instantly. He rubbed his eyes and stretched out his arms. "No Demock let them get closer. I want to take them by surprise."

Small blue blasts of energy started filling the radar screen. Demock thrust to port barely avoiding the shots. Making it look as if the ship was disabled.

The Titan fighters closed in to about five miles away. Jacob had Demock turn on all weapon systems and the cockpit lit up like a video game.

Jacob took aim and squeezed the trigger to the laser cannon. A White flash streaked across empty space towards the lead fighter like a flame reaching out to touch a moth.

The Titan fighter took the shot head on, instantly bursting into a fireball in front of the other two ships.

The explosion blinded the two surviving Titan fighters. They shot through the cloud of what used to be their commander and saw nothing but open space.

The one Titan warrior checked his radar in a panic. The Titan yelled to his comrade. "He's below us! He's below us! Split up! Split up!"

The two Titan fighters broke off from each other heading in opposite directions.

A red flash left the laser cannon muzzle of the Aderain fighter.

In less than a blink of an eye one of the two Titan fighters vaporized into small bits of light. Only one Titan fighter was left.

Demock steered himself for the last Titan fighter. "Jacob are you going to take out the last Titan fighter?"

Jacob thought about it for a second and check his radar screens. "No more blips."

Jacob focused his eyes on the last Titan fighter. "Not just yet Demock. We want him to get a signal back to Earth. We have to draw as many Titan fighters away from the planet as possible. Tail him but keep a safe distance. We'll follow him until we get some more blips on the screen."

The last Titan pilot was shaken and confused. His fighter had taken on some damage flying through his comrade's explosion. He signaled the moon base for more reinforcements. He topped out his speed at three quarter impulse heading back towards the moon base.

Jacob stayed behind him and peppered him with red laser fire to keep him on his toes.

Demock reported, "He's heading into the asteroid belt Jacob. It is possible we could lose him in there."

Jacob shook his head up and down realizing the Titan's plan. "I bet the Titans are setting up an ambush at the belt. Demock keep an eye out for reinforcements. Also start studying the belt for traveling at high velocity through it. I got a feeling we might need it to shake off some of theses fighters."

"I understand Jacob. I'm taking over all flying controls now. I'll start calculating all possible paths through the asteroid belt."

Jacob had his finger on the trigger of the laser cannon. His other hand gripped his comfortable chair tightly waiting for the ambush.

As the retreating Titan fighter reached the asteroid belt Jacob blasted him into space dust. Jacob reached to the top of his control board and pushed another button. Red laser blast sprinkled down a preprogrammed disperse pattern of laser fire into the asteroid belt. The pattern flooded the surrounding area where the retreating fighter was heading.

Six more Titan fighters emerged from the large moving asteroids. The random spread hit two of the Titan fighters. Jacob saw the other fighters break formation and abort the ambush.

Demock went to full impulse, heading for the asteroid belt pursuing the enemy. He slowed down and changed direction after passing the first large asteroid.

Exploding rocks in front of him suddenly blocked Jacob's view. The Titan fighters had turned around and fired on the Aderain fighter.

Jacob turned the laser cannon at the pursuing Titan fighters. He laid down a barrage of scattered red laser fire behind Demock.

Demock bucked down from two direct laser blasts. Jacob couldn't move in his seat when Demock took the ship into two spinning ninety-degree turns. Even Demock's stabilizers couldn't compensate fully from the "G" forces the space ship was creating.

Demock was making thousands of calculations a second. Eluding the Titans and avoiding the asteroids made the ride fast and furious. Jacob saw two more explosions behind him without firing a shot. Two Titan fighters had crashed into each other trying to adjust to Demock's maneuvers.

The Aderain ship started to gain distance, sliding in and out of the deadly flying rocks. Jacob tapped his console. "Demock its time to drop some mines."

Jacob went to the back of the ship and opened a small hatch in the floor by the cargo bay. He set the controls for deployment of four space mines. He programmed them so they would only be attracted to Titan fighter ships. He closed the hatch and pushed a button to release them into the asteroid belt. Four hydrogen mines spit out the back of the Aderain fighter.

Two more quick turns by Demock and the ship shot out of the asteroid belt. As they left the belt there was a bright burst of light. It was a large enough explosion to take out a couple of the fighters. Small rocks knocked up against Demock but none of them big enough to do any damage.

Jacob checked his radar, "Demock head straight for the Mars's moons."

Demock change direction again. "Jacob I'm not picking up anymore Titan fighters on the short range radar."

Jacob checked Demock's power supply. "Demock reduce power to shields and reroute it to long range radar. We're going to have to threaten the Moon base again and draw them out."

Demock reach Mars and headed for the small oblong moon, Phobos. Demock picked out a nice size crater and gently landed in it. "Jacob I've scanned six more Titan fighters leaving the Titan moon base. I'm also picking up three Titan fighters, who escaped your fire before, approaching from the asteroid belt."

Jacob scratched his chin. "Nine ships looking for us. What I need is a little distraction to split them up an even the odds a little."

Jacob looked at his weapon supply list. "Demock set three of the nuclear rockets to hit the Titan moon base in long arch trajectories. Maybe I can get some of those Moon base fighters off our tail for half a minute why we handle the other fighters."

Some lights flashed along the panel board. "Rockets armed and ready Jacob."

Jacob rubbed his hands together wiping the sweat from his palms. He grabbed the cannon controls again.

"Demock, I want a heading straight back towards the asteroid belt with Phobos directly behind us and the six Titan fighters behind Phobos."

"I'm afraid the Titans will see us soon after we leave the moon, Jacob. The moon doesn't have enough mass to cover our escape back to the asteroid belt."

Jacob pondered the problem.

"We'll take what we can get. As soon as we lift off we'll let the rockets go. The rockets will confuse them and buy us some time."

Demock lifted off Phobos and gently turned towards the asteroid belt. Jacob fired all three rockets as soon as they cleared the moon's surface.

The lead Titan fighter coming from the moon base saw the rockets appear from behind Mar's moon. He barked out a defense maneuver.

"Incoming! Attack formation zig-tem-five."

The six Titan fighters broke into three sets of pairs and approached faster spiraling as they approached their target. The Titan captain noticed the rockets weren't coming in their direction at all. He bit his lip and ground his sharp teeth when he realized what was going on. He called to his fighters, "Those rockets are heading back towards the moon base. The Aderain fighter is trying to deviate us from attacking him and send us back to protect the moon. He must have damage and be vulnerable."

The Titan's radio squelched on. Moon base control came over the speakers. "Captain Rodon we've been monitoring your battle. Your priority is to protect this moon base. You must intercept the rockets first then, go after the Aderain fighter. Acknowledge!"

The Titan captain hesitated. He then confirmed his orders to the moon base commander. He switched channels and issued his own orders to his squad, "Death shadow one three and five, go after the rockets. Two and four you're with me."

The captain focused his eyes back on the small Martian moon. "He's behind that moon."

Jacob saw that the rockets split the Titan forces. It was time to leave. "Demock calculate the quickest possible light jump we can make. Ready all weapons. This is going to be close."

The big screen in front of Jacob focused on the three Titan fighters coming in from the asteroid belt. "Jacob the quickest possible light jump we can make is in twenty seconds. We'll only be able to jump eight AUs away. We will have to head straight for the three Titan fighters coming in from the asteroid belt. If we can get by them and jump to light speed it will leave us without shields or sensors."

Jacob gripped the arms of his seat and snuggled himself deep in its cushions. "If it was easy Demock everybody would be doing it. Get ready to fire three missiles on the Titan space fighters coming in from the belt. We'll jump to light speed on detonation."

"Jacob we will be in the Titan fighter's range of fire before we reached light speed."

"Necessary risk. Prepare to fire,... fire!"

The three Titan fighters were in a staggered approach. Looking at their radar screens they saw the Aderain fighter heading right for them. They started firing right away, not taking notice of the smaller blips heading right at them.

Half of the barrage of blue laser fire was missing the Aderain fire. The other half of the shots ricocheted off Demock's shields. Just before the rockets reached their targets Demock started to form the jump gate.

All three fighters took direct hits. The three explosions blended into one great big fireball that almost instantly disappeared.

The bright light from Demock's stargate happened simultaneously with the destruction of the Titan fighters.

Then there was nothing but the blackness of the big empty after the explosion.

Captain Rodon and the other two Titan fighter pilots couldn't understand what their eyes had seen. "What happen to the Aderain fighter? Our comrades fired, there was a serious explosion and everybody disappeared."

The Aderain fighter now floated peacefully outside the asteroid belt, eight AUs away from the Titan fighters. Jacob asked Demock, "How are you doing Demock."

"We have no shields, no sensors and minimal firing capabilities. We're dead in the water Jacob. We have ten minutes before we start to get all power back to normal."

Jacob looked at the big screen full of space. "Not a bad view in the universe. It's so peaceful out here. You know Demock this has become my home. Space is the only place where I can relax."

Demock turned the walls of the ship transparent. "Technically Jacob you've always been in space. You just spent most of your life in one place, Earth. That's understandable though, it is your home world."

Jacob shrugged his shoulders. "The Earth I knew doesn't exist any more. It died a year ago when the Titans invaded. It's a totally new planet now. Demock you are my gold ring and I'm not letting you go."

Jacob stared out into space and took a slow deep breath enjoying the changing beauty. Suddenly a flash of blue light burned his eyes and he was momentarily blinded. The Aderain fighter rocked fiercely and started tumbling helplessly through space.

The walls of the Aderain fighter turned solid again. "Jacob, what was that?" There was concern in Demock's voice.

Jacob peered at the view screen in front of him. "We must have jumped near another patrol. How much longer till we get weapons back?"

"Five minutes Jacob."

Jacob relaxed in his comfortable command chair. "Demock, open up a channel to the Titan's ship."

Half a dozen lights blinked in front of Jacob. "You're on line Jacob"

"Titan captain, this is Lord Skyler of the Earth Defense Force. Do you read me?"

The transmission from the Titan captain was clear and crisp. "Human this is captain Gail, of the Titan war machine. Your ship is spinning out of control. You may take theses last couple of seconds of your life to reflect on your mistakes. Out of respect from one warrior to another."

Jacob hit a switch to turn off his radio. "You see Demock that wasn't hard." Jacob turned his radio back on. "Thank you captain Gail. I appreciate your warrior code ethic. I thought for sure that you would want to collect the large reward for my capture and the capture of an Aderain fighter, but I can understand hate."

Jacob let the idea sit for a couple of seconds. "I know I would want revenge for my comrades. After all, I killed and beheaded hundreds of Titan warriors. I thank you for my moment of prayer."

The Titan captain's reply was silence. Jacob had learned power and money always meant more than honor to a Titan.

Two of the Titan space fighters moved to take up positions behind the Aderain fighter, then captain Gail answered back, "Lord Skyler, I have decided to bring you back to Earth and let Titan justice have it's way with you. We will hold you in a tractor beam on the way back to Earth. Any sudden moves will be interpreted as an attempt to escape. We will destroy you and your ship if you make any attempt to escape."

Acting startled and a little afraid Jacob answered the captain. "Reconsider captain. I could be tortured for days under Titan justice. That's no way for a warrior to die."

The captain didn't reply. The Three Titan fighters engaged their tractor beams stabilizing the tumbling Aderain fighter and started back to Earth.

Jacob shut off communications to the Titans. "Demock how much longer until we're fully on line?"

"Ten more seconds Jacob."

"In twenty start a slow detonation of one of those nuclear missiles. Don't fire it until I give the word."

"I understand Jacob."

Jacob started rubbing his hands together. They always got a little sweaty just before a fight. "Say a prayer Demock. I hope this works."

"A prayer?"

Thirty seconds later the Titan captain called back to Jacob Skyler. "Lord Skyler I'm noticing a serious rise in energy on your ship. What are you trying to do?"

Jacob answered the Titan captain in a panic stricken voice. "I'm not going to let the Titans torture me for days. I'm going to die here in space. I'll be a martyr for my people."

The Titan captain screamed back, "No! You can't do that! They wouldn't give me the full reward if you're dead and the Aderain fighter is destroyed."

"Well captain, you have ten seconds to decide whether to join me in hell or not."

The Titans tractor beams disengaged. They turned ready to run even before the order was given.

Jacob gripped the joystick to the laser cannon. "Demock, weapons on."

Jacob aimed the laser cannon at the Titan captain's ship and put the small-arms lasers on automatic targeting at the other two Titan fighters.

Before the Titan fighters could thrust out of range Jacob opened fire. The white laser light struck the Titan captain's ship first. In a large explosion the Titan fighter was blown away like a white tidal wave.

The other two Titan fighters were ripped to shreds. Red laser blast knocked them around making them tumble in space, ripping them apart until they exploded.

"Demock fire that rocket and give me our best possible speed to Earth. We have to get those other three Titan fighters and the cruisers orbiting Earth before they can give air support to the Titan jamming station.

Jacob stared at Earth. "I'm on my way Leo. I won't let you down."

Chapter 22

The Titan transport space ship was the size of four school buses side by side. It could hold two hundred humans easily, with plenty of headroom to spare. It landed right in the Titan slave camp that the humans took over, behind the main building.

Matt Byrne was made temporary captain of the ship by Jacob. Doug was made second in command. Matt sat in the captain's chair of the transport ship studying his console with careful scrutiny.

Hitock sat at a console on Matt's right pounding on the keyboard. He had found an old video of the last Titan captain screaming at some poor officer. He was planning on using the video to help get on the moon base.

Tea Aurus and Gem Clip, two Debarrians sat down in front of the captain at the navigation and helm controls. They were handling the flying and navigating of the Titan transport.

Doug left the transport to get the codes from Leo. He returned quickly with a piece of paper and handed it to Matt on the bridge of the transport. "I explained to Leo that since we saw his smoke we might as well come join the party."

Matt took the paper and read the moon base code to Hitock. He looked back at Doug. "How did the battle go for Lord Ruzzi and Lord Leo?"

Doug stood behind Hitock and watched his tiny hands fly over the computer console. He turned back around to face Matt. "Five dead and ten wounded. We got nine Titan hover tanks and more laser rifles. They'll be moving out within the hour."

Danny a young excited rebel sat at Matt's side on the bridge. Matt noticed Danny's ear-to-ear grin. "You have a good attitude

Danny."

Danny's mind was elsewhere. He was busy absorbing all the alien switches and the video screens like some space movie adventure. "I've never flown in space before. Never been in an airplane for that matter."

Matt shook his head with a grin. He began studying the engineering specs on a computer screen and the different capabilities of the ship. He started figuring out ways to fix vital circuits when trouble begins.

"Danny, I hope you took that pill I gave you. I hope everybody took them. I hate to have you tough guys blow chow all over the Titan Commander when we take his moon base away from him."

Danny looked back at six of his friends standing around on the bridge trying to learn something from Hitock and the Debarrians. They were all nervous and excited. "What were those pills for? To keep us safe from the gas the Flarconeans left us to use on the Titans."

Matt stopped what he was doing and looked at Danny. "Yes, anybody who didn't take their pill will die if their exposed to the gas."

Danny shook his head yes. "Don't worry Lord Byrne we took the pills."

Danny walked over to one of the bridge's side portals and looked up into the sky. He was a young teenager but his voice took on a harder, older tone. "Nobody's playing games here Lord Byrne. Come on lets go. Let's get this thing air born again."

Matt smiled at Danny. "You got it man." He nodded at Doug, who now sat in the command chair next to Matt.

Doug gave a nod back. "Let's get going. Gem Clip take us to the moon base."

The Titan transport shook for the first couple of seconds as the engines slowly charged up. The shaking faded away into a light hum as the Titan transport slowly lifted off.

The Titan transport shot straight up four hundred feet then, banked left and headed south. It would leave the Earth's atmosphere gradually.

Danny was in awe of everything. He never stopped staring out the window. He looked back towards the planet and his eyes widened in amazement as they broke away from Earth's gravitational pull. "Look how thin Earth's atmosphere is. It's a wonder we don't use up all the air."

The Titan transport, filled with humans, circled the Earth once completely. Matt immediately noticed how there were no Titan fighter patrols in the area. They only caught a glimpse of the back of a Titan cruiser as it disappeared behind the edge of the Earth.

Matt looked out into space trying to sense Jacob with his enhanced feelings.

Jacob must have his hands full somewhere out here, he thought.

The Titan transport drifted through space until it caught sight of the moon. The sight of the moon captivated Danny.

"Lord Byrne, where's the Titan moon base?

Matt was concentrating on his computer readouts.

"It can't be seen from this distance, Danny. It's half buried in that sea of white dust called Archimedes crater."

The trip was short. The whole flight took three hours. The Titan Transport slowed down as it approached the moon's orbit. Matt watched as two other Titan transports left the Titan base heading out of the solar system.

The comlink light went on. It was the dreaded signal from the Titan moon base. A set of numbers appeared on Doug's screen. This was the crucial moment. Matt typed in the codes that Phil and Leo had captured from the mining camp. If they were wrong they would come under fire from the moon base instantly. Hitock transmitted the old Titan captain's video with out any audio.

Danny put his hand on Matt's shoulder. "Can we shoot our way in?"

Matt took in a deep breath. "These Titan shuttles have limited fire power Danny. We can't survive an attack from the moon base defenses."

A long tense moment passed as they waited for instructions from the moon base. Everybody on the ship waited in silence. The Debarrians kept their hands at the controls, in case they were found out.

The transport computer bleeped twice and the screen went black. Danny grabbed Matt's arm. At that, Matt bit his lip.

The screen flashed white then went black again. A series of numbers ran back and forth across the screen

A sigh of relief came from the Lords and the aliens when they recognized the approach vector coordinates to the Titan base.

Danny looked up at Matt. "What's that? What do those numbers mean?"

Gem Clip adjusted his course to the new coordinates.

Matt patted Danny's hand. "The first step was a successful one. The Titans think the shuttles are full of material harvested from Earth."

The human-filled transport approached Archimedes crater. Danny pressed his face up against the window. "It looks like a big silver basketball half buried in the sand."

The transport passed the rim of the crater and the silver dome cracked down the middle. The top of the dome opened up slowly. A bluish glow of light filtered out from inside the base. A flash of light around the base was the sign that the force field was down.

When the transport was half a mile from the base six Titan fighters spit out of the dome. They swarmed like bees toward the transport ship.

Doug stood up. "This doesn't look good."

Danny pointed a shaky finger at the on coming Titan fighters. "They're attacking! They're attacking!"

Doug studied the Titan fighters carefully. "They would have started firing already, but they're not." He hesitated another moment studying the fighters. "Nobody move, everybody stay quiet and calm."

The fighters approached circling in a counter clockwise motion towards the transport ship. Like a wave of bees they flowed in a corkscrew manner fast, and furious.

The Titan fighters flew right past them, completely ignoring the transport.

The Moon base kept opening its large sliding doors like a

largemouth bass ready to feed. Its electromagnetic shields never went back on. The path for the humans to land was clear.

The transport floated past the two colossal dome doors. The inside of the enormous dome was a landing bay. There where a dozen other transports in the blue section of the landing bay. When the human transport landed, more Titan fighters were being prepped for flight.

The dome doors closed and a rush of wind howled throughout the landing bay. The light changed to an orange color, signaling that the atmosphere had returned to the landing bay.

The Titans on the landing pad were busy. They were running around in almost a panic situation. No one was paying attention to the newly arrived transport ship.

Doug and Matt each made their way to the back of the transport to the big cargo door. Doug said softly to his soldiers: "No one move until the doors are completely down."

The humans crouched in the shadows of the transport as the large cargo bay door quietly lowered to the floor like a ramp.

A rush of cold air filled the ship. As soon as the transport doors were down human rebels poured out from the ship, firing lasers at anything that moved. The transport ship had some automatic laser weapons on it. Hitock preprogramed it to target the other Titan ships.

Matt yelled to his troops: "This way." He pointed to a door out of the landing bay. Matt and a hundred humans shuffled across the landing bay towards a very large closed door. The humans started throwing out a wall of laser fire in all directions.

The Titans were taken by total surprise. The Titans nearest to the humans were mowed down instantly.

The door that Matt was heading to began to open up as his people were running toward it. Two Titans walking through the door stopped in their tracks in disbelief. A herd of humans were charging at them.

One of the Titan warriors was close enough to grab a human by the chest and leg and slammed him above his head against the ceiling of the tunnel out of the landing bay. The force broke the human's back. Four more humans stopped and blasted the two Titans in the chest with laser fire.

The humans ran down the hall blasting any Titan in sight. Their mission was to secure the landing bay and the control room a few floors below it.

Doug and the humans who were with him ran to another door fifty feet away on the other side of the landing bay. The door was locked up tight.

His troops formed a circle around him as he worked at the control panel trying to jerry-rig the door open.

The humans picked their startled unsuspecting targets carefully. They started shooting all Titans that were on the landing pad systematically, as if they were playing a video game. Transports and Titan fighters started exploding.

It didn't take long and the Titans started returning fire, picking off humans before they could find cover.

Just as Doug got the doors that lead out of the hanger open he heard a large steady piercing howl. Doug turned and looked up at the dome doors. He turned to his people and yelled. "They're opening the dome doors! Everybody, inside, now!"

The air was escaping into space. The lights turned blue again. Titans and small machinery in the bay started sliding across the floor carried by the escaping air.

The human soldiers ran through the door and flooded into the corridor. Once everybody got inside, Doug blasted the door control panel and the doors shut.

"Split here. Lord Caesar, take your group and head down that corridor. My group will head down this way. Don't forget to drop a gas grenade down every other corridor."

The two groups ran through the Titan base. Blasting away any Titans that had the bad luck to turn the wrong corner and come face to face with a human. There was no hesitation, no second thought. The human soldiers were all young but had a lot of experience in confronting the Titans.

The humans made their way down into the inners of the moon base. They ran a hundred yards through the hallway before they found a maintenance door. One of the soldiers by the door whistled for attention. "I got a ladder going down further into the Titan base."

Doug split his group into three large squads. Some slid down the ladder while others took nearby elevators to the third and fourth floor. Demock had told them that the control room was on the third floor.

Doug slid down the ladder to the third floor. Several red laser blasts made him jump off the ladder for cover.

Doug took the opportunity to blasts two of three Titans shooting. One of the human soldiers coming out of the elevator threw out a gas grenade. The last Titan took off running and choking.

Doug led the troops to the control room. The soldiers threw more gas grenades into the main control room for the base. They proceeded to secure the control room and the floor with precise deadly laser blast to any Titan still able to move.

Doug ran to the base control consoles. He was locked out of the base defenses but was able to access the air vents. He opened air ducts from the two floors that were filled with the deadly gas. It spread to the rest of the Titan base.

A special team of humans started filling the ventilation ducks with the gas.

Doug contacted Matt over the intercom.

"Lord Byrne, the control room is secure."

Doug scanned the room to see Matt in one of the security cameras. "I have you on visual with the security camera. Is your position secure?"

Matt flipped a thumbs-up signal towards the camera. Doug responded right back. "Hold your position. I will be in visual contact if you need me."

A young dark haired woman in front of one of the monitors called every body's attention. "Lord Marcoux I have some Titan fighters on this screen leaving the base."

Doug searched frantically over his console. He hammered on the council keys with his fingers and flicked a couple of buttons.

The hanger bay doors started to close.

Four Titan fighters narrowly escaped the dome doors. Three more fighters crashed and exploded trying to squeeze out.

Doug ran over to another panel and typed out more commands to the computer like Hitock had instructed. "I can't control the outside laser cannons."

Hitock made his way into the control room with a human soldier as a bodyguard. He got on his back and did some rewiring and then some reprogramming. The base laser defenses went on-line.

Two escaping Titan fighters got caught in the base's laser crossfire. The last four laser batteries dug in on the upper crust of a crater had caught the fighters before they got out of range.

The other two fighters quickly fired at the defense batteries, destroying one of them. They headed directly away from the moon at a ninety-degree angle.

Matt smacked the console with his fist. "Damn it! They got away."

Chapter 23

Phil and Leo's troops reached a small horseshoe mountain range by two o'clock in the morning. Out of the five hundred human troops that attacked the slave camp only three hundred and fifty made it to the jamming station riding horses and on top of the stolen Titan hover tanks. A hundred humans stayed behind to take the blame for attacking the slave camp. If some Titans wandered in to the captured slave camp, a force of Titans would gather in search of the humans who liberated the camp.

The air was a few degrees past brisk and just short of ice in the dark pine forest. It would be a couple more hours before the sun would spill over the Appalachian Mountains into the Pennsylvania valleys.

In the night's shadows, the trees stood like massive black pillars, placed randomly into the ground. The forest at night was capable of making your soul shiver from fright. Long tree limbs leap out like arms of half dead zombies on a rampage.

The new Earth Defense Force now wrapped themselves up in blankets, like the little children they really were. The tried to keep the evil spirits and the cold morning chill away from their tired bodies and drained emotions. Some of the fortunate ones were able to get some sleep.

Leo sat down next to Phil on a log. "A handful of the soldiers can't sleep, being so pumped up from their victory at the Titan slave camp and the fight that's ahead of them.

Phil shifted his weight on the log and stared at the stars. "The most important couple of days in human history are happening around them. Their adrenaline surge through their bodies has played on their nerves."

Leo nodded his head in agreement. "The ones caught up in the historical moment came forward for guard duty, trying to keep busy. They didn't want to think of what was going to happen to them."

Phil pointed into the valley. "A few miles into the horseshoe valley is the jamming station. It's resting on a small plateau with a white marble wall surrounding it. It has the usual four Titan guard towers, and the three story marble buildings inside. More importantly it has a huge jamming dish hidden somewhere inside those thick white marble walls. The Titans also have a capable Titan force to protect it."

Leo stood and took in a deep breath. "Don't worry Phil we have a good plan and an army that believes in what it's fighting for. We will win."

The open end of the valley would soon face into the morning sun. Leo's rebels now sat in the cover of a pine forest, by the mouth of the valley. A hundred humans were just drudging over the crest of the mountain, on the southern side of the valley. Phil was leading the troops down the mountain to attack the backside of the jamming station.

Phil stopped, and leaned up against a tree. He took out a pair of binoculars to watch the opposite end of the valley. He watched for Leo's movement out of the pine forest by the mouth of the valley.

Three of Phil's fastest runners stopped beside him waiting for orders.

Phil paused and looked around at his companions. None of their facial expressions ever changed, always serious, concentrating on killing the Titans. They all had animosity burning deep in their eyes. Victory had made them even thirstier for revenge. This human army had nothing to lose. Their souls had become cold and hard.

Phil wanted retribution on a personal level, for being tortured. He growled through his teeth. "We will win this battle. There isn't an army in the galaxy that fights with the passion of a human. Alien races have become so advanced that they have no more passion."

His comrades stopped and listened to what he was saying.

"These Titan warriors are fighting on a planet light-years from their home. This place is our place. This planet is our home. After today, no Titan will look at humans as being slaves. We'll soon be known as the fiercest warriors in the galaxy."

Leo was coordinating the movements of the nine Titan hover tanks they had stolen from the Titans. He split them up into three squads of three. The hover tanks were each operated by three humans inside. Flying a Titan hover tank didn't take long for a human to master after they modified the control to fit the smaller bodies of humans. The controls were set up like a computer game. A huge command chair sat in the middle of the tank, where the driver sat. Right behind him, just a few feet higher, sat the main laser cannon controls. The right front side of the tank was reserved for the radio and the smaller laser guns.

The only experience any of the humans had with the tank was the trek to the jamming station from the slave camp.

Leo moved out of the woods gradually, being ever so cautious. The two tanks in his squad flanked him on both sides. They floated peacefully up into the Pennsylvanian valley.

The center strip of the horseshoe valley was clear of trees. There was tall yellow dead grass with some small shrubs scattered about an open field. Fifty human volunteers walked in front of the Titan hover tanks, looking like captives. All of Leo's soldiers volunteered for the duty. He felt proud of their courage, and cursed in having to select them himself.

The humans walked five yards apart from each other keeping spread out between the Titan hover tanks. They wore layers of rags, which made it easy to conceal their weapons. The soldiers approached the jamming station with the sun's rays just starting to touch their backs.

Leo learned how to speak Titan, without using the harmony translator. This was the only reason Phil couldn't lead this suicide run on the jamming station. Only Leo knew how to speak Titan.

Leo whacked the radio switch with his hand and punched in a set of code numbers that they retrieved from the slave camp. A Titan voice from the jamming station replied quickly.

"Name, rank and assigned mining station."

Leo didn't hesitate.

"Sindeck, captain, Mining Station eighty-two."

The Titan jamming station answered with no hint of mistrust.

"Captain, state your business. Why are you bringing those slaves here, and not to your slave camp?"

Leo spoke into his sleeve to help make his voice deeper so it would have a more Titan accent. "We were on patrol when we intercepted this herd. They had horses, and we chased them half a day before we could catch them all. This was the closest station to get supplies and reinforcements. We're going to need help in delivering them back to our station."

Operations at the jamming station were usually quite and boring. No human slaves to watch, there was no real threat. The Titan officer on duty had to think over this new problem.

Leo bit his lip at the long silence. "Hold your position, Captain Sindeck. We will send out two squads and three tanks. You will keep the humans away from the station."

Leo let out a breath of satisfaction. The girls in his tank relaxed when they saw him starting to grin. The fifty walking volunteers kept well spread out. Making sure that their hover tanks had an unobstructed path past them, straight at the jamming station.

Leo changed the radio frequency from the Jamming station to his people in the tanks. "Gunners ready. Wait for my signal."

Time seemed to stand still for the Earthlings. Leo could sense the tense feelings of everybody waiting for the Titan reinforcements to appear. It took ten agonizing minutes before three Titan hover tanks rolled out of the massive wooden gates of the jamming station. Two squads of Titan warriors rode on the angled steel of three Titan tanks.

Leo thought this ambush was going to be easier then he had arranged. His tank squad should be on the initial attack on the jamming station with "C" tank squad instead of engaging with the Titan reinforcements coming to escort the human prisoners.

He cautiously scratched his chin with one finger, and made his decision. He hit his radio button. "Squad "B" to squad "A" come in."

Ginger hovered in the lead tank in "A" squad. Her squad squeezed in between the trees on the northeastern edge of the valley. The woman manning the radio replied sharp as a nail. "Read you, go ahead"

Leo replied: "Hold your position and take aim at the Titan reinforcements. Squad "B" will accelerate pass the Titan tanks to support squad "C" on the primary attack. Open fire as soon as we past the Titan tanks."

Before Ginger could begin an argument, Leo broke in with a steadfast tone. "No time to discuss it Ginger! Just do it!" Then Leo directed his attention back to his squad. "Squad "B" follow me, gradually at first. When I say now, punch it up to full speed. We'll blow right pass these jerks."

Leo's squad slowly sneaked up through the crowd of human volunteers. A hundred yards away from the Titan reinforcements Leo saw the towers start blasting the woods on the backside with laser fire.

"Punch it now! Go straight for the jamming station."

The Titan reinforcement forces were taken entirely by surprise. The Titan hover tank commander didn't notice the increase in speed of the tanks, until Leo's squad was twenty feet in front of them. He yelled into the radio. "What the hell is going on?" The Titan tanks froze in confusion, while Leo's tank squad raced farther away from the Titan relief force.

Ginger coordinated the targeting of the Titan tanks with her squad. Each hover tank in her squad now targeted a different Titan hover tank. She saw Leo's squad race into the valley. "A" squad, Fire!"

A bright sharp ray of red light burst from the cover of the woods. Ginger's gunner took out the lead Titan hover tank, with one blast. The shot exploded between the turret and the main body of the tank.

Titan warriors sitting comfortably on the hover tank were ripped apart. Pieces of Titan were flung a hundred feet into the air.

The massive tank dropped like a twenty-ton rock. After it hit the ground it started to glow a bright red until it erupted into a massive explosion. The concussion knocked down half the humans who were exposed in the open field.

The second Titan tank was hit in the front side of the main body. The shot ricocheted off one of the many angles on the Titan hover tank. Most of the force was deflected into the ground. The Titans that were sitting at the front of the tank never had a chance to scream. Half of the Titan squad riding the tank was killed instantly. The Titan warriors on the backside of the tank were thrown thirty feet away.

The Titan hover tank stooped forward on an angle but still hovered above the ground. The muzzle of the laser cannon was pointing straight towards the ground.

Human volunteers were scattered fifty feet away from the wounded hover tank. The Titan hover tank turned towards the human rebels and opened fire. Rapid beams of red light pulsated out of the small lasers mounted on the front of the tank.

Everything transpired so abruptly that the human volunteers couldn't react fast enough. Instantly, three men and two women were pierced with half a dozen holes of red laser fire. The rest of the humans hit the dirt, or ran for the trees.

The inexperience of the human gunner on the third tank really showed. He had missed his target entirely. The shot blasted into the Earth, kicking up dirt. The dust cloud that formed gave some cover for the humans in the open.

The Titan soldiers left alive on the ground used the dust for cover. They jumped off the un-hit hover Tank, and charged towards the humans roaring battle cries and firing their laser rifles.

The humans reacted quickly, firing aimlessly into the dust as they lay on their stomachs. Smoke filled the battlefield with confusion.

Wounded humans and dying Titans were screaming out in painful agony.

The undamaged Titan tank spun around and headed back towards the jamming station, giving pursuit to Leo's tank squad. The human soldiers started picking off the stranded Titans as they charged out of the cloud of dust in a mad craze. The number of Titans alive started to dwindle quickly. As their numbers diminished, the shots on the live targets became all the more concentrated.

The humans were much better shots than the Titans. If they didn't have a laser they carried hunting rifles.

Ginger's tank broke away from the cover of the woods. She ordered her driver to chase after the surviving Titan tank. They had to intercept it before it caught up with Leo.

The other two hover tanks in her squad, rushed into the battlefield. They zeroed in on the remaining crippled Titan tank.

The Titan tank turned and fired two shots that fell short. It ripped up the ground in front of the two charging human-controlled tanks.

The two human hover tanks burst out of the dust cloud firing. The first shot blew the turret off the Titan tank. The turret shot into the air like a cork from a Champaign bottle. The second and third shot blasted through the wall of the Titan tank, setting off a series of explosions.

The remaining Titan warriors took cover near the smoldering remains of the first tank that was destroyed. They were quickly out flanked, and overwhelmed by continuous laser fire from all directions.

In a matter of seconds, three squads of Titan warriors, and two of their hover tanks were out of commission.

Ginger had her radio operator dispatch a message to Leo. " "A" squad to "B" squad, in pursuit of Titan tank on your tail."

Leo never acknowledged her transmission. He was arguing with the Titan Captain inside the Jamming Station, stalling for time. "Captain Sindeck, what's going on out there?"

Leo's voice was jittery, as if he was panicking. "We're being ambushed by another human herd."

The Titan officer responded. "Yes they're also attacking our rear, pretty insignificant attempt."

Leo continued, "They're over running us out here. We're coming back to regroup."

The Titan captain hollered back at Leo. "Regroup! You get your butt back out there and wipe out that insignificant alien force. Don't forget where you come from, captain."

Leo didn't bother to reply. In another hundred feet his squad would be a quarter mile from the jamming station. Close enough to do some real damage to those thick white marble walls.

The Titan tank following Leo started firing at Leo's squad. Laser shots streaked over his tank. Concussions were knocking Leo's squad side to side.

Leo quickly changed the Titan frequency. "Ginger get that tank off my ass, now!"

Ginger opened the hover tank to full throttle, making the tank's flight even bumpier. Her gunner already had the Titan hover tank in her sights. Ginger yelled, "Fire!"

The gunner squeezed the trigger as the tank bucked up then down. The shot blasted into the Earth, just beneath the Titan hover tank, flipping it forward, making it land upside down. It was as helpless as a turtle on it's back.

Ginger's gunner took two more shots and ripped apart the inverted Titan tank. Ginger sent a call back to Leo. "Lord Leo, you have no excuses. Good luck."

The Titan jamming station Captain kept screaming over the radio to Leo to turn and engage the human rebels. Leo ignored him and took aim at the front left tower nearest the main gate, where a laser cannon was mounted. A red ball of light shot out of the muzzle of his tank, and blasted a good section of the tower to dust.

The two front towers immediately turned their fire on Leo's squad, bombarding the advancing tanks. Leo's radio operator reported: "Squad 'C' has engaged on the other tower. They've lost one tank."

Leo grabbed the radio. "'C' squad, head around back to help out Lord Ruzzi."

Titans with laser rifles started firing at Leo from along the top of the white marbled wall. Each tower had several laser cannons at different levels firing at the human-controlled tanks.

Leo took aim on the other front tower. Before he squeezed the trigger again his tank viciously rocked backward from a laser blast.

Everybody in Leo's tank clutched onto his or her chairs. The lights flickered on and off inside the tank, as it rocked itself steady and came to a stop. Leo gave a quick scan around the tank, to make sure everyone was all right and still functional.

He adjusted himself back in his chair and took aim again. A bright red light blinded his view. Then everything went black.

Chapter 24

Phil stood on top of the part of the mountain that was the same elevation as the top of the Titan's thick marble walls. He looked to his left and gave a slight nod. A hundred human soldiers started slithering down the mountain on their stomachs.

Phil's brigade had no heavy armor. They had no chance of breaking through the back gate. Phil looked up to the two young men standing on either side of him. "Our mission is to divert the Titan's attention away from Lord Leo long enough for him to get close to the Titan jamming station."

The dark haired boy wiped his nose and added, "So, Lord Leo's tank squad can penetrate the station."

Phil placed the barrel of the laser rifle on a large smooth rock in front of him. He muttered a warning to the two runners next to him. "They'll be firing at us first, don't panic. Be ready to run and give the order to scatter."

Phil's soldiers ascended over the ridge of the mountain, and trickled their way down through the brush undetected. The soldiers blended in with the thick woods, behind rocks and trees. Some of them camouflaged themselves with red and orange leaves stuck to their clothes provided by the change of seasons.

Sliding on their stomachs, the floor of the forest seamed to pour slowly down the mountain like maple syrup. Concealment and surprise were their only defense. They stopped and took positions less than a hundred yards from the back wall of the jamming station.

Phil checked his watch; it was almost nine o'clock. He picked out a fat Titan on top of one of the towers. He had ordered his soldiers to concentrate their fire on the two back towers after he fired.

He studied his target's movements. "If I could sting them in the right place, I could get their attention."

He placed the bulky Titan in his sights and squeezed the trigger. A bolt of blue light instantly hit the unsuspecting Titan, blowing a huge chunk of his shoulder away. He dropped like the dead weight he had become.

Phil's soldiers opened fire on the towers. Titans along the wall and in the towers were swatting at the bullets like pesky bugs. There were ten laser rifles passed out to Phil's soldiers. Leo's infantry were issued most of the laser rifles.

Phil took aim at the other tower. He drilled another Titan in two. More Titans popped up along the back wall, quickly retaliating with multiple laser blasts. They randomly fired into the woods cutting down small patches of trees in one release. All four towers turned and focused their laser cannons into the wooded hillside behind the jamming station. The forest became the center of a deadly storm of laser fire. Deafening explosions shook the Earth. The ground seemed to spit trees and bushes into the air twenty to thirty feet high.

The wave of fire quickly shifted to a Titan dominance. Phil fired one more shot and yelled to the runners. "Scatter, tell them to scatter."

The runners headed in different directions yelling. "Scatter, scatter!" The humans stopped firing and scattered.

It didn't take long for the Titans to zero in on the humans filtering through the woods.

A barrage of blue laser fire swarmed the back right Titan tower. Two squads of humans targeted the back right tower making the Titans duck for cover so the first group could relocate.

The two runners ran back to Ruzzi's side. The first runner who ran towards the Titan laser fire reported while trying to catch his breath. "Sir, we've got a lot of wounded and more than ten dead."

The scared runner was interrupted by a loud thundering barroom. Three quarters up, on the front left tower. A big chunk of marble tumbled down to Earth in a large cloud of smoke. Phil smacked the one runner in the chest. "Lord Leo has started his attack."

The other runner pointed to the jamming station. "The two front towers have turned their laser fire out towards the valley."

The back gate flew opened. Two Titan hover tanks burst out at full speed, aimlessly firing into the woods.

The rebels set up small avalanches to roll down to the edge of the forest, blocking the Titan's paths trying to make it harder for the hover tanks to maneuver. The Titans blasted through the debris easily.

None of the humans' weapons had any effect on the hard angled steel, even the laser rifles. The Titan killing machines fired constantly up and down the mountain into the woods, scraping the woods full of death.

The humans started taking heavy loses. They were too busy running to fire back at the towers or the tanks. Phil Ruzzi sent word out to regroup in the pre-designated area.

Two tanks from "C" squad raced along the side of the jamming station and almost crashed head on with the two Titan tanks repelling Phil's forest attack. The human tank squad was along side them before firing on them point blank. A fast and furious exchange of laser cannons thundered rapidly like mountains colliding.

Both "C" tanks fired on the same Titan tank. The Titan tank exploded and flipped high into the air. It continued to explode into a million pieces of red-hot scrap metal.

The remaining Titan tank swung it's laser cannon around and took aim at one of the human tanks. It opened up with every laser weapon in their arsenal, turning the tank into a melting metal of Swiss cheese.

The other human tank kept moving. As it past the last Titan tank it turned its main laser cannon quicker than the last surviving Titan tank. It hit the Titan tank point blank. The explosion was so destructive it almost blew up the human's hover tank.

The humans' tank then opened up on one of the two back towers, drawing some of the heat off Lord Ruzzi's troops.

Chapter 25

Leo's soldiers rushed from the woods along side the jamming station. Screaming like crazed lunatics. They ran two hundred yards before dropping for cover. The humans laid down a massive amount of small arm's laser fire, peppering the walls and front towers.

At the same time, Phil's first group had regrouped and started attacking the rear of the jamming station again splitting the Titan firepower. They kept the Titans firing into the woods at phantom targets, using a hit and run strategy.

Ginger caught up with Leo's squad. The two remaining rebel tanks zigzagged slowly towards the jamming station's front gate.

Leo's tank was further back from the station lying on its side smoking, and not transmitting. His tank looked lifeless. Even the Titans stopped firing at it.

Ginger naturally took control. "Squad "B" this is Ginger, head straight for the main gate. We're taking a little tour of the station. Squad "C" concentrate your fire on the two front towers."

The tanks kept moving in a serpentine fashion as Ginger came along side of squad "B" forty feet to their left. The ride was fast and bumpy. The tank drivers were barely able to control the Titan hover tanks.

Suddenly one of the tanks took a direct hit from the right front tower. The large concussion from the rebel tank's explosion shook Ginger's tank back and forth out of control. Ginger mumbled to herself, "Things are starting to look bad."

She looked at Mary her driver. "Step on it, we've got to get inside of that station."

Ginger looked to her screen to see two Titan tanks appear at the gate of the jamming station. They started firing repeatedly at the two on coming tanks. Sue, Ginger's radio operator reported, "Squad "C" reports four Titan fighters overhead."

Ginger whispered under her breath. "This is it. We're dead. The Titan fighters must've taken out Lord Skyler. Now we're all sitting ducks."

Ginger looked through her targeting systems and saw one of the Titan fighters blow up. Two Titan fighters broke off their attack. The other Titan fighter was diving in towards the jamming station firing on the Titans. The base defenses turned on the Titan fighter. It overwhelmed the fighter and it turned away from the jamming station.

Ginger heard Doug's voice over her radio.

"Jim Kelly, Jim Kelly. Hey, you humans down there, don't shoot at the Titan fighters, one of them is me, Lord Marcoux."

Ginger nodded to her radio operator. "Read you, Lord Marcoux."

Doug circled around the base. "Somebody has to take out some of those defensives. I can't get close enough to the base to hit the dish."

Ginger and one other Titan hover tank stormed towards the gate firing. A ball of red light struck one of the Titan tanks taking it out of commission.

Doug swooped by and blasted away the gates of the jamming station.

The remaining Titan tank fired and missed both tanks. The red ball of light flashed down the valley and crashed into the trees.

The other tank in "B" squad blasted the last Titan tank. Mary scanned her radar. "The gate and the Titan hover tanks guarding the gate are gone."

Two human-controlled hover tanks flew through the smoke into the Jamming station. They hovered straight down the main road firing as fast as their weapons would allow. Ginger screamed into her radio to the other tank. "Keep firing and head straight out the back."

The two tanks faced their guns in opposite directions and fired. Blue laser fire filled the compound. Red laser fire was shooting out of the human's tanks as fast as they could recharge. They hit most targets point blank.

Buildings flew apart in repeated explosions. A chain reaction started ripping the mighty Titan buildings apart. One of the towers blew up at its base and toppled over knocking down part of the wall.

The two human-controlled tanks ran through the camp unanswered until they reached the end of the road. Mary yelled out, "Two Titan hover tanks just turned onto the street blocking our way."

Ginger fired at the same time as one o the Titan hover tanks did. The Titan's shot whizzed passed her, and hit the other human controlled tank head on. The tank stopped dead in its tracks, and blew up.

Ginger's shot hit the Titan tank on the side pushing it to the left side of the road into the other Titan tank. Ginger targeted small arms lasers on the Titan Tanks turret keeping it from turning its main laser cannon.

Ginger got the red light that the main cannon was charged again. She aimed the main laser cannon at the wounded tank.

The shot flipped the one tank on top of the other.

Ginger turned the small lasers back into the main part of the station. They traveled another hundred yards when Mary yelled out. "Ginger there is no back gate."

Ginger re-targeted the small-armed lasers on the back wall and riddled a hundred holes through the back wall. Ginger screamed, "Floor it Mary."

At top hover speed, Ginger's tank burst through the weakened wall, spinning out of control into the woods.

Chapter 26

"Jacob Skyler, are you out there? We have a situation here." Matt's voice was shaken. He sat in the Titan control room next to Hitock, who was working furiously on the Titan computer program. "Hitock have you gotten the base defensive system back on line yet?"

Hitock never took his eyes off his work. "The Titan commander has put in a special blocker on the base defenses. It's going to take some time unless we find him."

Matt looked at the base's internal scanner. "We haven't found him yet. He's either dead or has escaped to one of the cruisers. We don't have time Hitock. A Titan cruiser is coming into range."

Hitock paused and looked at Matt. "Our only chance is the Aderain fighter. Try calling Lord Skyler again."

Matt nodded and tapped his keyboard. "Jim Kelly, Jim Kelly. Jacob Skyler, this is being broadcast on an unsecured Titan frequency. We need help at the moon base."

Caesar was monitoring one of the radar systems. He gripped the console and turned to Matt. "Lord Byrne' we have a tackyon field in sector "D" forty-five point nine. It's got to be Lord Skyler"

The Aderain fighter burst out of a flash of white light. "Jim Kelly to you Lord Byrne. This is Jacob Skyler how can I assist?"

Matt smiled at Hitock. "Jacob we got an angry Titan cruiser heading our way and we haven't got the base defenses up yet. Hitock is still working on it."

Jacob responded, "I'll see what we can do Matt. Have you seen the second cruiser?"

Matt's eyebrows rose up and he looked at Caesar, who was just as surprised and shook his head. Apologetically, Matt answered: "No Jacob, there is no sign of a second Titan cruiser."

Jacob searched his radar screens. "I don't see it either. Keep your eyes open and get those defenses up."

Demock cautioned Jacob. "Two cruisers can be a dangerous thing Jacob Skyler. We are only tracking the one Titan cruiser coming away from Earth's orbit heading right towards the moon base."

Jacob wiggled himself deep in his chair. "Take control of navigation Demock. Give me full power on the laser cannon and head for the Titan cruiser."

The Aderain fighter weaved towards the Titan cruiser. A wave of blue laser fire came at Demock and he bobbed and weaved avoiding the fire.

Jacob took aim at the cruiser when a red ball of laser fire spit out of its main gun. Demock quickly compensated and avoided the shot.

Jacob fired back. A white bolt of laser fire hit the Titan cruiser's electronic shield and the cruiser went dark and started spinning out of control. Jacob smacked the arm of his chair. "Demock, "Is it dead?"

Demock took a moment to analyze his sensor readings. "It's shields absorbed the blast and shorted out the ships electronic system. They have no power or control of the ship."

Jacob gripped the joystick and took aim. "I'm going to finish her off before she charges back up."

Matt's voice cut in over Demock's radio. "Jacob behind you. The Titan cruiser is breaking over the moon's horizon."

Jacob looked at his bottom left screen and saw a red ball of light heading right at him. "Get us out of here Demock."

The red laser blast hit the Aderain fighter's shields in the rear of the ship. The lights flickered on the bridge and the Aderain fighter went spinning end over end out of control. Jacob was disorientated for a moment before he was able to speak. "Demock damage report."

Demock's lights flickered on and off. "Jacob Skyler we have

lost half our power. My shield was able to absorb the blast but we don't have enough power for the white laser cannon or a jump gate."

Jacob put his head in his hands and tried to concentrate. "Take us behind the moon. Get us out of firing site of the cruiser."

The Aderain fighter stopped spinning and headed for the moon in a large arc avoiding the Titan cruiser. Jacob shook off his disorientation. "What kind of weapons do we have left?"

Demock displayed the diagnostics on the four smaller screens. "We are low on power. We have red laser capability but with a thirty second recharge. We also have blue laser capability. Shields are at sixty percent. Another hit like that and we are defenseless."

Matt's voice cut through the air. "Jacob are you all right? The cruiser is heading right for the moon base."

Jacob took a moment to think. "Hang on Matt, we're on our way."

Jacob checked his view screens. "Demock head at top speed to the Titan cruiser. Stay low to the moon's surface and come up behind them."

Jacob leaned forward in his chair. "Once I've fire, bank away from the cruiser and head back to the moon's surface."

Jacob watched his view screen carefully. He caught site of the cruiser firing a red ball of light down at the moon base. "Hurry Demock, take us behind and over top of the cruiser. I'm going to target the main laser cannon."

Matt's voice came back over the radio. "Jacob they've blasted a huge hole in one of the dome's doors we've lost all atmosphere on the landing pad."

The Aderain fighter sprang off the surface of the moon right behind the Titan cruiser.

Jacob shot a red laser ball at the cruisers main laser cannon that was mounted on top. The Titan's shields absorbed the blast. Jacob followed up with repeated blue laser blast that made a hole in what was left of the cruiser's electronic shield.

The Titan cruiser fired a massive spray of red laser fire back at the Aderain fighter. Demock dodge most of the fire and his shields absorbed the rest.

Jacob took careful aim at the Titan laser cannon with the small-arms lasers. Several blue laser blasts and one red laser blast ripped up the spine of the Titan cruiser shattering the cannon into space dust. The cruiser headed down and turned away from the Aderain fighter and the moon base.

Demock turned ninety degrees in a long arc and headed for the moon's surface. Jacob stood up and checked his screens. What's going on Demock? Where are you going? Go back after the cruiser. Let's finish him off."

Demock displayed a damage report on one of his smaller screens. "Jacob our shields are down to thirty-five percent. I need time to reroute circuits and repair."

Jacob looked at his view screen. "They're heading for the stargate. They're retreating. Where's the other Titan cruiser?"

The screens changed to a view of the Titan moon base. "They're firing on the moon base. It appears the Titan cruiser has regained power."

A red ball of laser fire hit the moon base's electronic shield and the shot dissipated. The moon base started firing back with a flurry of red laser shots.

The cruiser took another shot that was absorbed by the moon base's shields.

The moon base shot a red ball of light across the cruiser's bow. The Titan cruiser steered away and headed for the stargate.

"Jacob Skyler we've done it." Matt's voice was full of joy.

Jacob acknowledged Matt and relaxed in his chair. "Don't get too excited Matt, they'll be back."

Chapter 27

Matt was checking the radar screens monitoring Earth. Leo and Phil's attack was a hot one. The heat sensors were picking up all sorts of laser fire. Matt reached for the communication link. "Jacob Skyler, do you read me, this is Matt Byrne'"

Jacob's voice was strong and confident over the speaker, "I read you, Matt. How did the takeover go?"

Matt took a moment to look around the large control room. Two humans stood guard at the control room door. They were alert and full of confidence.

"Well executed, although we did lose a handful. We are still sweeping the station, adding to the Titan death count. It seems the gas did the trick. Hitock has rewired most of the controls to work for us."

Matt cleared his throat: "I'm at the main monitoring board looking at a radar screen of the jamming station on Earth. It looks to me that Leo and Phil could use some more air support. Doug is in a Titan fighter engaging three other Titan fighters now over the jamming station."

Jacob snapped back.

"I read you, Matt. I'm on my way. Secure the base and check long-range radar for Titan reinforcements. Send a signal to the Galactic Community to help us maintain our hold on Earth."

Matt nodded his head with enthusiasm. "I'm on top of it Jacob. Oh, by the way, how did it go out there?"

Jacob took a second to think of all the fighting he's been through. He stared at Earth with its thin layer of atmosphere, now exposed and vulnerable to the rest of the Universe. "Skin of my teeth Matt, skin of my teeth."

Matt's voice went solemn, "I hear you Jacob. As soon as we're secure here we'll get more Lords into Titan fighters and we'll clean up the rest of Earth."

Jacob took control of navigation and grabbed the controls. He headed Demock back towards Earth. He could see the fire works as he broke through the atmosphere, blue and red laser shots blinking in between the passing clouds.

Jacob dove close to the ground, hugging the terrain as they approached the battle. "Demock, you got navigation."

Everything immediately got faster. The trees and rocks became a blur as they rolled over the countryside. They came over one mountain and a burst of red laser fire streaked over their heads from the jamming station.

Jacob ducked from the near hit, "The Titans have picked us up on their radar."

Jacob zeroed in on the source of the shot. "Demock do I have enough power for the blue laser?"

"You have enough power for one shot but then you won't have the use of the white or blue laser for ten minutes."

Jacob rubbed his hands together. "I think the sound and destruction of our first shot will affect the Titans morale."

Jacob fired the shot from the main laser cannon to announce their arrival. It echoed like thunder in the canyon. The shot boomed twice as loud as any other weapon on the battlefield. Warriors on both sides of the battle dove to the ground for cover.

The shot tore through one of the front Titan towers. The blue ball of energy continued through the station to hit a Titan tank inside the Titan base. The explosion was three times the size of any other explosion during the battle.

Jacob ordered Demock to head directly east, keeping low to the ground. Hugging the rolling hills of Pennsylvania, Demock spit out a report, "Jacob sensors are picking up a large explosion from the jamming station. A direct hit on one of their towers, and wait, we got two Titan space fighters coming in fast, behind us."

Two blue laser shots immediately hit the Flarconean fighter, shoving the ship down into the trees, creaming off the tops of a hundred trees.

The Aderain fighter shuffled to one side then back to the other regaining some altitude. "Jacob I think we missed a couple of fighters up there in the big empty. The two Titan fighters are heading back to the Titan jamming station."

Jacob yelled urgently, "Get us back there Demock. It's vital that we destroy that jamming station now. We have to win this battle."

Demock banked hard and turned the ship around and headed back to the jamming station. Jacob could see the Titan fighters in the distance firing on Leo and Phil's ground assault.

The two Titan fighters flared out away from the battle and turned to attack the Aderain fighter again. They almost completed their turns when one was plucked out of the sky.

Another Titan fighter had fired on it's own.

Doug's voice broke out over the radio, "Jim Kelly, Jim Kelly, Jacob this is Doug. I'm in the Titan fighter. Don't kill me."

Jacob sighed a breath of relief. "Doug, go help Leo and Phil finish up that jamming station. I'll get this other clown."

The Titan fighter was running scared heading out into space. Jacob aimed carefully and let go several red laser shots. The fighter's shields absorbed the first three shots. The last four burned through the weakened shields and hit its target.

The last Titan fighter was gone.

Doug approached the jamming station on a high angle again. The jamming station's air defenses were just about gone. He fired continuously for a full twenty seconds at the large jamming dish, pulling up at the last moment.

A large fireball from the explosion chased after him. Doug whispered, "That was for you Gram."

Demock and Jacob charged towards the station, trees and hills zipping past them like a movie on fast-forward. Five miles away, Jacob could see Doug pulling out of a dive just above the jamming station. He barely got away as the whole station went up behind him. A huge red and black fireball chased him into the sky.

A series of explosions echoed through the valley for a whole minute, then a strange motionless calm settled.

Jacob hovered close to the burning jamming station looking for Titan survivors, when Demock gave a report. "Jacob I'm monitoring multiple radio distress calls all around the planet. It seems your mission is a success. My congratulations to you."

Jacob Skyler watched Leo and Phil's troops start to overrun the jamming station.

Jacob rubbed his eyes. He felt for one small moment a sense of peace. "We've taken back our planet."

Then a flash of the possible future and the burden set in front of him popped into his head. The feeling of peace went away. "Demock send a signal to the moon base. I want to talk to Lord Byrne. Set us down in front of the jamming station."

The Aderain ship floated softly down onto the field just outside a group of wounded humans. Before the ship's door could open, Matt's voice came over the speaker. "Jacob, this is Matt. How can I help you?"

Jacob was checking his monitor. "Matt, Demock is picking up distress calls all around the planet. I want you to get in touch with them especially the Lords in Paris. Send some Lords in Titan fighters there.

We have to liberate the rest of the slave camps on Earth as quickly as possible. Also, send back the transport ship. I have to get these wounded where they can be taken care of properly."

"Read you loud and clear Jacob."

Demock's back door opened and Phil greeted Jacob with a satisfied grin and a great big bear hug. "We did it Jacob. We kick their Titan asses off our planet."

Jacob gave Phil an easy slap on the back. "Not all of them Phil, but we're getting there." Jacob took a sobering look at all the wounded humans lying in the field. "Where's Leo?"

Phil's voice got humble. "I'm not to sure Jacob. I heard his tank got shot up pretty bad. I haven't heard from him yet."

Phil pointed to the meadow in front of the jamming station. "I told everyone to bring the wounded into the field. If Leo survived he would've been brought out into the field with the other wounded.

I've just started looking for him now."

Phil continued with the situation update. "I ordered all the hover tanks that are left to patrol around the edge of the forest. I told them to keep looking for Titans and secure the area. Anything else you can think of Jacob?"

Jacob took a slow careful look around. "Yeah, get word out. We're going to have a big feast in the middle of the field tonight. Kind of let everyone know on the planet where we are in this war. They need it."

Phil turned and nodded to one of his men that was standing close by. The man took off to spread the word, "Good idea Jacob. It's good to celebrate the victories of battle when you have a long way to go in the war. Could be the only time we might smile until the whole thing is over."

The two lords started walking, searching through the wounded looking for Leo. They gave encouragement wherever it looked as if it would do some good. A hundred humans lay in pain as pup tents erected around them, a sort of small tent town sprung up quickly. Everybody seemed to have something to do. They forgot about the Titans while they were helping each other.

Two young girls covered in blood and dirt ran up to the two lords. "Lord Ruzzi, this way, this way. Lord Leo is badly wounded and he is asking for you both. Follow us we'll take you to him."

The two girls ran off and the Lords chased after them. They ran to the far side of the field both men wondering what condition they would find him in.

The two girls disappeared into a big brown tent. Jacob and Phil threw open the tent flap and rushed in to see Ginger and a handful of Leo's female captains standing around his cot with their heads down.

Leo lay in his cot with his hands over his bleeding belly and his eyes close. Jacob threw his arms up in the air.

"Everybody out, everybody out now," said Phil, helping the captains out of the tent.

The women looked at the lords like they were going to attack them.

Jacob felt Leo's pulse. "Lord Leo can sense your sorrow and your grief for him. Do him a favor right now and think of sex or any happy feeling you can think of."

Jacob looked at Phil. "We got to get him out of here. Away from this battle field."

Jacob yelled, "Demock, Demock can you hear me. I need you here with me right now."

Phil reached for the end of the cot by Leo's feet. Jacob grabbed the other end and lifted him up. They carried him outside near the Aderain fighter.

Jacob looked at Phil's raised eyebrow. "The Aderain fighter can pick out a particular voice a mile away, even in a crowd of talking people."

Jacob stopped at Demock's back hatch. "Demock start analyzing Terry McGuire's wounds. I want you to transport him and two of his captains to the moon base. Tell Lord Byrne what's wrong with him, and what they have to do to heal him. Then come back here."

Jacob waved at Leo's inspecting captains. "I need two of you to go with Lord Leo to the moon base."

Ginger step forward right away. "I'll go, Lord Skyler."

Jacob put a hand on her shoulder. "Sorry, Ginger, you're in charge of Lord Leo's brigade now. I need you here with your troops."

A man and a woman stepped up and stood at attention. "Lord Skyler we will be honored to go with Lord Leo to the moon base."

Jacob stepped away from Leo. "Fine, go and listen to what Demock tells you. He'll fly the ship and take you to the moon base. Carry Lord Leo off once you've landed and remember this, Lord Leo can sense your feelings. Think happy thoughts. Think of the freedom we've just achieved. It will bring his spirit up."

The two captains picked up the cot that Leo rested on and carried him into the Aderain fighter.

One bagpiper started playing Amazing Grace. Once he finished the first verse a drummer joined in. All of Leo's troops stood up, even the ones that were badly wounded. They all stood very still and watched as the stretcher bearers carefully walked inside the Aderain fighter. Everybody watched Demock take off with the music humming in the back round and wondered if they would ever see their lord laugh again.

Phil and Jacob started organizing the camp. They talked to all the captains and arrange guard duty and sent people out to gather food. Within a two hours all the seriously wounded were transported to the moon base.

Demock returned with a report from Matt. "More than forty slave camps are situated around the world. None of them are close to your position. I can keep an eye on the Titans from here. They are playing possum all around the planet.

The Galactic Community praised our victory and its sending a military task force of space ships for assistance."

Jacob looked at Phil and sighed. "I hope they arrive before the Titans do. "

Ginger looked up at Jacob. "I hope they're nicer than the Titans."

It was a little past noon and it turned into a beautiful fall day in the horseshoe Pennsylvania valley. The humans set up down wind from the burning jamming station, so they wouldn't smell the stench of dead Titans.

Demock surveyed and patrolled the area and reported back to Jacob. "Lord Skyler it seems the Titans are standing still hoping not to be noticed. They're reinforcing their camp's defensives."

Jacob scratched his beard, "Will they be a problem?"

Demock reported, "I've seen the Titans in this position before. They will bargain with the humans for their freedom with their captives."

Jacob shook his head in disgust. "We'll have to deal with that next."

The soldiers around the make shift camp started relaxing more and slowly started enjoying their victory. Jacob climbed on top of Demock and had him hover a few feet off the ground. Everyone in the field started cheering. Jacob tried to calm them down by slowly waving his arms and showing a thankful smile.

Demock opened up his microphones and speakers so Jacob could talk to everyone in the camp and across the world and on the moon base at the same time. "This is the most humans I've seen in one place since the last rock concert I went to. It's like Woodstock or something."

The crowd went wild with cheers, and Jacob had to calm them down again. The crowd came to a soft hush. Jacob thrust his fist in the air and yelled: "Today, we have taken back our planet."

Again people started jumping for joy, dancing around like little children.

Jacob put his hands out like he was patting the ground. "We now control the Earth under our feet and, the surrounding nine planets and their moons. We celebrate now, because in the future there wouldn't be much time for celebrating."

Jacob drew in a deep breath. "Today the battle is ours, tomorrow the fight continues. We will exterminate all Titan influence on Earth. There are still many slave camps still operating. By the end of the week they will all be shut down."

The crowd was pumped full of adrenaline. Screams of uncontrollable joyous jubilation roared back from the crowd.

"We are not alone in our fight against the Titans. A number of worlds have formed a coalition. They call it the Galactic Community. They are sending a military task force to help us defend Earth."

The crowd cheered again.

"We will retrain with new technology and new tactics. The Titans will try to come back, but next time we'll be ready."

Jacob Skyler raised his fist high in the air. Pumping it up and down, he chanted: *"Humans, humans, humans."*

The crowd in front of Jacob joined in. *"Humans, humans."*

Soon the whole world was chanting together.

The End